Th... bol... ...—ready to fight for what they believe is right ... their homes, their families, and the women they love ...

Juliet Crowley had the most voluptuous lips Noble had ever seen. Full, soft, kissable lips that firmed into an uncompromising line when she noticed his attention lingering there.

"Major, I'm sorry to say it's not a pleasure to meet you."

"But the pleasure is indeed mine," he replied smoothly.

"Are you being honest, Major Banning? I thought Southern men liked their women docile."

"I can't speak for all Southern men, Miss Crowley. But I prefer my women spirited."

She lifted one honey-colored brow. "My, my, such a bold claim."

"Tell me," he drawled. "Is it me you dislike, or my former uniform?"

She glanced back over her shoulder to skewer him with a look. "Oh, it's you sir." But she knew she was lying, for it wasn't dislike she was feeling, but something far more disconcerting ...

Other **AVON ROMANCES**

THE BELOVED ONE *by Danelle Harmon*
ENCHANTED BY YOU *by Kathleen Harrington*
HER NORMAN CONQUEROR *by Malia Martin*
HIGHLAND BRIDES: HIGHLAND SCOUNDREL
by Lois Greiman
PROMISED TO A STRANGER *by Linda O'Brien*
THROUGH THE STORM *by Beverly Jenkins*
WILD CAT CAIT *by Rachelle Morgan*

Coming Soon

KISSING A STRANGER *by Margaret Evans Porter*
THE MACKENZIES: PETER *by Ana Leigh*

And Don't Miss These
ROMANTIC TREASURES
from Avon Books

A RAKE'S VOW *by Stephanie Laurens*
SO WILD A KISS *by Nancy Richards-Akers*
TO TAME A RENEGADE *by Connie Mason*

Avon Books are available at special quantity discounts for bulk purchases for sales promotions, premiums, fund raising or educational use. Special books, or book excerpts, can also be created to fit specific needs.

For details write or telephone the office of the Director of Special Markets, Avon Books, Inc., Dept. FP, 1350 Avenue of the Americas, New York, New York 10019, 1-800-238-0658.

THE MEN OF PRIDE COUNTY

THE REBEL

ROSALYN WEST

AVON BOOKS · NEW YORK

This is a work of fiction. Names, characters, places, and incidents either are the product of the author's imagination or are used fictitiously. Any resemblance to actual events, locales, organizations, or persons, living or dead, is entirely coincidental and beyond the intent of either the author or the publisher.

AVON BOOKS, INC.
1350 Avenue of the Americas
New York, New York 10019

Copyright © 1998 by Nancy Gideon
Inside cover author photo by McLain Images
Published by arrangement with the author
Visit our website at http://www.AvonBooks.com
Library of Congress Catalog Card Number: 98-93121
ISBN: 0-380-80301-1

All rights reserved, which includes the right to reproduce this book or portions thereof in any form whatsoever except as provided by the U.S. Copyright Law. For information address Avon Books, Inc.

First Avon Books Printing: November 1998

AVON TRADEMARK REG. U.S. PAT. OFF. AND IN OTHER COUNTRIES, MARCA REGISTRADA, HECHO EN U.S.A.

Printed in the U.S.A.

WCD 10 9 8 7 6 5 4 3 2 1

> If you purchased this book without a cover, you should be aware that this book is stolen property. It was reported as "unsold and destroyed" to the publisher, and neither the author nor the publisher has received any payment for this "stripped book."

In memory of my mother,
who taught me how to dream

Prologue

1864

Almost time...

A lone rider stared down upon the tracks below. The tip of his cockaded hat provided little protection from the chill sleet lashing weary features. He made a single move, to check his pocket watch, clearing away the fog from the crystal with his sleeve.

7:58.

Almost time, if time was something one could count on in these interminable days of war.

As if in answer, the forlorn wail of the train's whistle sounded in the distance.

The mounted man's attention was drawn away from the stretch of track by movement beside him.

"Right on time. Must be a sign that things are going our way."

Major Noble Banning didn't answer.

Though he wasn't particularly superstitious, a part of him didn't want to jinx their mission with words of false confidence.

"Are the men ready?"

"Ready and anxious to bite some Yankee butt, sir."

"Tell 'em to look sharp and stay alert. We'll move on my signal."

The slicker-shrouded figure faded back into the mist as he continued to watch. To wait.

He'd planned this attack on the Union rail for weeks, using coded snippets gleaned by their network of telegraph spies to discover where the supplies would be shipped and when. If their information was right, the train appearing in the next few minutes would be loaded with enough food and powder to further the Confederate effort through the long winter months ahead. If it was wrong, it would still give his men a chance to work off some dangerous tension. It was always worse when the holidays grew near. His men wanted to be home with family. Hell, so did he. This would be his third year away.

He shook off the moment of melancholy to focus on the immediate goal. A success on this miserable morning would go far toward boosting their wavering morale. And it would prolong the costly confrontation perhaps through another Christmas.

Then it crossed his mind unbidden, a brief, traitorous thought.

Was he crazy to want to do such a thing?

Another year of hardship and death with loneliness and fear as a constant companion. If they all were just to lay down their arms and go home now . . .

The train appeared at the bend in the track, clearing his mind of all but the immediate objective. He and his men had a job to do. Union flags fluttered boldly on the laboring engine. The incline would slow it just enough to give them the opportunity they'd need to—

"Ambush!"

Minié balls chopped through the thicket like an axe through kindling, sending branches flying. For a moment, Noble was disoriented, shocked that the bullets were coming from behind him. Federal troops poured out of the dense woods, ringing his men with deadly gunfire. In the confusion that followed, one thought came with agonizing clarity.

How had the enemy known to be there?

Grabbing up his reins, Noble brought his mount around as he reached for his sidearm and sought a target. He never had the chance to fire, for he was already in an infantryman's sights.

He heard his brave horse's scream of pain and at first didn't realize that the ball had passed through his own leg before plowing into the animal's lung. The stallion went down, he with it, rolling, toppling down the embankment toward the train, which would continue to its final destination.

Chapter 1

"Major Banning, you got a visitor."

Clutching the threadbare blanket about his shoulders as if it could keep the penetrating cold of the blustery Maryland winter from rattling through his bones, Noble shuffled to the door of his tent. Until last week, he'd shared the meager quarters with a planter from Alabama. After they'd carried the man's wasted corpse away, he'd had the place to himself. But with Point Lookout overflowing with his fellow Southerners, he knew the privacy wouldn't last long. Perhaps this was to be his new tentmate.

He paused for a moment at the closed flap. Drawing a deep breath that felt as if ice was coating the lining of his lungs, he forced his stiffened form to straighten into a proud military bearing. As a defiant gesture, he tossed the blanket onto the cot behind him and took a moment to align his ragged uniform. Only then did he throw back the canvas flap.

The Union officer waiting in the cold gave him a quick once-over glance, unable to stop the pity from stealing into his expression. Then his manner became crisp.

"Major Banning?"

"Sir?"

"I'm Lieutenant Horvath. Might I have a word with you?"

Noble stepped back. "Come in, Lieutenant. I'm afraid I can't offer you much in the way of hospitality except to cut the wind a little."

His drawling sarcasm drew a wince from the other officer, who entered, then waved for his aide to wait in the cold.

"What can I do for you, Lieutenant?"

"I'll get right to it."

"I'd appreciate that. I'd like to get back to my Dickens before the pages freeze together."

Another grimace quickly concealed. Noble understood the man's situation. One couldn't afford to show sympathy for one's enemy, even when that enemy was humbled in defeat.

"Major, do you know a Colonel Crowley?"

His features hardened, but his tone remained coolly civil. "By reputation, sir." By more than that. Crowley was responsible for his incarceration in the Union prison along with the men who'd managed to survive the ambush.

"Colonel Crowley speaks highly of you, sir. So highly, in fact, that he asked me to put forward his request."

Noble turned and made his way back to the

cot, his gait hindered by a slow-healing wound. He lowered himself gingerly. "If the colonel would like an invitation to dinner, he's welcome as long as he brings the meal and is prepared for delousing afterward. Lice seem to be the only things that thrive in this place." Lice and despair.

"The colonel would like to offer you the means to leave these surroundings."

Leave? Noble's interest leaped but his manner remained purposefully indolent. "Really? Is he proposing to surrender to me, then?"

The lieutenant caught his grin with some difficulty. "I don't think so, sir."

"Then what does he have in mind?" Refusing to seem eager, he began to wind a loose thread from his fraying jacket cuff about his forefinger. He glanced up idly for an answer.

"The colonel is on his way to a frontier post. He was impressed enough with you and your men to ask specifically that you be allowed to accompany him."

"Accompany him?" Unable to maintain the pretense of disinterest, Noble's demand slashed saber-sharp. "Accompany him as what?"

"As part of his troop."

"As part of the Union Army?" The question was posed incredulously.

"Yes, sir. You are undoubtedly aware of the parole program—"

"Sir, my men and I were never part of the regular Union army before the war, and we've no plans to change our allegiance now."

"Major Banning, your men are dying here. I would think that you, as their commander, would be willing to do just about anything to spare them another day in this hellhole."

Noble said nothing. His glare emitted frost.

The lieutenant's tone softened. "You lost two more of them just this morning."

"Who?"

"Burns and Cable."

For a moment, the prideful disdain crumpled. Noble's head bowed, his eyes closed as he fought for the strength to find some reply, some words to make sense of the senseless loss. "The fortunes of war," he said at last.

"It doesn't have to be yours, sir."

The man's angry claim brought Noble's attention back to him. "What does the colonel offer?" he asked wearily but with no less wariness.

"That you and your men serve under him on the western frontier for the duration of this—this damned conflict. Then you will be free to return home with honor."

Home . . . The temptation of it nearly made him tremble.

"What kind of honor is there in betraying one's homeland?" he asked quietly.

"What kind of honor is there in a useless sacrifice to a lost cause?"

"It's our cause, sir. One we held highly enough to be brought into your . . . care."

"You wouldn't be fighting against your fellow Southerners, so how can you see it as betrayal? It's survival, that's all. And none of you is going to survive if you stay here. Is that your definition of honor? If it is, it's a poor one."

Noble rose, rubbing absently at his thigh before crossing to the tent flap and flinging it open. He needed air to clear the seditious whispers from his head. Home. Bitter cold rushed in along with the bitter sight of what lay around him.

Unlike most Northern prisoner of war camps, Point Lookout had no permanent barracks. Prisoners were housed in tents and died daily from sickness on half rations of beef and hardtack. Those who had the questionably good fortune of surviving lacked fuel and clothing and suffered from the brutal cold. He'd heard the death toll was close to thirty percent, though prison officials denied it.

Burns and Cable. That made eleven brave men who'd sworn to fight an enemy they could see, not one that drained away their vitality day by miserable day.

Noble sighed. How many of his remaining men would last through spring, some sleeping on the ground without blankets? They were still his responsibility, and he suffered from the knowledge of their hardships even as he suffered beside them.

He was being offered a chance to save them, because if he went, the others would follow.

Then his stare narrowed as his mind latched

onto another truth. He was being offered a chance to save them—and also something else, something extra that tempted him even more than the thought of freedom.

Justice.

"I would like to speak to my men first."

"Of course, Major. I'll have them gathered for you."

For a long while after the lieutenant had gone, Noble stood in the opening at the tent, not feeling the cold, not considering what he'd say.

He was lost in thoughts of retribution. In the unexpected opportunity of discovering who among his own men had betrayed them to their enemy.

"What you're asking is treasonous, sir."

"No, sir. We can get along just fine on these bastards' hospitality."

"I say we stick it out here. Why should we do them any favors?"

"I ain't serving under no Yankee, even if it means freezing for another winter."

"Even if it means none of us seeing another winter?" Noble put in softly.

His men muttered, but agitation and fear trickled under their resentment, a cold sweat, as they huddled together in scarecrow tatters. All of them were afraid what he said was true. That they'd never leave Point Lookout alive. That they'd never see their families, their homes again.

"I'd rather die here for what we believe in than die out there for them."

Captain Donald Bartholomew's sentiments were echoed by the others. Noble focused his argument on his second in command, knowing that in swaying him, he'd turn the others.

"Donald, I don't like this, either, but I don't want to die here. That's not going to do a damn thing for the Confederate cause. They're going to need men to rebuild after this thing is over. If we all die here, who's going to do that back home? Who's going to take care of our families? Our vanity? Our nobility?" He shook his head. "What difference does it make if we sit out the war here in this deathtrap or as free men out in the West? Neither is going to make a bit of difference to the outcome of this war. We're not going to see battle again. The only thing we can hope for now is to see a future once this is over."

"He's right."

Red-headed George Allen was the unit's chaplain. His words cut through the mumbling, through the grumbles.

"Staying here proves nothing. But by surviving out in the western territories, we can bring honor to ourselves and return home free men. Men with nothing to be ashamed of."

"As cowards, you mean," Bartholomew snarled.

"Cowards would choose to sit out the war shivering in tents, being fed like dogs," Noble told them. "Brave men would seize their own future, standing with pride."

No one said anything for a long moment, considering both sides, until a lowly private spoke what they all were thinking.

"I don't want to die here and be buried on Northern soil without ever seeing my mama again. I guess that means I'll follow you, Major Banning. I mean, we already done followed you into hell, why not back out again?"

A couple of men laughed halfheartedly.

Noble looked to Donald Bartholomew. "Don? Are you with me, too? I want your word as a gentleman that you'll serve and serve honorably."

Bartholomew scowled. Finally he muttered, "Ah, hell, Noble. I'd rather be straddling a horse than one of these frozen latrines for another year. I'm with you."

Even as he shook each man's hand, Noble could sense their confusion and divided loyalties. But he knew his men and knew that once they'd given their word, they'd stand by it. They'd follow him even if it went against everything they held sacred. Because none of them believed dying helplessly of cold and scurvy could earn them any glory.

He'd asked for their allegiance to an enemy they loathed. He got it, and he hated himself for having to do it. But one thing convinced him that what he was doing was right in selling out their loyalty to save their lives.

In serving under Crowley, he would find out who among his men had betrayed them all.

He'd find out. And if that man still lived, justice would be done, sure and swift, for the eighteen who'd fallen in the field, for the eleven who lay interred in frozen Northern graves. For the sake of his own tormented soul, a soul that cried out nightly for those twenty-nine men who'd trusted him and put their lives in his hands.

"You're going to lead Southern troops? Papa, are you mad?"

"I've been accused of being crazy as a fox. Is that the same thing?"

Juliet Crowley ignored her father's teasing, unwilling to be sidetracked from what she considered his sudden lunacy. "You're taking enemy soldiers with you to Fort Blair."

"Not enemies, Jules. Just soldiers. Some of the best soldiers I've ever seen. Wait until you see them on horseback. Why, half our men sit a saddle like clothespins, falling off at every unplanned turn. We need men—riders—who can match the hostiles on their own terms. Men like these. Then maybe we'll have a chance."

"But who's the more dangerous? The Indians or the men who'll be in your own command? I prefer to trust an enemy I can see, not one that poses as my friend."

"Jules—"

"*Et tu Brute?*"

John Crowley shook his head. "'Tis my own fault for providing you with an education—now you can best me in an argument."

Juliet brightened. "Does that mean you see my point?"

"Of course, I do, my dear. But that doesn't mean I'll surrender to it."

"Oh, Papa, you are so vexing!"

Then her father flanked her with an attack against which she had no defense. "If you are so against it, perhaps it would be better if you stayed here in the East."

Juliet shut her mouth with a snap. Her glare decried an unfair advantage taken, but when she spoke, her tone was demure.

"My place is with you, Papa. Whether I think you are foolish or not does not matter."

Crowley smiled. "So like your mama. Even in your concessions, you act the victor. What am I to do with you, child?"

"Take me with you."

"I would not have it otherwise, Jules. If I've never said so before, I depend upon you for your strength and counsel. I've missed you sorely while in the field of this civil war. I look forward to returning to the West, where we know, even if we don't understand, our enemies."

Pleased by his words, Juliet embraced her father, but her misgivings didn't lessen. "At least I'll be there to watch your back, should any of your own men try to stick something in it."

"I am comforted in that knowledge."

Later, Juliet paced her Maryland hotel room, fretting over the situation. She was a born campaigner, taking up where her mother had left off. She knew no other life than the hard one she led, accompanying her father to isolated posts on the frontier. She didn't think to complain of the loneliness, the difficulties, or the continual danger. She considered those a part of daily living. What worried her was the men her father would command for the next year or two, men he'd faced in battle and had secured in a Northern prison—men her father would have to trust to follow his instructions and not desert at the earliest opportunity.

She had no fondness for Southerners. There had been a few in her father's last command in Texas before the war began. She thought them vain, arrogant, and more than a little lazy. The were used to lackeys doing their work and to women who'd fawn and faint to earn their favor—pompous fools, all of them, severing the Union for their own selfish purposes at the cost of innocent soldiers' lives, and forcing her to spend three long years in a prison of her own while her father was pulled from her life to fight in the Western Theater.

She'd hoped to put all that behind her when her father was reassigned to Fort Blair in the New Mexico territory. She had more tolerance for Indians defending their land than for *beaux galants* defending their self-indulgent ideals. How could her father trust such shallow aristocrats to cover his flank when under hostile fire?

She had a very bad feeling about the whole thing.

Juliet's feeling only worsened when she got her first glimpse of the recalcitrant troops.

They formed a ragged line just inside the gates of Point Lookout Prison, shivering with cold in thin uniforms. Mere skeletons, less than men, she thought—until she saw their eyes. Those eyes burned with a fever of pride and indomitable will.

Her father was going to have his hands full.

And it didn't take more than a second to figure out who was going to cause the most grief.

He wore the insignia of major, but even without it, there could be no mistaking him for anything but the Confederates' leader. Even weakened by the harsh conditions of the camp, he braced the blustery weather with a posture as stiff as a Stars-and-Bars-bearing flagpole. His ice-blue stare was fixed upon her father with an unblinking intensity, his look not one of arrogance or hostility, as it was with many others, but with a wary gauging, a careful studying. This man was no soft Southern fop. She read intelligence in those unswerving eyes, confidence in his rigid stance, and authority in the way the others deferred to him as her father spoke.

"I am Colonel John Crowley. From what

you know of me, I'm sure it's a name you've cursed since your incarceration in this... facility. From what I know of you, you are men deserving of more respect than this place allows you—a respect you have already earned by your cunning and valor in the field. It's my wish to put you in that field again, not here in this theater of brother against brother, but in the West, where we can all rally together against a common foe."

He scanned the impassive troop, looking for a reaction, finding none. Juliet wondered if he'd expected any from these hard and hostile men.

"I don't expect you to thank me. In fact, I am certain you'll have even more cause to curse me. A U.S. soldier on western duty has little to be grateful for. I have heard it said that where we are going, everything that grows pricks and everything that breathes bites. You will be facing an enemy tougher and more ferocious than you can imagine, and if you are foolish enough to think of them contemptuously as simple savages who are no match for our military acumen, they will be wearing your hair on their lances. The danger is ever-present. The pay is rotten, a miserly sixteen dollars a month for most of you, and you'll earn every nickel of it ten times over. So don't thank me for taking you out of this hellhole. You haven't seen hell yet. But you will. You will."

A rousing speech sure to win these sullen

troops over. Her father was not one to sugar-coat any given situation. He was forcing them to swallow a bitter pill while saying it was for their own good as they choked on it. She found herself studying the Rebel major, watching for any sign of response. His whiskered features might well have been slashed from stone. Juliet smiled. He probably thought, just as his men must think, that they'd endured the worst life could offer. How quickly they'd discover they were wrong!

As if he felt her interest, the major's steely gaze cut over to where she sat, bundled in a rented hack. Though protected from the weather, she felt vulnerable to the sudden penetrating cold of his stare. A tremor raced through her, but instead of a chill, she was suffused by heat, a confusing warmth of response and unbidden reaction.

Confusing because she wasn't one to be intimidated by a man. She'd grown up in the army and considered herself the mental and in many cases the physical equal of a man in uniform. Not understanding her own emotions, she looked away, embarrassed, then back, angered that she should feel guilty. But she no longer had his attention. It was riveted on her father. A strange shiver rattled her sensibilities. The man unsettled her. And for that reason, she disliked the Confederate officer before they'd exchanged a single word.

"I've told you what you have to look forward to," her father said with his typical brusqueness. "Now, there's something I want from each of you. I would have you swear allegiance to our United States of America and will take your word as gentlemen that you will not raise your hand against her for the duration of this war and that you will carry out the duties placed upon you by our Federal government, for which, in return, you will be paroled from this prison."

Juliet expected the Southerners to balk and they did. Rebellion, resentment, and open defiance flared in their hollowed eyes, in the tight flexing of their stubbled jaws, in the fisting of their hands.

Her father ignored the signs of approaching mutiny with a calm demand. "Major Banning, I would have an oath from you and your fellow officers, then you may turn the task over to your sergeant to relay to the rest of your men."

He wasn't going to do it. Juliet read refusal in the prideful narrowing of his glare and knew a moment of relief.

"Major?"

At her father's prompting, other emotions played over the lean and dangerously set features, strong emotions that challenged and humbled an inherent arrogance. She saw in that raw moment the cost of bowing to her father's command: a sacrifice of conscience, the crushing of loyalty and honor beneath the heel of desperate circumstance, the bending of an independent will for the good of many.

And for just that instant, she felt sympathy for the proud soldiers and their conviction-torn leader.

"Major?" her father repeated.

A tense pause was followed by the reluctant lift of Banning's right hand. The gesture was repeated by his two captains. Clearly, fiercely, they spoke the words binding themselves to the very nation they'd parted from with bloodshed and bitterness. Then the same oath was spoken by the enlisted men, their sentiments more apparent, their phrases more grudging. Juliet listened. And didn't believe a word.

They were traitors. They would go back on their vows the first chance they got.

How on earth were they all going to survive the trip to New Mexico?

But her father appeared satisfied with the pledges of loyalty, for he turned to his aide and ordered, "Secure the release of these men from the prison commandant. I want them bathed, clean shaven, issued uniforms, and fed all they can hold. Is that understood?"

"Yes, sir, Colonel Crowley."

Then, in a lower aside, the colonel said, "And don't take your eyes off them for a minute."

Chapter 2

Nothing felt as good as washing off three months of captivity. Noble scrubbed until his skin was as raw as his emotions and stinging like his conscience.

Because theirs wasn't a freedom without cost. A cost dear to pay.

The mood in the washhouse was strangely subdued. If his men had strong opinions, they kept them in check as baths were filled, then the filthy contents emptied, and razors scraped pallid faces bare.

His own reflection startled him. He didn't recognize the gaunt features at first, all hollowed by constant hunger, worries, and weariness. Not a vain man, he'd never put much store in looks, so it wasn't his haggardness that alarmed him. It was the guilt shadowing his stare. He had the look of a man who was haunted.

"You did the right thing, Noble."

George Allen's freckled face appeared in the

glass alongside his. Allen was close to twenty and looked all of maybe fourteen. An innate innocence kept his features free of harsh experience, even after the horrors he'd seen. A small-town boy, his only ambitions were to return to the church where he was baptized and to lead its congregation of fewer than four dozen. Allen's spiritual optimism had pulled the men through more than one dismal night.

And now the young reverend thought to apply that same gentle tolerance in the hope of quieting his commander's regrets. Noble didn't envy him the impossible task.

"You've your men to think of before military pride," Allen told him with conviction. "It wasn't an easy choice, but it was the right choice."

"I wonder."

"Don't second-guess your instincts, Noble. They're all that's kept us alive."

"I thought you believed it was divine intervention."

Used to his teasing mockery, George took no offense. "God works in a variety of ways."

Noble's smile took a wry turn. "My reasons aren't all that divine, George."

"Saving men at the sacrifice of your own honor?" His tone grew hushed, almost reverent. "I can't think of a more unselfish motive—or one that will cause more personal pain."

"That's only part of it. The rest—the rest is more inspired by darkness than divinity."

George's unblemished brow puckered in concern. "I don't understand."

Noble stared into those haunted eyes, trying to find the cocky confidence of the man who'd once stared back at him. "No, you wouldn't, George. You're a good, decent fellow with his mind on higher goals. I'm afraid mine are a bit more grounded in earthly pursuits."

"Such as?" He stared at his superior with a look akin to you-could-do-no-wrong worship. Noble hated to destroy that naïveté. But he did so with a single cutting claim.

"Finding out who in our unit betrayed us to Crowley."

"Betrayed?" George whispered the word. "Noble, are you sure? I can't believe that—that one of us—" He couldn't finish, the idea too abhorrent.

Noble cleaned off his razor with quick flicks of his hand, his mood as lethal as that bared blade. "I didn't want to believe it, either, but there's no other answer. Only our own men were privy to the details of the raid. There's no other way Crowley could have been prepared and waiting for us. They sprang that trap before we could fire a shot. Someone told them to be there, George. And I intend to find out who."

There was a moment's silence as the younger man absorbed the fierceness of his impassioned claim. He seemed shocked, alarmed—because his god had suddenly shown he had feet of clay? "And then what?"

George asked at last, obviously disturbed. "Take matters into your own hands? Noble, there are higher courts than those of man."

"You mean leave the traitor's judgment to God? I'm not that patient, my friend. Justice will be done here, by me." He glanced at the young reverend's furrowed brow. "I can see that troubles you, George." Again the cynical smile. "Have I fallen in your estimation?"

"No. No, of course not. It's not up to me to determine who falls where and why. My influence is limited in that area."

"Well, use that influence on my behalf. Even if I'm not acting as the right hand of God, I'm dealing out his laws as only I know how."

"I'll do my best, Noble." He said that with all seriousness, and Noble didn't chide him for the depth of his belief. It didn't hurt to have God in his corner. This wasn't a complex matter, like that which called Him to choose between North and South. It was a simple case of right and wrong, of trust and betrayal. Surely God wouldn't have any trouble siding with him.

"Major Banning?"

Noble turned to face Crowley's aide.

"The colonel would like you to join him for drinks at his hotel. I'm to wait and escort you."

"Is he afraid I'll try to run off?" Noble shrugged into the fresh uniform shirt, his lip curling at the color. Blue. Annoyance crisped his question. His word was something he didn't care to have doubted.

"It's more for your protection, sir. Your accent, sir. It might cause—difficulties were I not with you."

"Ah. A Samaritan effort, eh, George?" He looked back at the mirror and rubbed his gaunt cheeks. "I wouldn't want to be mistaken for an escapee from the prison camp. I suppose next he'll be ordering me not to speak in public. I've already traded away my allegiance, why not my birthright?"

"Noble—"

Noble brushed off Allen's concern by adopting a tight smile.

"I'll be ready in a moment, Corporal. And don't look so alarmed. I may be bitter but I'm not suicidal."

Strange how one took for granted the simple freedom of moving through a crowded room. With his Union escort trailing behind him, Noble crossed the busy hotel lobby, aware of the admiring looks he drew in his crisply pressed Northern uniform. He tried not to let it matter that the stamp on his buckle was USA instead of CSA or that the fabric was blue instead of butternut—tried, but wasn't very successful, especially when approached by a gray-haired matron who seized his hand, forcing him to pause.

"God bless you, young man," she cried in a fragile tone. "Are you off to fight those damn

Rebels? My husband and sons are in the middle of it. McNamara. Maybe you know them."

"No, ma'am. I'm sorry, I don't." He spoke quietly, slowly, to de-emphasize his accent, not so much to protect himself but to spare the poor woman clutching at his hand. "I'm on my way to the western frontier."

She sighed in aggravation. "Why are we wasting fine officers out there when they are so desperately needed on our own home front? Let the Indians have their deserts. I want my family home for Christmas."

"I sympathize with you, ma'am."

When the woman began to frown at the sound of his drawn-out *is*, Crowley's aide cut in with a prompting. "Sir, the colonel is waiting."

Noble nodded then smiled at the woman even as she jerked her hand free, as if his touch was suddenly repellent. "I shall hold your family in my thoughts, ma'am."

He reared back as her spittle stung his cheek.

"At least you won't be shooting at them, you damned Sesesh. You dishonor the uniform, sir."

Noble wiped off the dampness of her scorn as she swept away through the crowd. A wife, a mother, not an enemy to be despised, as she obviously despised him. That made her attack all the more personal. He was unable to move until the corporal prodded impassively, "This way, Major Banning."

Crowley had an elegant suite on the hotel's second floor. Noble was directed into the posh sitting room that joined the two bedchambers. There he was greeted by the scent of a good cigar and a hearty handshake from the man who until hours ago had been his greatest nemesis.

"Major, you're looking much better than when last I saw you. It must be the uniform."

"It's probably the bath."

Crowley laughed, a rich, full-bodied sound of genuine delight. "Have a drink, Major. I should like to toast our new alliance."

"No, thank you, sir. I prefer a clear head about me when I'm discussing business, military or otherwise."

Crowley wasn't stupid. He read between the lines of Noble's refusal. There was nothing the Southerner cared to drink to—not with the man responsible for having him imprisoned for the last three months.

"Very well. Shall we get right to that business then?"

"I wouldn't refuse a cigar if it was offered."

Crowley smiled and gestured to a box on one of the side tables. "Help yourself."

While Noble trimmed and lit the aromatic cigar, he used the time to study the other man. He knew his reputation, but he'd never seen the colonel until just that day at the prison. He knew Crowley as a shrewd tactician in the field. In person, Crowley conveyed the kind of directness and confidence that led others to follow without question. But Noble had plenty of questions and he began them without delay.

"Why my unit, Colonel? Surely if you needed a troop of galvanized Yankees, you could have requested one that held you in less personal animosity."

"So true. Have a seat, Major, and don't be so modest. I've seen your men in action. I don't mind their hostility just as long as they can direct some of it to the enemy we'll be facing together."

Noble settled into one of the plush chairs and drew deeply on his smoke before continuing bluntly, "They're not going to like taking orders from the man who's responsible for the deaths of a good number of their friends, both in the field and in that prison."

"You're not going to like it, is that what you're saying, Major?"

Noble's icy stare was his answer.

Crowley's demeanor toughened. "I don't give a damn if you like it or not just as long as you follow the orders you're issued. You've given your oath that you would."

"Not of my own free will, sir. Your case of blackmail was quite convincing."

Crowley didn't look particularly pleased, but he didn't try to refute Noble's claim. He couldn't. "I'm not ashamed of the means I employed. The government has given me every right to demand your service, coerced or no. What I need to know is will you obey those orders once given? Are you a man of your word, Major Banning?"

"My men and I are yours to command for the duration of this war, Colonel," Noble stated through gritted teeth. "I will personally guarantee the behavior of my men, but I would have something from you in return."

Intrigued, Crowley leaned forward. "And what is that?"

"I want the name of the informer who turned his own comrades over to you."

Crowley sat back, his mood growing granite-hard. "No. That I can't give you."

"I will not take my men into the field with a traitor in our midst. Give me the name and let us take care of our own dealings."

"You will not. You are under my command now, and such matters of quasi-justice are no longer yours to claim."

"The name, Colonel, or I promise I will do my best to make your western tour a living hell."

"Threats, Major?"

"No, sir."

"Let me set you straight right now. I will not be manipulated and I will not betray a confidence."

"You only encourage others to betray theirs, is that it?" Noble sneered. "And that leaves you blameless. Is that what you think, Colonel?"

Narrowing his gaze at the insubordinate tone, Crowley said, "I will not apologize for things done under the dictates of war. That war no longer applies to us, Major. Put it behind you, for if you cannot, I will have you and your men back at the Point before sunrise. Is that clear?"

Before Noble could answer, a low, whiskey-throated voice intruded.

"Excuse me, gentlemen. Am I interrupting?"

Both men rose as the woman Noble remembered seeing at the prison entered from one of the suite's bedchambers.

"Major Banning, my daughter, Juliet."

Except for a voice that made a man's skin tighten in anticipation of equally dusky pleasures, Juliet Crowley wasn't a woman to excite a man into an immediate passion. She was no conventional beauty. Nothing about her was conventional. Tall enough to meet most men eye to eye and beyond the bud of youth by several years, she possessed the same steely gaze her father used to put inferiors in their place.

Against deeply and unfashionably bronzed skin, her hair was a pale blush of gold, swept back and tied with a simple ribbon at her nape. Her gown was of modestly cut calico, the lack of hoops adding to the illusion of intimidating height. Combined with her no-nonsense stare were strongly cut features that spoke of intelligence and stubbornness. She might have been dismissed as handsome yet unremarkable if not for a pair of the most voluptuous lips Noble had ever seen. Full, soft, kissable lips that firmed into an uncompromising line when she noticed his attention lingering there.

"Major, I'm sorry to say it's not a pleasure to meet you."

"Forgive her, Major Banning," Crowley said quickly to cover his daughter's lack of manners. "I fear I'm to blame for Juliet thinking honesty takes precedence over politeness. I've led her to believe that men admire openness in a woman."

"You are not mistaken, Colonel." Then to the unapologetic Juliet, Noble said, "Let me assure you that the pleasure is indeed mine."

"Are you being honest, Major Banning?" she chided. "I thought Southern men liked their women as docile as their slaves."

"I can't speak for all Southern men, Miz Crowley, only for myself. And I, for one, have never owned a slave and prefer both my horses and my women spirited."

With the lift of one honey-colored brow, she drawled, "My, my, such bold claims."

"Tell me, Miz Crowley," Noble asked as she swept by him with a haughty indifference, "is it me you dislike or my former uniform?"

She glanced back over her shoulder to skewer him with a look. "Oh, it's you, sir."

He blinked, momentarily unsettled. "And why is that, ma'am?"

"Aside from your smug Southern platitudes, sir, I've grown sick of hearing your name in my father's every letter. That wily major, that clever Reb, that cunning Confederate." She made an uncharitable noise. "I feel as though we've been living together for the past three years and it's a familiarity that's bred contempt."

"Strange. Others who've lived with me for far longer have had many fewer complaints."

In the brief pause during which she scanned his left hand for sign of a wedding band, her father jumped in to head off another volley.

"Juliet, sheathe your sword. The major can hardly be blamed for my canonizing him for his brilliance in the field."

It was Noble's turn to go all flinty. "Were I so brilliant, I would not be here, sir."

Juliet smiled at him, pleased that she'd managed to ruffle his temper. That was enough to force him to wrestle it back under control. He regarded her with his own bland smile and a lift of one brow that conveyed a wry "Touché."

"Major, it's that brilliance in command that made me ask for your company," Crowley said, either oblivious to or ignoring the interplay between his guest and his daughter. "I've followed your career with interest. I've known men trained at West Point who could use some of your daring and initiative."

Juliet made another unkind sound. "Please, Father. He hardly needs your praise to feed his vanity. I'm sure he's quite insufferable already."

"It's not empty praise, my dear, as well you know. The major and his men have been a particularly annoying thorn in the Union's side, which is why I need them at Fort Blair. Now, Major Banning, I believe you were going to tell me where you plan to spend the next year or so, as a guest of our government or in service to it."

Noble couldn't make a decision that would force his men back to the oppressive harshness of Point Lookout, not after allowing them to stand as free men again.

And damn him, Crowley knew it.

With all the dignity he could muster, Noble said, "I'll take that drink now, Colonel."

Crowley accepted his answer with a satisfied nod. "My dear, would you please pour. The major and I have particulars to discuss."

What was it about the silky-voiced Southerner that worked her into such a lather? Juliet wondered as she sat quietly watching the two men talk. She knew she'd gone far beyond the latitude of good behavior. She'd been rude and confrontational, and was still bristly as a wild boar where the major was concerned. She told herself it was out of worry for her father—a comforting excuse but not the truth.

The truth had to do with how much better looking Noble Banning was up close, with his freshly shaven face and his black hair clean and trimmed. It had to do with the way her blood pounded in anticipation at the thought of bandying words with him and the way her palms had grown suddenly damp when he spoke of desiring spirit in his women. *His* women. And she was sure there were many.

She couldn't think why that would rankle, but it did.

She was a woman given to plain, outspoken opinion and not to flatteries—especially where she herself was concerned. She knew well what she was and was not. She was a well-educated female given unusual liberties. And she was not a beauty.

She had several pleasant features, and was aware that any number of her father's men would have her for a wife if only she'd give the nod of approval. But women were scarce in the West, and she'd prove a capable helpmate. Their admiration had nothing to do with her intelligence, her good-heartedness, or any of her natural talents. Not one of them would consider her as any more than a convenient servant and available bed warmer. And because those reasons weren't enough, she'd refused to give that nod.

Noble Banning, with his sophistication and bold claim that he admired a woman's independence even as he eyed her like a prospective brood mare, doubled the insult.

"Won't you, my dear?"

Juliet blinked at the intrusion of her father's voice into her dark musings. "What was that?"

"I told Major Banning that you would make

his men's wives feel welcome if any of them are able to join us at the railhead."

Blushing beneath her father's quelling stare, Juliet murmured, "Yes, of course." Then her flusters were gone as she looked at the unnervingly handsome Confederate. "But understand, it's no life of luxury. Few men can afford to keep a wife on what the army pays. We may have nothing more than tents to live in after the most miserable travel imaginable. The food is poor, the boredom is constant, the danger ever-present."

"Yet you've managed, Miz Crowley."

"I was born to it. Can your soft Southern ladies say the same?"

Noble's reply was cold enough to match the chill of her demeanor. "I don't think there are any soft, pampered ladies left in the Confederacy, Miz Crowley. To many, a tent and bad food would be a luxury."

Unwilling to look chagrined, Juliet said, "If they're willing, I'll teach them how to survive. A little female company is always appreciated."

"Even Southern company?" he challenged.

Her gaze narrowed. "This is not a woman's war, Major. We choose our causes more carefully."

He almost smiled.

Then, for some reason she didn't wish to consider, she asked, "Will your wife be joining you, Major?"

"I'm unmarried, Miz Crowley. I wouldn't

expect my family to uproot themselves for what I hope to be a short military career. I have plans waiting for me at home."

"And where is home, sir?"

"Kentucky. Pride County." He said that with a soft longing that made Juliet ache for a place she could call home with such deep fondness. She'd never known one. Then she frowned slightly in confusion.

"I thought Kentucky had cast its lot with the North?"

"Not all of it, ma'am. This conflict tore right through our midsection. Some of my best friends are wearing Union blue."

His gaze dropped, but not before she witnessed the pain of regret clouding his pale eyes. So his past loyalties were as divided as his future called him to be. It would take a man of strong convictions to survive such tearing upheavals. She took Noble Banning to be a man of convictions.

But were his dangerous convictions?

Could a man of divided loyalties be trusted on the frontier with a gun in his hand and a force of men riding at his command? Would his word be enough to tie him to a hated uniform a world away from where his friends and family were fighting an altogether different war against a country he was now pledged to serve?

She wondered. And she worried. Because in the West, one faced a vicious enemy and couldn't afford to fear one's supposed comrades.

"You'll be leaving all those friends behind, Major, and *their* causes, as well. If you don't stand together in the West, you fall separately. And I don't intend to fall because you don't keep your word." Let him think about that.

"You have nothing to fear, Miz Crowley," Noble assured her tightly. "My word is one of the few points of honor I've been allowed to retain, and I will keep it, as an officer and a gentleman. You may hold to it as zealously as you do your own virtue."

"You can't imagine my relief, sir," was her dry retort.

Noble placed his empty glass on the table and turned to Crowley. "Colonel, if there's nothing else, I'd like to return to my men. They asked if you could find a way to see their letters safely home. Their families deserve to know their whereabouts."

"I'll do what I can, Major. See my aide gets them in the morning. Our train leaves at nine. When you get off, it will be in a world unlike any you've ever seen. Prepare yourself and your men."

"We are ready for anything, sir."

Crowley smiled. "I trust you will be. Or the next letters sent home to their families will be sent by me."

Chapter 3

Upon leaving the train in the New Mexico Territory, Juliet abandoned all hope of comfort and peace of mind. It wasn't the lack of personal comfort in the overland miles ahead that alarmed her. It was the thought of sharing those miles with Maisy Bartholomew.

The Southern captain's wife epitomized all Juliet's preconceived notions of the plantation belle: pale, helpless, spoiled, and superior. During the long train ride, Juliet added several more qualities to that unpleasant list. The woman was also lazy, stupid, and mean-spirited. The brunt of that temper was borne by Colleen McDonnal, a gentle Irish girl hastily hired in St. Louis to tend to the aristocrat's every whim.

Maisy Bartholomew made complaining into an art. Nothing suited her. The air was too cold, too humid, too dry. The food too spicy, too salty, too bland. Her maid was too slow, too hurried, too clumsy. And for bringing her with him, her husband was too insensitive for words.

And after days together in the same rail coach, Juliet was ready to strangle her.

She gave the woman a week, maybe two at most. Perhaps not that long if she surrendered to her overwhelming urge to shove the nasty female from the platform beneath the steel wheels of the train.

But Juliet felt a sudden stab of sympathy for even this loathsome creature, because upon her first view of the Southwest, the woman was clearly terrified.

While on the train, there remained an air of civility. Standing on the sand-bleached platform, looking out over miles of desert, all traces of civilization were stripped away.

"Oh, Lord help us," Maisy whispered in dismay. Surely she must have thought they were entering the gates of hell.

In a way, she was right.

Panic sent her scurrying to her husband as the troops approached in a ragtag order.

"Donald," she pleaded frantically. "Donald, you must send me home. This is not what I imagined."

"Maisy, darlin', it's too late for that, I'm afraid. Calm yourself, my dear."

She wouldn't be quieted. To his embarrassment, she dragged the captain out of the ranks before his men.

"But Donald, please! You can't mean to take

me out into that savage country. I won't go. I'll wait here for the next train—"

His claim was firm, his reasoning unarguable. "You cannot wait here, Maisy. I've no money for the ticket back to the Carolinas. I spent it all to bring you this far. There's no going back. I'm sorry."

She stared up at him in horror, her delicate chin quivering. "But Donald, I shall perish."

"I'm sorry, my dear," he said more forcefully. Then, the matter concluded in his mind, disengaging himself from her clutching hands, he rejoined his men, marching away without looking back to witness her devastation.

That's when Noble Banning stepped in.

While Juliet watched, unable to move away because of the small size of the platform, he approached the near-hysterical woman and gently took her hand.

"Mrs. Bartholomew—Miz Maisy—don't fret. It's just the strangeness that has you so upset. You're made of sterner stuff than you realize."

The frightened female clung to his soothing words as desperately as she clutched at his hand. "Do you think so, Major?"

"I'm certain, ma'am. You know how much your husband depends on you to be strong for him."

A tremulous smile. "Yes, yes, he does at that."

"Why, coming home from a hard march to

your lovely face is all the medicine a man needs to cure his ills."

A blush accompanied the small smile.

"I can understand a fine woman like yourself being flustered under the circumstances," he continued in the same silky tone, flattering and calming the nervous female like a highstrung horse. "But you'll be all right, ma'am. You have my word on that. Miz Crowley here can take care of you and put your mind at ease."

Caught by his unexpected claim and the sudden pinning shift of his stare, Juliet managed a stiff smile. She made herself come over to put a consoling arm about the trembling Southerner's shoulders.

"Now, Mrs. Bartholomew," she began with a coaxing authority, "I want you to look over at your husband right now and give him your sunniest smile and wave. You can't expect him to do his duty if he's worried about you. Do it now."

Maisy lifted a soft hand and conjured a wan smile to earn a grin of relief from the captain before he directed his unit around the side of the station and out of sight.

"I'll leave you in good hands, Miz Maisy," Noble crooned. As he placed a light kiss on the woman's knuckles, his gaze slipped to Juliet to convey his thanks. She pursed her lips in wry acknowledgment.

If only he know she'd considered tightening those good hands about the lady's neck...

The minute the handsome officer was out of sight, Maisy Bartholomew flung off Juliet's arm.

"I'll thank you to mind your own business," she snapped. All traces of vulnerability had disappeared. "I do not need you to tell me how to handle my husband."

Juliet washed her hands of the situation with a dry, "No, I'm sure you don't."

She was relieved from further discourse by the arrival of her father. He was swaggering about, happily in his element.

"Jules, we'll be a few hours getting the men outfitted for the journey to Fort Blair. Do you think you can manage your own baggage and that of Mrs. Bartholomew? I can't spare anyone at the moment."

"Of course, Papa." Didn't she always?

"Very good. I'll have your conveyance brought 'round as soon as possible and someone to help with the loading."

With a nod and a sigh, Juliet cheerfully abandoned Maisy Bartholomew to see to the unloading of her worldly goods.

After a dusty forty-five-minute wait, their transportation arrived. The mule-drawn army ambulance commonly used to carry wives overland was without a doubt the most uncomfortable means ever created for that purpose. Fitted like a cowboy's chuck wagon, it had an outside seat for the driver and two seats facing each other inside. Canvas sides and ends could be rolled up to allow the hot wind to blow through or lowered for stifling privacy. Water kegs hung underneath for both passengers and beasts, and a chain-supported platform was suspended in the rear for storing luggage.

"Can I give you a hand, Miz Crowley?"

She turned from the mountain of bags to the Confederate major, suppressing her desire to sweep him from top to toe with an appreciative gaze. He grinned, as if aware of her dilemma. "Surely you've more important things to do than serve as baggage handler."

"Not at the moment. I thought I'd check on Mrs. Bartholomew."

Juliet sniffed. "She's fine. She's busy haranguing her poor maid, so you needn't worry that the troops' morale will suffer from any more of her outbursts."

"I appreciate you stepping in as you did." His sudden earnestness shocked her from her indignation but left a wry aftertaste.

"I wasn't given much choice, Major."

His smile acknowledged her lack of volunteer spirit, and Juliet was beset with a sudden breathlessness. My, but he was an eyeful up close in his dapper blue uniform with the hot western breeze ruffling through his black hair. A steady diet on the trip west had filled in the deeper hollows of his face while leaving the dramatic angles to sculpt a lean perfection. And his eyes were so searingly blue they dazzled like the cloudless New Mexico sky. The cool, intelligent eyes of her enemy.

"Are *all* these bags yours, ma'am?"

"Mine and Mrs. Bartholomew's. We're setting up households at Fort Blair." She wondered why she felt it necessary to explain but heard herself making excuses. "There's no telling if they have a decent sutler's store, so I've grown used to carrying everything we might need."

"A resourceful lady."

"I try to be, sir."

He began loading the wagon boot with trunks, bags, and bandboxes, the last belonging to the style-conscious Maisy. Juliet traveled with a practical wardrobe pared down for utility.

Noble gave a sudden groan as he struggled to get under one of the battered boxes. "What are you carrying in this? Gold bars?"

"Something more precious than gold, Major. My books. Be careful."

"Don't worry. I don't plan to strain anything."

"I meant be careful not to drop them."

"Of course. What was I thinking?" He shoved the heavy crate into the boot and straightened slowly, rubbing at his lower back. "What kind of books, if you don't mind me asking?"

"A little of everything. Poetry, philosophy, history. My interest is in the Napoleonic Wars and anything French at the moment."

"Really."

"You sound surprised, Major. That I am

well read, or by my topics of interest?"

"Not surprised, Miz Crowley. Just hoping you'll be willing to loan out some of your volumes once we get established at the fort."

"I am not a library, sir. I place considerable value on my books."

"Of course you do. Forgive me for asking."

He bent to continue the loading and Juliet took a moment to consider her reaction. She was being rude and miserly, and neither trait pleased her.

"Once I'm set up, you may borrow whatever you like, Major Banning."

He glanced up at the offer. "Thank you, Miz Crowley. I look forward to examining your volumes." He was smiling as he grabbed the next crate, then reared back in alarm at the sudden loud squawking. Juliet rushed forward.

"Oh, do be careful. That's Hortense. She and Hernando will ride up with me."

Noble regarded the crated poultry with a blink of surprise. "Dinner?"

She snatched the crate away as if he'd planned on roasting them up right there. "Fresh eggs, Major Banning."

He turned to look at the spotted goat that had begun chewing on the hem of his jacket. Pulling the fabric free, he said, "Don't tell me—"

"Fresh milk. Things you take for granted until you have none."

"And what's this fellow's name? Billy?"

"Willamina."

"Does she ride with you, too?"

"Don't be silly. Tie her behind. She's a regular trooper and can make the walk easily."

"And these things?"

She took the potted plants from him and placed them gently inside the wagon. "These are mine as well. They've been traveling with me for years."

"A strange group of companions, Miz Crowley."

"The only ones I have, sir."

On that melancholy note, she strode away, leaving Noble bemused and more intrigued than he cared to be by the quixotic female who considered houseplants and barnyard creatures her only friends.

Looking ahead over the vast miles of desert, Noble agreed with Colonel Crowley's assessment. It was like nothing he'd ever seen.

Born and bred in the lush green of middle Kentucky, Noble was used to thick grasses under his feet and to leafy trees casting a relieving shade, to hills that were forested and water aplenty.

New Mexico was a different world.

Under a sky of unbroken blue, sand and scrub stretched from horizon to horizon. Plant life crouched low to the ground, none growing high enough to shade a jackrabbit. A harsh, wild landscape, offering little, forgiving nothing. His new home for the next months or maybe years.

Noting his misgivings, Crowley angled his horse closer.

"Humbling, isn't it?"

Unwilling to admit to intimidation, Noble asked, "When do my men get proper sidearms? I think you've led us far enough away from civilization to trust us with the means to save our own lives."

Without hesitation, Crowley swiveled in his saddle. "Corporal, break out the armaments."

A change came over the thirty-two former Confederate soldiers when they took possession of the seven-round Spencer carbines and Navy Colt revolvers. They became fighting men again, sitting tall in the saddle, in control of their own destinies. In that moment, Noble realized he could never regret his decision to free them from Point Lookout. These were men meant to battle for survival, not to huddle helplessly beneath an enemy's reluctant charity. At least on these cruel plains, they would have the opportunity to strike back against a bitter fate, and if they were to die, would die as free men. He might have thanked Crowley for that chance, but he wouldn't. Nor would Crowley have expected him to.

Armed and in columns of four, they set out for Fort Blair. Thirty-two sullen Southerners, twelve raw recruits, three seasoned sergeants, and five officers escorting an army ambulance and a supply wagon.

Riding straight into hell.

* * *

The wagon struck a deep rut, throwing the three occupants back and forth. Juliet dodged the penduluming plant pots as frantic clucking was followed by a filtering of chicken feathers. Maisy Bartholomew's strained temper cracked.

"Must those creatures be inside with us?"

"The travel is as hard on them as it is on us," Juliet said with what she hoped was a calming sensibility. But her companion wouldn't be soothed.

"I did not expect to have to share my accommodations with barnyard refugees. I insist you put them out this instant."

Juliet's demeanor hardened into a likeness of her father's. "Mrs. Bartholomew, I agreed to put up with your squawking, so the least you can do is reciprocate."

The woman drew an indignant breath, but seeing the steel in the other's glare, thought better of releasing more protests. Instead, she began a fierce fluttering of her fan within the ovenlike heat of the closed wagon. They'd had to drop the flaps when Maisy complained continually of the dust. To Juliet, the dust was preferable to the stifling temperature.

Sweltering minutes ticked by, slowly adding up to hours. Had Maisy been the least bit interested in what lay ahead, Juliet could have filled the time by educating her about frontier life: where to hang laundry to dry so that it wouldn't be ripped to ribbons by the wind-driven sand, putting tin cans underneath bed legs to keep ants from crawling up them, how to deal with niggardly quartermasters who doled out every nail as if it came from their own pockets and that sour milk made a passable skin bleach and borax would soften water for a hair rinse. She would have even shared her own secret—a mixture of castor oil and pure whiskey scented with lavender for a fine homemade shampoo. But any attempts on her part led to a quick dismissal.

"Colleen will take care of those matters," was the captain's wife's answer to everything.

So Juliet gave up and stayed silent, sympathizing with the freckled girl who would have the miserable task of pleasing her impossible mistress.

By late afternoon, Juliet could no longer stand the oppressive heat inside the ambulance. Across from her, Maisy and Colleen were dozing fitfully, leaving her to face her discomfort alone. Impulsively, she threw open one of the canvas sides to address the driver.

"Private, see if you can find me a mount. I'd like to ride for a while, if I can."

"Yes, ma'am."

It was no cooler in the saddle. The desert air lay in heavy waves that rippled the distant scenery. But just the freedom of sitting a horse made the journey more comfortable. She tucked her skirts to assume an unladylike straddle, and nudged the animal forward, cantering along the ranks to where her father rode flanked by the three Southern officers.

"Hello, my dear. I wondered how long it would be before you tired of civilian travel."

She smiled, too aware of Captain Bartholomew to say it was the company she'd tired of. "How much farther?"

"We'll put in another hour before making camp. We'll see Fort Blair day after tomorrow."

Juliet rode on in contented silence. This was the life she was used to, the sound of men on the march with sabers rattling to the rhythm of hoofbeats, on the move from post to post. Her thoughts were already far ahead to the things she'd have to do to make the isolated post a home for herself and her father. Looking upon it as a challenge rather than a hardship was something her mother had taught her as they migrated the length of Texas as army nomads. She'd never heard her mother complain, despite conditions unfit for man, let alone a woman with a child. And that was the example Juliet swore to follow as the monotonous drum led her farther into the New Mexico wasteland at her father's side.

Needing daylight to accomplish the task of setting up camp, the column halted early and began the complicated routine of preparing for the night. Picket lines were strung and the animals fed and watered. After guards were posted, water and fuel details were assigned and two-man tents erected on the sandy soil. Without cooks while on march, the men did for themselves, parboiling their ration of salt pork and roasting green coffee beans in their own skillets before settling in for the evening.

Exhausted in body and mind, Juliet retired early, the sound of her father's voice outside their tent as he spoke to his officers comforting her like a sonorous lullaby, just as it had since she was a baby. Accompanying his low tones were the soft, drawling syllables of the Southerners, making a quiet night music as she drifted off to sleep. The last image to dance traitorously through her weary thoughts was that of a certain Southern major.

Reveille came before daybreak so that they could be on the march before the light. It was a routine Juliet followed instinctively: first call roll out at 4:45, reveille and stable call at 4:55, mess call at 5:00 followed by thirty minutes in which to prepare and eat a hurried meal. The camp was struck at 5:30, boots and saddles at 5:45, fall in at 5:55, and forward march at 6:00. It was a rhythm as predictable as the tides.

Choosing to ride over the dubious pleasure of listening to how Maisy Bartholomew spent her first night rough camping, Juliet bound her hair back in a heavy knot and secured a flat cavalry hat on her head to shade her eyes against the glare of daybreak.

As she fell in with the precision of a veteran campaigner, it was impossible for Juliet not to notice the change in the Southern soldiers. Seemingly overnight, with the aid of their campfire fraternity and the extra weight of steel riding on their hips, all of their cocky bravado had returned. Hints of their former allegiance were evident in the knotting of a butternut-colored sash here, in a CSA buckle there, in the jaunty cockade tucked into the band of a regulation hat. Small jabs of defiance that her father chose to overlook, but that Juliet feared were symptoms of a greater, more dangerous outbreak of sentiment. She watched them warily.

As the day progressed, those subtle shades of rebellion grew more blatant. Orders issued by Northern sergeants were ignored until repeated by a Southern counterpart. Ranks shifted, forming a division like the separation rending a nation apart, with Rebs bunching together in front and Yanks eating their dust in the rear. Again, nothing was said, but Juliet knew her father too well to think him ignorant of what was happening. Perhaps he preferred to let them stage their little insurrections in hopes that it would soothe a pride rubbed raw by defeat and incarceration. Perhaps he feared a reprisal now would end in an overt refusal to comply. If that was the case, he was wise to wait until they were closer to the reinforcements at Fort Blair.

Still, it made for an uneasy ride as tensions chafed across a razor edge of distrust.

"How are you faring, daughter?"
Juliet glanced up from her tin of bitter coffee

to smile at her father's concern. "Better than Mrs. Bartholomew."

The entire camp had been privy to an argument between husband and wife that the thin canvas walls of a tent couldn't contain. Though Juliet couldn't sympathize with the woman for her accusations, she could understand her fears—fears of the unknown, of being without home or permanent shelter, the fear of vulnerability—fears Juliet suffered from in silence because speaking them aloud made them all too real.

"Now, Jules, don't be unkind. Not every female has your fortitude."

She could have pointed out that not every female grew up trailing behind a column of fours. She and Maisy Bartholomew were as different as the sun and moon. And she was suddenly angry with the captain for not showing a whit of common sense where his wife was concerned.

"He never should have brought her out here. Perhaps she's right in calling him insensitive. You'd think a man would know his own wife well enough to realize her shortcomings. She'll never be frontier stock."

Crowley sighed at his daughter's cool assessment. "That's not for us to judge. It's their business."

"Well, if they want to keep it private business, they'd best discuss it at lower registers." She set aside her cup and bent to tug off her father's boots, standing them at the flap of the tent as ready sentinels.

"I'd hoped the company of another woman would keep the journey from being quite so tedious."

"Mrs. Bartholomew and I have little in common. She's made it clear that she prefers it that way."

"Perhaps things will improve between you when we get to Fort Blair."

She didn't share his optimism but offered a quiet, "Perhaps."

Crowley studied his daughter's solemn features for a moment then asked, "Regrets?"

"About what?"

"Coming along."

Her smile was genuine. "No."

"I know I promised you a home and a yard and regular neighbors. When this campaign is over—"

"There'll be another." She placed her hand on his arm before he could protest. "It's all right, Papa. I understand your devotion to the army, just like Mama did. You'll never settle for a yard and nosy neighbors."

"But you'd like to, wouldn't you?"

"Of course not, Papa. My place is with you. You know I'd have it no other way."

Having said that, Juliet glanced away. She could fool him with a cheery voice and false smile, but her eyes would give her away. He could read volumes in her gaze, he'd always told her, and this was one chapter she wanted to keep to herself, the chapter that would give her the happily-ever-after ending she'd always longed for.

Her answer satisfied him, either because he believed it to be the truth or because it was what he wanted to hear—probably a bit of both. He touched her hair, the gesture brief yet filled with grateful fondness.

"You get some sleep, my dear. Tomorrow we reach Fort Blair."

"And I'll be busy making another home for us."

Thankfully, he'd turned away and didn't catch the hint of bitter melancholy in her tone.

Because Juliet knew that though she'd try her best, Fort Blair would be nothing more than another temporary stop, not the home she desired.

Chapter 4

By noon the next day, John Crowley had had quite enough of the dissension in his ranks. He'd chosen to overlook the minor digressions at first. But now, though they were several hours out of Fort Blair, soaring temperatures and sore new recruits forced a midday stop for a cold meal of hardtack and salt pork. Now, the tensions were unmistakable.

"Sir, the Southern boys won't fall into ranks."

Crowley looked up at his sergeant, his irritation plain. "Won't? For what reason?"

"They say they're suffering from heat exhaustion."

"But you don't believe them."

"The only thing they're exhausting is my patience, sir. They've been dogging all morning, late to strike camp, slow to form columns, refusing to heed orders."

"Any orders?"

"Just *our* orders, sir."

Crowley dashed the remains of his meal to the ground and stood. Though he didn't look in her direction, he was well aware of his daughter's pointed stare. *I told you so*. At least she was wise enough not to speak it aloud in front of his subordinates.

That chiding would wait until they were alone.

"Where is Major Banning?"

"I believe he's tending to an ill-fitting shoe on his horse, sir."

"I'll be fitting my shoe to his arrogant—" The colonel broke off his mutterings as Juliet cleared her throat in a diplomatic reminder. "Fetch the major, Sergeant."

"Yes, sir."

Then Crowley shot his daughter a withering glare. "Don't say anything."

Her sandy brow lifted in a blameless arch.

"How can I command the respect of my men when my own child mocks me?" he mumbled direly, to earn Juliet's chuckle. Glowering at her unrepentant air, he strode to the nearest lounging Southerner to vent his annoyance.

"Private, why aren't you preparing to march?"

The solider glanced up indolently and drawled, "I ain't heard no order given, sir."

"Have you some hearing problem, soldier?"

"Nossir. My hearing's jus' fine."

"Then hear me when I tell you that if you aren't off that ground and saddled up in thirty seconds, you'll be walking the rest of the way to Fort Blair—in your socks. Did you hear me that time?"

"Yes, sir." The private jumped to his feet but made no immediate move toward his horse. Instead, he stood frozen, his expression one of infinite surprise.

"Private?"

Crowley caught the boy as he toppled forward, the shaft of an Apache arrow jutting out from between his thin shoulder blades.

"Indians!"

The cry brought Juliet to her feet, terror shooting up her spine in a stiffening bolt. For a moment, her mind was blank to all but the horrible memories of a girl of nine—to the vivid images of faces bright with menacing paint thrusting between the flaps of their wagon. To the sounds of her mother's screams. Even though her hands flew up to cover her ears, those anguished cries echoed through her head—cries that sounded like her own. . . .

A sudden impact sent her sprawling headlong to the ground, her cheek grinding against hard-packed sand, her breath knocked from her by the force of a man's covering weight. Her first thought was to struggle, but the wind-sapping fall had disconnected mind from body.

"Stay down."

There was no mistaking the source of the curt command. It was Noble Banning's prostrated form pinning her to the desert floor. For a moment, her awareness of him swallowed up all else. She could hear the harsh intake of his breath as it fanned her face, could feel the powerful drum of his heartbeats, could smell the hot wool of his uniform jacket and see the blueing of his Navy Colt next to her head as its barrel sought out targets. The reality of him helped push the other, darker memories back into perspective, allowing her to get a grip upon her fear.

And suddenly the danger of the man holding her close, the man who'd witnessed her weakness, was greater than the threat she couldn't see.

"Get off me," she wheezed.

"We're under attack."

His words were direct, punctuated by the bark of carbines, yet the softness of his tone held a purposeful comfort, relaying a message that she had nothing to fear. An empty comfort. Because she knew better. And she knew how to defend herself.

"I have a gun in the wagon."

Her no-nonsense reply told him that she'd recovered from the momentary shock. His embrace loosened and she was able to wriggle free. Without so much as a thank-you or a second glance at her savior, she started running. Staying low to the ground, she scrambled for the safety of the wagon, refusing to pause even when clods of dirt spit up in front of her from bursts of enemy rifle fire.

Maisy and Colleen clung together in the belly of the wagon, squealing in terror. Their petrified features rose up when Juliet tossed back the canvas, giving her another shock of remembrance. She shook off the image of a woman and her child, then hurriedly climbed inside.

"Stay low," she warned the frightened pair as she reached under her seat for the solid feel of her Spencer repeater. At the sight of the rifle, the two women quieted to an anxious whimpering. After checking the chambers, Juliet turned back the canvas side just far enough to give her an unrestricted view of their surroundings.

There was nothing to see. The Apache knew how to make themselves invisible amongst the mesquite and thorny shrubs that didn't look as though they would hide so much as a feather. From their concealment, the Indians fired at their leisure, using single-shot rifles and the more deadly bow and arrow to pick off any careless soldier who made himself a target. Maisy screamed as an arrowhead thudded into the side of the ambulance, but Juliet didn't flinch. Then Colleen edged up beside her with a huge dragoon pistol braced in both trembling hands.

"I'll not make it easy for them unholy savages to make off with me hair."

Juliet praised her bravado with a tight smile, then continued to scan the thickets. Panic beat in her breast when she thought of her father out in the open. She'd seen several men fall. Had he been among them? She didn't dare to seek him out.

A taut silence settled over those lying belly down in the dirt and those hunching down in the wagon as minutes crept by without the fateful twang of the bowstring sounding.

"Why have they stopped?" Maisy asked in a quavering voice, not rising up so much as an inch from her crouched position on the floorboards.

"I don't know."

"Have they run off?" Colleen asked, hopeful yet cautious, too. "We were sitting ducks. Why would they leave?"

"I don't know," Juliet said again. She, too, was wondering. Though she didn't think they'd been attacked by a force of more than three or four, that was a large enough number to whittle them down to a like-sized group.

Then Juliet gave a gusty sigh of relief when she heard a beautiful sound wafting on the dusty air.

The bugle from Fort Blair.

So that's Indian-fighting.

Until that moment, Noble hadn't realized how truly ignorant he was about the situation he'd committed himself and his men to.

Cautiously, he lifted himself out of the dirt. His system hummed from the familiar rush of excitement and horror that came after battle, but those sensations were now mixed with a feeling of awe. He and his men had come up against some of the best military forces known to history. They themselves were no strangers to hit-and-run warfare. But he'd never engaged an enemy he couldn't even see in territory so wild and foreign. All his knowledge of conflict came from set-piece battles fought on wooded terrain against an opponent he could second-guess. Nothing prepared him for this wily enemy, who struck without warning from a seemingly empty wasteland, then disappeared when the fight was no longer to his advantage.

Holstering his pistol, its chambers still warm, Noble suppressed his uneasiness when presenting his unprotected back to the wasteland, but he allowed himself to slip into the mode of efficient commander. Forgetting that he was not in charge, he called to his second.

"What are our casualties, Captain?"

Bartholomew's count was far from good news. "Privates Washburn, Morgan, Long, and LeRoy. Corporal Stevens."

Refusing to let himself feel for those men or even to conjure up their faces until it was safe to do so, Noble ordered, "Have a detail prepare them for travel. We'll pay our respects to them once we get to the fort."

"Yes, sir."

The fast-approaching dust cloud became an identifiable force of men on the horizon. A company from Fort Blair, no doubt, come to the rescue of raw recruits and Southern fools who were equally scared and ignorant of how to keep themselves safe on the frontier.

The column of dusty soldiers drew up, and its major dismounted to address Crowley with a sharp salute and a crisp, "We came as fast as we could once we heard gunfire."

"I applaud your haste, Major. And I welcome your escort back to Fort Blair."

No sooner had the major replied with a "Yes, sir, thank you, sir" than there was a delighted feminine cry.

"Miles!"

Juliet Crowley threw herself into the arms of the grinning major, who hugged her up and whirled her about unashamedly. Noble blinked in surprise, the unseen hostiles, the bundled bodies that were once friends momentarily forgotten.

He'd never thought . . . He'd never considered . . .

When he'd seen Juliet standing in shock, lost in an hysterical daze, an easy target for an Apache arrow, something had snapped inside him. Enough. He'd seen enough innocents die, and he could not bear to see Juliet Crowley's indomitable spirit added to that number. Without thought to his own safety, he'd raced across open ground to push her out of harm's way, but that's where honor ended.

How good she'd felt in his arms. Soft where a woman was meant to be soft, yet strong with the lean, hard muscle of an active life, a combination that sent all sorts of arousing signals through him.

He'd grown up around and had courted his share of women, the most beautiful, dainty, and refined creatures the Middle States had to offer, women trained to reflect well upon the men they married. He was used to gentle blushes and coquettish manners and had thought that was what he desired in the opposite sex—until he'd met the colonel's headstrong daughter and she'd knocked all his notions of desirability askew.

Not that he was in the market for a wife. His life was carefully regimented, meticulously planned down to the slightest detail. Once he got out of this army, he'd return to Pride County and set up his law practice, then he'd pick an appropriate hostess from the neighboring elite. It didn't really matter which he chose. The why was more important than the who. A woman of breeding and a background of power. A woman who would understand her place in his life and ask no questions. One who would be an asset to his career and his home—in that order.

Though he admired a woman of opinion and brain, he knew the practicality of having a docile and domestic bride who would do nothing to jeopardize his community standing. Nowhere was there room for a distraction like Juliet Crowley, not in his future, not in his present. He had specific goals in mind from which conscience could not be tempted if he meant to succeed within the narrow confines of Pride.

He knew that.

He accepted that.

So why was the sight of her twirling in another man's embrace enough to make him bristle protectively?

He'd never considered that Juliet Crowley might have someone waiting.

But why that should bother him, he didn't know. And it irritated him almost as much as the Yankee major's skewering glare when those narrowed eyes rested on him.

The tension was immediate, man to man, the staking of territory as basic as it was momentarily blatant. *She's mine, hands off*, was the message clearly conveyed by that one chill stare.

Wondering why he was perceived as a threat, Noble returned the look with a cool impassivity. Though he had no designs of his own on the bold Miss Crowley, he'd let the other sweat over his intentions.

"Miles, see that the dead and wounded are taken care of," Crowley instructed, apparently unaffected by the sight of his daughter in the major's arms. That casual acceptance made the situation somehow much more significant. "I'd like to get to the fort as soon as possible."

"I'll see to it, sir." He set Juliet away from him, giving her a quick smile and a softer, "We'll talk later."

And the way she leaned in close to whisper,

"We have much to discuss," did funny things to Noble's reason.

It wasn't Juliet Crowley, he told himself. It was the war. He'd been without female companionship for over three years. Any woman—not just the colonel's confrontational daughter—would scramble his thinking and excite his imagination.

He told himself that while his gaze followed her aggressive stride back to the wagon and he thought of her courage in the face of a threat that had his own men cowering in terror. Quite a woman, by any standard, the kind of woman a man would count himself lucky to have at his side in this wilderness—or anywhere else.

But not as his woman. And he reminded himself, just in case he was tempted to forget, his future had no place for the daughter of his enemy.

Even if she did present an intriguing challenge.

Chapter 5

They reached Fort Blair by midafternoon. Unlike the stockaded posts of the plains, Fort Blair was a collection of loosely assembled adobe buildings crouching low to the earth. The site was picked for strategic location rather than comfort. There was sufficient water to sustain the men, sufficient grass for the animals, enough timber for firewood situated on land level enough to support barracks, officers' quarters, stables, storehouses, and a parade ground. In the center of the drill ground rose the flag, its colors drooping listlessly, unstirred by the stifling air.

Juliet had lived in dozens like it.

Once her father reported and officially took command of the fort, the men were dismissed from ranks and shown to their accommodations. The enlisted men were crowded into barracks, where rows of bunks stood head-in to the walls. Even in the noncommissioned ranks, there was a definite hierarchy, with the senior enlisted men securing the best spots near the windows in summer and the stoves in winter. The sergeants had the luxury of small rooms off the barracks. Any privacy was a luxury. The privies were outside and bathhouses nonexistent, since there was no water to spare. Enlisted men with wives were allowed to live outside the barracks in their own tiny homes, but the best quarters were reserved by seniority of service. But even the best was little more than a small house with two to four rooms.

Juliet stood in the doorway of her new home and surveyed the interior dispassionately. A sheet-iron stove stood in the middle of the main room surrounded by scant furnishings: several campstools and unpainted chairs, and a dining table composed of three planks stretched across carpenter horses. Gray government blankets held down the dust on the floor, and curtains fashioned from unbleached cotton sheeting hung limply at the windows. A grim and uninviting welcome. She'd seen better. She'd also survived worse. Her mind hummed with possibilities. Some beet juice to dye the curtains. Colorful calico to tack over the packing-crate shelves. She'd crochet rugs for the floor from strips of an old gown. The extra touch of greenery from her plants would almost create the appearance of a real home.

Almost.

A sudden commotion from outside interrupted her musings. Juliet wasn't surprised to hear Maisy Bartholomew's strident tones rising in a shrill crescendo. Though she would have preferred to close her door and leave those troubles to another, as the daughter of the ranking officer, she knew it was her duty to make peace and restore a tenuous harmony.

"Mrs. Bartholomew," Miles Dougherty explained reasonably, "Captain Folley has a wife and three children. They would have to move from four rooms to two. Surely you can see how uncomfortable that would be for them, especially when we're dealing with a matter of only a few months."

But Maisy's jaw was set and her eyes flashed indignantly. "Does or does not my husband's earlier commission date entitle him to those quarters?"

"Of course it does," Pauline Folley answered with a resigned smile. She'd followed her husband from post to post long enough to understand the practice of "ranking out," which evicted a military family if an officer of superior service wanted the house. It was an often barbaric system, but an officer wouldn't be respected if he didn't demand his due. And Maisy Bartholomew was demanding. Loudly. There was nothing the Yankee captain's wife could do but back down gracefully. "We'll have our belongings removed immediately."

The situation was grossly unfair, but Juliet had no grounds to interfere. The military caste system was rigidly adhered to, regardless of inconvenience or personal sacrifice. It was a case of rank value, not family size, or in this case, a favoritism of North over South. But Maisy Bartholomew's attitude left a bad taste in the mouths of the occupants of Fort Blair. Juliet could read it in their closed expressions. And she feared subtle repercussions.

Apparently, she wasn't alone.

"Miz Folley?"

The matronly woman turned toward Noble Banning, probably wondering if she was about to be bumped from those two rooms to a tent.

"Ma'am, as a bachelor, I've no need for the four rooms I've been given. I'd gladly surrender them to Captain and Miz Bartholomew so that you and yours don't have to uproot yourselves to move two doors down. I'm sure Miz Bartholomew will agree to the logic of that, won't you, ma'am?"

Put on the spot, Maisy was forced to swallow down her bid for superiority by accepting a show of generosity. "Why that's fine by me, Major Banning. It wasn't my desire to put anyone out."

A true gentleman, Noble didn't allow his wry smile to escape, though Juliet caught the glint of amusement in his eyes. He waited outside her door until the others dispersed to settle into their appointed lodgings. Only when they were alone did he display a toothsome grin.

"Very diplomatically done, Major."

"Thank you, ma'am. Can't see that it'd do

anyone any good to get folks at cross purposes so early in our stay."

"And that's all that motivated your gesture?" She'd hoped there'd be more. The quick downward cant of his gaze said there was.

"A family shouldn't be put out on a vain woman's whim, regardless of rank."

"I quite agree."

"Then we've found some common ground at last." His words were teasing, but his sudden penetrating stare was not. It conveyed all sorts of deeper meaning, giving Juliet a start of alarm.

"A small patch, Major," she conceded gruffly, then turned away. On second thought, she looked over her shoulder. "I should have my books in order by tomorrow. Then consider the library open."

His dazzling smile shot a quiver to her soul. "Yes, ma'am. I look forward to looking under your covers." Again his grin took a devilish twist that both annoyed and aroused her sensibilities with its unspoken subtext.

"Rogue," she muttered to herself as she shut the door between them. A rogue and a rebel. She couldn't afford to forget the latter.

John Crowley stepped into the small adobe house hours later and felt instantly at home. Familiar touches already filled the stark rooms. A lacy cloth covered the plain pine board tabletop, where two place settings of well-traveled china were laid out for dinner.

His wife's woven shawl was folded over the back of a reassembled rocker set at an inviting angle next to the stove. His pipe and humidor and tattered leather slippers waited there as well. Plain daubed walls were adorned with a portrait of his late wife and the military citations that highlighted his long career. And those ferny green things his daughter insisted on carrying wherever they went leaned toward the harsh light at the windows. In his bedroom, he knew he'd find his shaving mirror on the wall and a tin basin next to his toiletries.

Like her mother before her, Juliet knew how to make a man feel welcome.

And while he selfishly enjoyed being that man for the moment, he also thought it high time she found one of her own to cater to.

"Dinner's almost ready."

Juliet stood in the doorway of the small kitchen. An apron covered her practical gown, and her features were flushed by the heat of the stove. Not a beauty, but a handsome girl, her father observed. One who would make some deserving officer a fine wife.

"If it's no trouble, set two extra plates. I thought the dinner table would be a good, informal place for my seconds to get to know each other."

A deeper color rose to his daughter's cheeks, but her reply was automatic. "No trouble."

Crowley knew better. Something was bothering her, and he didn't think it was worrying over how to divide their beef into two extra portions. It was one of the guests who flustered her, and by evening's end, he hoped to learn which one.

No trouble.

Juliet grumbled to herself as she diced more potatoes for her stew. Most of her ill-temper was because it ordinarily wouldn't have been any trouble. She was used to stretching meals to accommodate her father's last-minute invitations to their table. But this time it irritated her.

And she knew it had to do with Noble Banning.

The thought of sitting down to a meal with him disconcerted her. She'd have only enough time to set two more services and dish the meal, none to freshen her appearance or change into another dress. Such sprucing-up details wouldn't have occurred to her if Miles had been their only guest. The knowledge that she wanted to fuss in order to please the smug Kentuckian galled her no end.

After all, he wasn't coming to dinner to ogle her.

But obviously, that was Miles's intention.

Miles Dougherty had been her father's second in command at his last post in Texas, before the War between the States pulled the Crowleys back East. Miles had gone on to serve under another at Fort Blair until that unfortunate commander had taken a bad turn after a sudden, unexplained fever. So her father's return had the comfortable feel of a reunion.

Miles Dougherty was a fine man. Everything about the tawny-haired major was solid as stone—his build, his character, his ideals. He was career Army, a volunteer who wished for nothing more than to lead his own command. Her father had been impressed by his unflagging devotion to duty, and Juliet, by his devotion to her.

He met her at the door with a warm kiss of welcome that grazed her cheek. And when he stepped back, she saw something new in his eyes. Before there had been fondness and friendship. Now there was more. More like confident ownership. Her smile of greeting faded.

"Hello, Miles. How good to have you back to sit at our table."

"Always a pleasure to be invited."

He stepped inside, and before she could close the door, Noble Banning slipped across the threshold behind him.

"Good evening, Miz Crowley." He leaned closer to croon *sotto voce*, "I don't suppose you'd allow me a quick kiss, too."

Though her pulse was suddenly thrumming, her reply was cool. "I don't think so, Major. Were I you, I'd be grateful for the supper."

Her tart reply earned a sober response. "Oh, I am, ma'am, truly I am, considering most of the meals I've sat down to in the past three years weren't fit for human consumption. This is the first table I've seen since '61."

Unbidden, her tone gentled. "Then I trust you'll have no complaints."

"No, ma'am. I don't imagine you'd accept them kindly."

"No easier than your compliments, sir."

He gave a low chuckle, then strode past her to greet her father. "Good evening, sir. I hope you've gone to no trouble on our behalf."

"No trouble," Juliet supplied with enough vinegar to earn a quick glance from the colonel. She forced a smile. "Excuse me, gentlemen. I must tend the stove."

All three waited at polite attention until she'd left the room. Once in the kitchen, she dished the stew with a vengeance.

"A quick kiss, indeed. Maybe you can turn the heads of your vacuous Southern girls with such nonsense, but you'll find me immune to your empty flattery."

But for all her angry mutterings, her heart beat faster just considering what a kiss from Noble Banning might be like.

Perhaps she could blame her limited experience of kissing for her senses being all aquiver. Otherwise, why would such intimacies with a stranger hold an appeal? Her knowledge of kissing, at least mouth to mouth, was based on one brief moment beneath the mistletoe four years ago. She'd been so surprised by Miles's sudden demonstration that she'd had no time to decide whether or not she enjoyed it. A stiff, dry pressure against her alarm-slackened lips—a gesture that hadn't stirred half the excitement as the mere thought of experimenting with Noble Banning.

Annoyed with herself for getting worked up over the Southerner's teasing remark, Juliet deposited the meal on the table with unnecessary force, then assumed her seat. Conversation between the men resumed almost at once, the topic Army business. Used to being excluded, Juliet ate in silence, keeping her attention focused on her plate and suppressing a desire to study Noble Banning's mouth.

"The horses should be arriving tomorrow, unless those damned Apache thieves snatch them," Miles reported. "We don't have an animal on this post that's worth a ration of grain."

"Or a rider, either. Until now," Crowley amended with a nod toward Noble. "Major Banning, my experience with livestock purchased locally is that it's green and wild. I trust you have men who can break them to the saddle."

"All of my men are capable, sir. Most of us were practically born in the saddle."

"As soon as the beasts are marginally agreeable, I want you to set up a schedule for drilling. I want this company turned out as proper cavalry. I'm sick of having the Indians riding circles around us. Until we can come close to matching them in the saddle, we've no hope of maintaining a balance here in the West."

"Sir, my men don't need to be drilled on how to sit a horse," Miles protested with a cutting glance at Noble.

"Miles, no offense to you or your men, but you're more suited to a wagon seat than a saddle."

"But sir, I don't think there's anything these Seseshes can teach us."

Crowley chuckled. "That's because you haven't seen them ride." His mood chilled slightly. "And I would remind you to watch your language, Major Dougherty."

The two majors exchanged cool stares for a long moment, then Noble returned to his meal. He paused after a few bites to say, "This is excellent fare, Miz Crowley. You'll hear no complaints from me."

The colonel beamed proudly at his child. "Jules is a fine cook. She can make hardtack into a delicacy. We've no shortage of men seeking invitations to dinner."

"Particularly once she puts Hortense and Willamina to work I'd guess."

Miles scowled when Juliet and Noble traded small smiles. He felt moved to state, "You've an exceptional daughter, John. I've always said so."

"Yes, you have," Crowley conceded, but his attention was pulled between Juliet and his new major. Slowly, he smiled. "A woman like Jules is a treasure out here on the frontier. She knows a man's wants before he needs express them. I shall hate to lose her."

Blushing awkwardly, Juliet glowered at him. "Really, Papa, such things you say. You're not going to lose me."

He sighed dramatically. "Kind of you to say, daughter, but totally untrue. You'll find some dashing young man to replace me in your heart, and I shall be back to eating from the army kitchen."

Her stare riveted to her chipped china plate, Juliet struggled against the humiliation heating her face. "If you continue embarrassing me like this, Father, you may find yourself standing in line with a plate tomorrow."

"She means it, too," Crowley laughed. "Gentlemen, for the sake of my palate, let's turn our talk to something else."

While Miles went on to give a detailed report on raiding party activities, Juliet risked a quick glance at Noble. He was listening intently to the conversation between the other two men and unaware of her interest. Feeling safe to allow a longer minute of study, Juliet's gaze lingered over the symmetry of his features: the lean, sculpted line of cheek and jaw, the raven blackness of cropped hair and heavy brows, the startling blue of his pale eyes. And the surprising soft and supple bend of lips that shifted expressively in response to what was being said—pursing, curling, thinning, even as his stare remained unblinking.

And as she watched, fascinated by those

mobile twists, the tip of his tongue edged out to slide along the seam of his mouth, leaving a moist trail that had her breath suddenly shuddering. There would be nothing stiff or dry if he were to . . .

The corners of his mouth took a slight upward turn.

Aghast, Juliet lifted her gaze to find him staring directly at her from across the table. How could he have missed the hungering way she perused his lips as she imaged the feel of them upon her own? Caught in the midst of her fantasizing, she had only two choices. She could look away in shame or she could brazen it out as if she'd done nothing wrong.

She'd never learned to stomach a skulking retreat.

When she met his stare with an unapologetic one of her own, a gleam of appreciation heated the chill blue depths of his eyes. That warmth increased to an uncomfortable level, which finally forced Juliet into turning away as if indifferent. While she returned to her potatoes, he covered his chuckle with what might have been the clearing of his throat.

She didn't make the mistake of risking eye contact with him again.

Keeping her imagination tightly leashed through the remainder of their meal, Juliet had recovered enough of her composure to extend her hand and offer a faint smile when Noble thanked her for the dinner as he readied to leave.

Instead of a polite press of her fingers, Noble lifted them, bending to meet them half way. His breath blew warm over the back of her hand, exciting a shiver from wrist to shoulder. He did more than touch a proper kiss to her knuckles. Beneath the leisurely caress of his lips, he drew lightly on her skin, then devastated her with the slow stroke of his tongue behind the ridge of her knuckles. It was all discreetly done under her father's nose.

By the time Noble straightened, Juliet could scarcely control her trembling. She stared into his eyes, mesmerized by his unblinking intensity. Her fingers curled about his in an almost desperate panic until he smiled with a formal remoteness and said, "Good night, Miz Crowley. Again, my thanks for the hospitality."

It was an effort to force her fingers open so that he could slip his hand free. If they'd been alone, she'd have never let him go until his actions had been explained. What explanation could there be? He was mocking her for her attitude of uninterest, making her weaken before her own desires.

And she did desire him. For all the wrong reasons. And perhaps for some of the right ones.

If her father chose to be blind to her dazed behavior, Miles wasn't as obliging. She intercepted his tight scrutinizing glare and tried to defuse it with a wan smile. He wasn't fooled.

"Excuse me, gentlemen," she managed in a

somewhat normal voice. "I'll clear the table and leave you to your cigars."

Her china plates almost didn't survive the distance between the main room and the kitchen. The shaking of her hands had them clattering together by the time she slid them into a basin of soapy water. She leaned there against the dry sink for a long moment, as chills rattled along her bones and her skin felt feverishly hot.

So this was what it was like to lust after a man. She took a deep breath and tried to observe the sensations dispassionately. Her heart pounded and her chest felt tight. The rhythm of her breathing came out of sync. All because she'd imagined the taste of his lips and was teased by his indecent kiss upon her hand. There the skin still tingled and the reason why made her all the more breathless.

She'd read about it, of course, in books her father never would have ordered for her had he known of their content. She knew one could expect basic man-woman responses on a level both powerful and primitive, but she'd been unprepared to experience those feelings herself—at least not with a man like Noble Banning, a man she'd sworn to dislike on general principles alone.

But the truth was, she didn't dislike him. She didn't trust him, but she couldn't despise him. Whether that was because of her weakness for his handsome face or her respect for his sharp mind didn't matter. What mattered was that the feelings were totally inappropriate and her father would most likely lock her away if he knew of them. When he spoke of losing her to another man, he certainly hadn't meant a man like his Southern second in command.

With her thoughts under control and when her hands were steady, Juliet returned for the glassware and table services only to be caught up in the topic of discussion.

"You plan to keep them under guard, of course."

Her father gave Miles a bland look. "They've done nothing to deserve such treatment."

"They're Southerners, sir, traitors. That sly devil sat here all during dinner measuring you for the best place to put a bullet."

"Miles," rumbled a word of warning. But he refused to heed it.

"We've given them guns, horses, the very means to slay us and escape into the night. What's to stop them from killing us all in order to return to their homes?"

"Banning gave me his word."

"His word? John, are you insane?"

"Careful, Major Dougherty. My daughter asked the same thing, but it's not within my power to court martial *her*."

"What makes you think you can take that man's word? He's betrayed the very Union we fight to protect. What makes you believe he'll risk his life for it now?"

"He told me he would. And I choose to believe him until he gives me reason to believe otherwise."

"Colonel, you're placing your men in danger, and your daughter as well."

Crowley's features darkened. "You are out of line, sir. I have the utmost respect for Banning, as do his men for him. Please do not force this issue further or I will lose mine for you."

Dougherty immediately snapped to stiff attention. "I beg your pardon, sir. And I wish you a good evening." He unbent slightly. "Thank you for the meal, Juliet."

Juliet nodded, but her silence gave Miles no excuse to linger.

"Papa, he's concerned for us all," Juliet said when they were alone. "Haven't you wondered if he's right to worry? You know I do."

"No, Jules. I can't afford to second-guess my decisions. Banning gave me his word—and I then gave him mine that he and his men would be treated with the respect due soldiers of our United States Army. I'll not leg-shackle them like criminals and be suspicious of their every move. Miles is just—"

"Just what?"

Crowley sighed. "He's jealous of an officer who outranks him and who he fears may surpass him in my favor."

"And would he be right?" She posed the question casually, as if she spoke only of rank and not of other areas of competition.

"Miles Dougherty is a fine officer. I wish I had ten more like him."

"And Banning?"

"If I had ten more like him, I could bring the hostiles to their knees."

And so answered her question of whom he favored.

"Be careful, Papa."

"You think Banning would like me dead?"

She looked uncomfortable but that didn't curb her observation. It never did. "I'm saying he has every reason to wish it."

Crowley nodded. He wasn't a careless or a foolish man. He had to know the danger of housing the enemy under their same roof. Caution and wisdom went hand in hand.

"And you would be right." He bent to kiss her cheek. "Good night, my dear. Try to put your fears aside for a good night's sleep."

"Don't worry," she said wryly. "I don't think Major Banning has any intention of sneaking into my room to slit my throat tonight."

She wouldn't admit it, even to herself.

What she feared was his ability to slip into her dreams to do worse.

Chapter 6

The unmistakable sound of a gunshot echoing too loudly to have come from anywhere but inside the house woke Juliet from a restless dream of ice-blue eyes and tempting kisses.

Papa!

She rolled from bed and snatched her Navy Colt off the floor, checking the chambers as she raced into the front room. Experience had taught her to be ready for anything, and with her heart in her throat, she greeted whatever waited pistol barrel first.

Her father was lifting himself up off the army-blanket rug. He, too, had pistol in hand. A quick assessment revealed a broken front window and no threatening assailant.

"Papa, are you all right? What happened?"

The colonel studied her for a long, silent moment, then managed a chagrined smile. About that time, Miles, Noble Banning, and the colonel's aide crowded in through the front door, each armed and alert. Their superior's embarrassment increased as he included them all in the explanation.

"I feel like a green fool," he muttered. "I was cleaning my revolver, tripped on that damned rug, and threw a shot through the window."

Juliet rushed to embrace him, holding tight to control her own trembling as she scolded, "Papa, how could you be so careless? You nearly scared ten years off us."

"I'm sorry, daughter. Gentlemen, you may return to your rooms. Please assure the men that all is well and tell them to go back to sleep."

As the group of officers drew relieved breaths and her own frantic fears eased, Juliet's attention was drawn to the splendid sight of Noble Banning wearing nothing more than his uniform trousers. What made her heart race then had nothing to do with distress. Her wide gaze canvassed the rugged expanse of muscled shoulders and heavily black-furred chest, her hands itching to survey that awesome terrain with the same leisure her stare allowed.

Then she glanced up into his face and salacious thoughts were derailed. Curiously, she followed the direction of his intense focus to a littering of glass shards upon the floor. She looked for a moment, not making sense of what she saw, until she realized that with the glass on the inside, the bullet would have had to come from without.

Her father hadn't fired the shot she heard. It had been fired at him.

So why hadn't he said so?

Juliet took the revolver from the colonel's hand, saying, "I'll just take this before you shoot off your own foot." He released it with reluctance and she immediately knew why.

The chamber was cool, its rounds in place, its cartridges never discharged.

He'd lied not only to his men, but also to her. And she was anxious to hear his explanation. Who was her father trying to protect with his silence? And why?

She was left to draw her own conclusions, for as soon as the others left, her father held up a hand to forestall her questions.

"To bed, Jules. It's been a long, trying day for us all. Tomorrow is soon enough to plague me for my carelessness." There was no mistaking the finality in his tone. The matter was closed.

But even as she lay back on her thin mattress, her thoughts were spinning in defiance of sleep. Who would have anything to gain from shooting her father? Only one answer came readily to mind, one disturbing answer as apparent as it was prophetic. Only the Southerners would have a reason to hate her father enough to wish him dead. But which Southerner? One hiding in the shadows? Or the one who came boldly to their door?

Had she been flirting with the man who even as he teased her was planning to murder her father?

In the morning, she learned her father's intention of sweeping the incident away, just as the window glass had quietly been disposed of. When she tried to bring it up again over a brief breakfast of coffee and biscuits, he made himself very clear.

"We won't discuss this matter any further, Jules. I'll not have your vivid imagination making any more of it than it is. An accident."

"But Papa—"

"No more, I said."

His tone brooked no argument, his look, no quarter. So Juliet finished her coffee in silence, hurt by his exclusion and worrying over what might prove serious enough for her father to wish her insulated from it. Was it personal embarrassment? He'd made such a strong stand on the side of the Rebels keeping their word. Did that keep him from naming them in the attack? How foolish to place one's pride above one's life. The more she considered, the more likely it became as the answer to his silence. If he were to admit an attack took place, all his Southerners would fall under suspicion. If a report were made, it could result in all of them going back to their incarceration at Point Lookout.

But why was he willing to suppress the truth in order to protect these treacherous men? Why was he willing to put his own life at risk?

Had she the right to go against his wishes?

Juliet wondered as she watched him sponge his uniform to restore a fresh appearance. She'd always thought him at his most handsome when turned out in a crisp uniform, his shoes blacked, his buttons gleaming, saber strapped to his side. She couldn't picture him any other way, not as a clerk going to work in a city store nor as a government employee heading for his comfortable desk and reams of paperwork. This was her father, the vital, fighting man before her, the man her mother had fallen in love with and followed throughout the West at the cost of her own life. Not a man of pride but one of honor.

A man who would not condemn an entire company for the action of one coward.

For him to be safe, that one coward would have to be ferreted out. If her father meant to let the matter pass, she could not afford to. Even if the bullet was meant to be a warning rather than a killing shot, she could take it no less seriously. Threats had a way of becoming actions, and those consequences were ones she planned to avoid.

The guard mount was the most important event of the average soldiering day. At 8:30 call, those assigned to guard duty assembled in front of the barracks for inspection by the company's first sergeant. Ten minutes later, they marched to the parade ground for an inspection by the sergeant major, who then announced the duty roster. The men were then turned over to the officer of the day, who inspected again and put them through an exacting manual-of-arms drill.

Juliet leaned on the porch rail outside their small house to watch Miles Dougherty bark out orders. Usually, those under his command were sharp as a military crease, but this morning, with half the ranks made up of Banning's men, the routine went poorly, a show of sloppy discipline that had Miles red-faced and seething.

"What the hell kind of soldiers do you call these, Major Banning?"

Noble stared at him straight on. "They aren't soldiers, Dougherty. They were men fighting for their homeland, and for that task, they had no equal. If you want tin soldiers to line up at your command, you'll have to train 'em yourself. I've no fault with their behavior."

Miles glared at him, furious at his lack of support, then returned his attention to the men. "I give you a choice, the only one you'll get from me. Act like soldiers going on guard duty or you'll all be in the guard house. Let's run through the drill again, like men this time instead of little girls."

The routine was repeated, this time with a greater degree of cooperation but no less obvious reluctance on the part of the Southern troopers. That done, Miles snapped a crisp salute and dismissed the men to the guard house, from which they would begin their two-hour tours of sentry duty.

"A less than impressive display," Juliet remarked as her father came to stand beside her on the porch. He made a noncommittal sound.

"I didn't request them for their ability to perform close-order drill. Miles will have them shaped up in no time. No one takes their soldiering more seriously than Miles."

Juliet glanced up at him in surprise. "You make that sound like a less than admirable trait."

"This kind of warfare requires some degree of initiative and imagination. Miles is an extraordinary by-the-book soldier. But he lacks a certain . . . flexibility."

Juliet blinked. She'd never heard him find fault with Miles before. Perhaps it was because he never had anyone to compare him to before Noble Banning arrived.

"And I suppose your bold Kentuckian has that desired *flexibility*."

He smiled at her tart assessment. "Major Banning is a survivor at any cost—short of acting without honor. He has a fine mind and a shrewd cunning that should do quite well up against our nemeses. The Apache aren't hampered by an excess of rules, either."

"You sound as if you can't wait to pit them against one another."

Her dismay forced him to cool his enthusiasm. "I can wait, my dear, but in the meantime, I can anticipate."

There was little for a woman to do on an army post unless she was doing laundry for the company at five dollar a month for officers and two dollars for enlisted men, or else serving as a midwife. It was a ritual for all women to turn out for the guard mount, and most professed a love for the flashy show of brass buttons. But after that, there came endless idle hours.

The strict caste system prevented socializing through the ranks. Though Juliet liked Pauline Folley, they had little in common. Pauline was wrapped up in her children and husband with scant time for or interest in much else. The only other officer's wife was Maisy Bartholomew, and Juliet knew more about her than she cared to already.

That left her to her own company. Juliet was no stranger to solitude. She'd spend her days devoted to self-betterment, improvement of her mind through reading and of her health by the cultivation of a garden.

She was in the midst of arranging her books when a soft throat-clearing alerted her. Her breath caught when she saw Noble Banning standing in the doorway. She forced herself to remember he might be a co-conspirator in the attempt on her father's life. That chilled her manner in a hurry.

"Major, can I help you with something?"

If he noticed the frigid plunge in temperature, he didn't react. His attention was on the dozens of leather-bound volumes.

"Just wondering if the library was open yet."

She gestured to the books scattered across the floor in teetering stacks. "I haven't sorted through them all yet, but I can make a couple of recommendations." She ran her forefinger down the gold-leaf type and selected two weighty editions. Noble took them and scanned the titles impassively.

"Brutus and Benedict Arnold. Renowned betrayers. Interesting topic. Is there some message I should be looking for?"

"You wouldn't have to look far, Major."

His mouth thinned as he studied the woman kneeling on the floor in what should have been, but wasn't, a submissive pose. "Is there something on your mind, Miz Crowley?"

She wasted no time with discretion. "If I'd taken your pistol last night, would I have found it had been recently fired?"

"Fired at your father?"

Her unswerving stare was her answer.

"No, it was not, and no, I did not. But I don't expect you'll take my word for it, will you?"

"I haven't my father's blanket trust in your sincerity, sir."

"Then what about something else you can believe in? Something like retribution. Your father has information I need. Until I find out what he knows, I need him alive. There. Does that satisfy you?"

She seized on his answer. "What information?"

"That's between him and me."

She accepted that reluctantly. But her questions weren't done. "You were quick to appear at our door after the shot was fired. Did you, perhaps, see anyone else out on the parade ground?"

"Meaning any of my men, I assume."

"Assume what you will, Major."

His expression closed down tight, becoming all lean angles and harsh hollows. "All my men were in their barracks. The only one I saw anywhere near your quarters was your friend Dougherty. Maybe you should be asking him these questions."

"That's absurd!"

"That's your opinion." He hefted the books. "I shall enjoy these. Hopefully fact will be as entertaining as the fiction you're creating." He nodded to her and was gone before she could come up with a suitably cutting reply.

The horses arrived in a flurry of dust and commotion just before the afternoon fatigue detail went out to forage for wood and water. The men broke ranks in an effort to wave them around, giving the weary wranglers a chance to herd the bony broomtails in with the rest of the fort's animals. One of the sergeants stood at the gate, counting, as the foam-flecked furies entered the corral. Thirty-four creatures as wild as the terrain milled about, inciting the milder company mounts to stomp and snort at the new arrivals.

"What a collection of teeth and ribs," Noble remarked as he met Crowley and his daughter at the corral.

"Nothing oats and rest won't restore at five dollars a head," one of the wranglers stated as he rolled down out of his damp saddle. "Know we'd promised you'uns forty head, but them damned A-paches nabbed six of 'em last night. We're lucky they was just interested in the horses instead of our hair."

"They'd have done better taking your hair," Noble said as he sized up the wayworn mustangs.

"Any of those animals worth five dollars, Major?" Crowley asked, deferring to the Kentuckian's expertise.

"Maybe for the whole lot."

"Now hold on a minute, pard," the wrangler sputtered. "We was pledged five dollars apiece."

"It'll cost us twice that to get them fit enough to carry a man any distance. If they recover at all."

That dire prediction had the wrangler twisting his hat in his hands. Juliet was glad to see he recognized Noble as a man who knew horseflesh, something the officers were usually ignorant of. He'd probably thought he'd have an easy sale. He was realizing he was wrong and didn't like it. Trying to salvage something, he wheedled, "Now lookee here, it ain't our fault them animals look so lean. We've had Injuns on our backs all the way here. After risking our very lives, you gonna go and welsh out on our deal?"

Crowley studied the scanty-tailed beasts. "My major says they're not worth five dollars. I trust his judgment. I won't put my men on animals that'll collapse ten miles into the desert. A man's only as good as his horse out here, and I happen to think quite a lot of my men."

Seeing the whole deal going sour, the wrangler looked to his scowling comrades, then sighed. "Since you've got to nurse 'em a bit, how 'bout we say four dollars a head."

"Three would be a lot more reasonable," Noble claimed as he watched the animals canter the circumference of the corral.

Juliet smiled to herself as the wrangler beat his hat against his thigh, sending up a choking cloud of dust, but he forced a smile and said, "You're stealing from us, but we can't afford to go back empty-handed. Three apiece it is."

Crowley nodded, satisfied a good bargain had been made. "If you'll follow the sergeant, he'll see you receive army scrip—and a good meal."

"Thankee for that much," the wrangler grumbled, then motioned to his two companions. When they were gone, Crowley looked to his major.

"Are they worth three dollars?"

"Probably, by the time we break 'em and fill in their ribs."

Crowley smiled. "When do you think they'll be ready to ride? Our mounts are about played out."

"Grain 'em and rest 'em good today and they'll be ready to kick up their heels in about a week."

Juliet leaned against the corral rail to watch the mangy beasts. She refused to admit her pleasure at the way Noble's cunning had saved them money, casually saying instead, "Is that when we'll discover if you're worth the trouble my father went through for you?"

Noble grinned. "That's where the seat meets saddle leather, ma'am."

"Well, what do you think of him?"

Juliet gave a start, then continued to serve their supper, pretending not to know whom her father referred to.

"Of whom?"

"Major Banning."

"I can't say my opinion of him has been much changed." She sat down and tucked in her skirt with atypical fussiness.

Watching her a bit too closely for comfort, her father asked, "And what *is* that opinion?"

"The one I've expressed often and loudly, only to have you ignore it. That he, like all of his kind, is arrogant, spoiled by luxury, and too full of himself to be much good to anyone else."

"His men thought highly enough of him to change their colors."

Juliet considered that, then said, "Perhaps his men are fools, as well. Or change colors as easily as a chameleon, just for camouflage."

Crowley chuckled. "Time will tell."

But how much time did they safely have with an assassin roaming loose upon their post?

Juliet's glance flew to the open window. It framed them in interior light where they sat at their table. Easy targets. Casually, she crossed to it and pulled the canvas curtains closed.

"I'd like to eat one meal without a seasoning of dust," she announced upon returning to her seat. Her father stared at her but said nothing. Eventually, he returned to his food. After a moment, Juliet continued.

"The major did say something earlier which has me puzzled. Perhaps you could explain."

"Oh? And what is that?"

"He said you were withholding some information from him. He wouldn't elaborate, so I thought you might."

Crowley's gaze lifted from his plate, his stare fixed and flintlike. "You thought wrong, my dear. What's between Major Banning and me is our business and none of yours."

Taken aback, Juliet snatched a hurtful breath. Though she tried to keep her tone light, the weight of his words tugged at her heart. "There was a time when you felt free to share everything with me. I'm wondering if something has happened to change that, Papa. Do you feel you have some reason to distrust me?"

He answered with the expected reassurances. "Nonsense. I trust you more than a confessor."

Using his own claim against him, she asked, "Then what makes this business off-limits, if I'm still considered a trusted confidante?"

Realizing how easily she'd trapped him, Crowley pursed his lips ruefully. "Such a clever girl. It's a complicated matter, Jules. All I can tell you is that Banning believes I know the identity of the man in his command whose information led to their capture."

She leaned forward, intrigued. "And do you?"

"That's all I can say."

Could say or would say?

She sat back with a snort of disgust. "How unfair to lead me on with tidbits, then refuse the final facts."

"I won't have Banning using you to get that information should he think you have it."

The sternness of his tone had an immediate effect on Juliet. She wondered aloud, "Do you think he would do that?"

"Banning is a man of serious convictions. I would not put anything past his doing if he thinks it will gain him what he wants."

Juliet fell silent for the remainder of the

meal. Were Noble's flirtations motivated by something so coldly calculating? Was he hoping to worm his way into her affections to get her to betray her father's trust? If so, what a cruel way to use her.

She told herself savagely that she should have known better than to think him driven by honest emotion. Why would a man like Banning pay special court to a prickly and ungainly woman? Here was the harsh yet completely logical truth. A painful truth, but one she would survive. Better to learn of it now than to have already lost her heart in the matter.

She blinked rapidly, using the bitterness of the coffee to explain the sudden haze of tears in her eyes.

Across the parade ground, the glowing tip of a cigar flared against the chill of Noble Banning's stare. He smiled wryly as he watched Juliet draw the window curtains shut with a snap, sealing the intimacy of the Crowleys' dinner from his intrusive view. It was almost as if she'd guessed he was standing there, but he knew that was not the reason.

A smart woman.

A difficult and possibly dangerous woman because of the way she distracted him from his cause.

He wasn't at Fort Blair to play tin soldier for the Union Army. He had another agenda, one he'd foolishly let slip out to the wrong person over volumes on history's greatest traitors. He wasn't at Fort Blair to play patty finger games with the daughter of the Federal officer who'd turned one of his own against him. Juliet Crowley couldn't matter to him. He couldn't afford to care if she was witty and bright and parried insults like a fencing foil. He couldn't afford to note that he found her piercing honesty more appealing than the cultivated charms of all the women he'd known.

He couldn't afford to let her get under his skin, because what he was doing was probably going to hurt her. He didn't want to suffer for her disillusionment.

He'd let down too many before her, and they were the ones that had to matter to him now, because they could not defend themselves from the grave against the one who had betrayed them.

Juliet Crowley's pain was a small price to pay for the eternal peace of those he'd seen buried.

And so was his own.

Chapter 7

In the relative cool of the morning, at a sandy riverbed within sight of the post, the men of Fort Blair began the bone-rattling job of saddle-breaking their new mounts. There was nothing elegant or tidy about the process.

Since Banning and the other new arrivals had come on fresh horses, the mustangs were paired with the Union regulars at the fort. These men were expected to get on and ride until the animals were subjugated. It seemed a simple task, considering how worn and wobbly the beasts appeared only days before.

How quickly the harmless-looking creatures reverted to seething masses of manes and flying hooves when the foreign weight of a man climbed onto its back.

Drawn by the explosive drama, Juliet stood off to one side, enjoying the show of man's attempt to dominate the wild. And the three-dollar broomtails were the wildest things on four legs that she'd ever seen. Once roped, the horses were blindfolded, then bridled and saddled. When they stood trembling and twitching, a soldier slipped onto saddle leather for the often short-lived ride of his life. Squealing, biting, kicking, whirling in defiance of gravity, the animals bucked and shimmied until their riders ploughed sand with their chins.

Along the ridge of the dry creekbed, the Southerners lounged in amusement, placing bets and jeering at the clumsiness of their Northern counterparts, who had no idea of how to best a green horse. Noble Banning loitered with them, sharing their humor, as the bruised and disheartened riders picked themselves up time after time, their tempers growing ever shorter.

Miles Dougherty was one of the men becoming annoyed by their goading audience. He'd picked a big smoke-colored stallion and wore an expression that brooked no nonsense. After glaring at Noble, he gave Juliet a tight-lipped smile, then climbed aboard for a jarring four-second ride. As he picked himself up from the dust, he bristled at the sound of Noble's laughter.

"Sure you don't want me and my boys to show you how it's done, Major? No sense you all getting your uniforms dirty. Why, those critters are probably so tuckered out from tossing you in the air that we could sit 'em like hobbyhorses and never break a sweat."

Miles beat the dust from his hat against his

thigh. "No thank you, Banning. We'll manage just fine."

"Manage to end up with half your men in the infirmary, you mean." His men whooped in appreciation. Noble grinned to encourage them. "Why don't we take the starch out of them for you?"

"We'll manage," he repeated through grinding teeth, trying not to limp.

Unwilling to just sit by and ignore the heckling, Juliet thought it time to insert her opinion.

"Miles, Papa wouldn't want you to take any risks with the welfare of your men," Juliet suggested practically, earning his stabbing glare. "As Major Banning has said often enough, his men were raised on horseback. Why not let them entertain you for a while. After all, it's *their* bruised . . . pride."

Miles considered her logic, then lifted a challenging brow along with the reins of the snorting gray to Noble. "Show me how easy it is, Major."

At the loud cheering of his men, Noble slid down the embankment to take the leads. Miles and the other Northern soldiers quickly scrambled clear, hoping to give Noble enough room to break his fool neck. Grinning at his men, Noble then turned to salute Juliet as Miles had done. She answered him with cool disdain, refusing to accept him as champion even as her pulse accelerated.

His easy air of confidence wouldn't help but

inspire admiration as he carefully fitted one boot into a stirrup and swung astride, touching off a powder keg of furious energy. Despite all the animal's jerky leaps and dizzying revolutions, Noble clung like a burr, refusing to be parted from saddle leather. Moving as one with the fiery stallion, he made the ride look more like a graceful dance than a display of brutal mastery.

Soon, the animal knew it had been bested, its jumps growing less frequent, less high, its struggles more subdued, until finally it circled the sandy wash at a snorting canter while Noble's men hollered and waved their hats in the air.

The breath gushed from Juliet. She was dangerously close to forgetting herself in the thrill of the moment. She found she was quivering just as much as the vanquished beast. The man was liquid poetry in the way he rode—strong, fluid, in control. Exciting. Too exciting for her vow of disinterest.

Noble's triumphant grin eased to a subtle curve as their eyes met and held. How could he not notice her vivacious coloring and the jewel-like brilliance of her gaze that suggested everything she couldn't say?

And how could Miles Dougherty miss the same display?

"A right fancy ride, Major Banning." Miles's retort broke the exchange of questing looks between the Southerner and his colonel's daughter. "But just because the animal's tired out now doesn't mean he's fit for a soldier to take into the field tomorrow."

Noble's smile took a wry bend. "Why, Major Dougherty, this here animal is tame enough for a lady's pet. Or are you afraid to find out for yourself?"

Hoots of laughter came from the Southerners while Miles flushed at the insult.

Seeing the potential for trouble brewing, Juliet stepped forward to intercede.

"If that animal is docile enough for a lady, I should have no difficulty, should I, Major Banning?"

Noble's amusement ebbed as he read the challenge in her stare. His smile grew indolent. "I guess you'll just have to take my word for it, ma'am."

Juliet began tugging on her gloves. "Since I seem to have some problem in that area, I guess I'll just have to find out for myself, won't I?"

Realizing her intent, Miles tried to still her stubbornness with a hand on her arm. "Jules, you don't have to prove his case for him. Or disprove it at a risk to yourself."

Juliet never looked away from Noble's steady stare. "Unless Major Banning is a complete liar who's trying to make fools of us all, I shall be perfectly safe. Which is it, sir? Liar or gentleman?"

Noble swung down from the sweaty stallion and extended the reins. "At your service, Miz Crowley."

More worried now, Miles tightened his grip. "Jules—"

She placed her hand over his in what looked like a tender gesture but was actually a way to pry his fingers loose. "Now, Miles, by your very attitude you are questioning Major Banning's word."

"You're damned right I am. Jules, this is madness. Your father—"

"Would trust my judgment. And you," she concluded coolly, "are not my father." She peeled away his hand and slid down the crumbling embankment to where Noble Banning waited to call her bluff.

She smiled at him thinly, knowing he thought she was playing some game to make Miles jealous. If she was indeed playing a game, it was not for Miles's benefit. She came to a stop between Noble and the nervous stallion.

"Would you like me to help you extricate yourself from this silly attempt to impress your . . . friend?" Noble asked her.

She matched the cynical softness of his words. "I'd like you to help me into the saddle."

He frowned slightly, aware at last that she meant to go through with her impulsive plan. He took a step back. "I'm not going to help you break your neck."

Her smile was killingly sweet. "But I thought you said you'd made this beast into a docile lamb—the perfect ladies' mount. Are you saying now that I am not a lady?"

"You are that, ma'am. And reckless to boot."

She lifted her foot and arched an impatient brow. "Sir? Will you help, or not?"

He cupped his hands beneath her boot and gave a powerful boost that almost sent her over the animal's back. Experience helped her catch her balance and right herself in the saddle. She gathered the reins, feeling the stallion bunch in anticipation.

"Stand clear, Major Banning. Let's see if you are a man of your word."

The moment he moved back, Juliet set her heels into the animal's flanks. The horse lunged forward, surging up the embankment in a pair of mighty leaps. And horse and rider were gone.

"Son of a—"

Noble glanced around for a ready mount, snatching the reins of a half-wild horse from a startled corporal. He rolled up into the saddle, and before the animal could think to protest, Noble kicked it into a galloping pursuit.

As the horse's wild plunging leveled out into an all-out run, Juliet gave it its head and lifted her own to the rip of the wind. Her hat tore loose, freeing her hair to stream out behind her in a rippling golden banner. The sense of glorious abandon was worth the thought of Miles's distress and even her father's scolding that was sure to follow. Worth anything to humble the smug Noble Banning. Imagining his chagrin, she nudged the gray into stretching his legs.

They thundered across the open desert, scaring up the occasional jackrabbit and vaulting over rainwater runoff cracks. The wild race let her throw off the remnants of city life, the feeling of being hemmed in and restrained while living in another's house, living by another's rules for three long years. There she hadn't been able to shake out her hair or taunt fate or do anything that made her revel in the joy of simply being alive.

Feeling as though she and the horse were the only beings within miles, Juliet was startled by the sudden shadow of a man and another horse drawing alongside them. Before she could react, Noble reached fearlessly out to snag her reins, yanking back on hers and his at the same time to slow their mounts together.

Noble Banning didn't look impressed by her skill in the saddle.

He looked furious.

"Are you crazy?" he yelled at her. "What are you trying to do, get yourself killed, pulling a stunt like that?"

She jerked her reins away from him and snapped back, "If you thought I'd be in danger, why did you goad me into it?"

"Because I didn't think you'd be insane enough to go through with it."

She bristled up in her own defense. "I am

hardly insane. I've probably been riding as long as you have. Did you think I'd spent my last twenty years huddling in a wagon?"

"I don't know what to think where you're concerned," he admitted angrily. "Other than that a man'd have to be crazy himself to tangle with you."

Her voice lowered to a husky rumble. "Then why did you follow me, Major Banning?"

Her question took him off guard. The furious pace of his breathing faltered, then resumed with a raspy chuckle as he shook his head. "I guess I must be crazy. Now be a good girl, Miz Crowley, and come back to the fort with me before we end up with our hair on some Indian's lodgepole."

She smirked at him, showing off her superior knowledge. "Indians don't venture this close to the fort unless it's to steal livestock. And that's not likely to happen in broad daylight."

"But maybe they *are* as crazy as we are. Did you ever think of that?"

"Then after you, Major Banning."

"After you, Miz Crowley."

"Why, sir, don't you trust me?"

He laughed at her attempted drawl. "We'll ride together," was his solution.

They started back toward the post, letting the horses catch their breath at an easy lope.

"You're a fine horsewoman, Juliet." His compliment would have been enough, but the way he said her name caressed like a drip of warm honey. He took advantage of her silence to add, "You're accomplished in many unusual areas."

"Compared to your dainty girls back home?"

He didn't miss her searing sarcasm. "Compared to just about any lady I've ever known, and I met quite a few Northern girls while attending Harvard."

Her quick turn toward him set her mount prancing to one side. She controlled it more easily than she did her own surprise. "Harvard?"

"Do you find it so hard to believe that this disreputable liar should have a passion for the law and seek to learn it in the best possible arena?"

She considered his shrewd intelligence and his unswerving directness. "No."

But then why was a man who professed to love the law determined to pursue the one he thought guilty of treason outside its parameters? She stewed on that for a moment, but her mood was too buoyant to dwell on it for long.

"What made you choose the law, Major?"

"Call me Noble. There's no one out here to protest the informality."

"Do you come from a family of lawyers—Noble?"

He laughed, a soft mocking sound. "My father knows all about the law, all right. As a politician, he knows his way around all of them."

"So you went into the legal profession to

THE REBEL   111

help him?" She couldn't keep the disappointment from abrading her tone or suppress her wish that he'd prove her wrong in this.

"Not to help him. To spite him. I've seen enough injustice in my day to make me sick of the way things are done in my hometown. Those with money and power pretty much make the laws, laws they don't have to abide by. I plan to change that." He grinned at her, the dazzling gesture making her pulse leap. "Not exactly what you expected to hear from a slave-holding secessionist, eh?"

"Not exactly."

"I don't believe in this war, Juliet, but I believe in the reasons behind it. I believe in the right of states to make decisions on their own behalf, but beyond that, I believe in the right of men to be treated as men."

"I should think *that* would be an unpopular view with your plantation neighbors."

"And with your father and those like him who are just as determined to dominate the rightful owners of all that we see. Supremacy of the rich white man isn't exclusive to the South, Miz Crowley."

"Nor is compassion and open-mindedness exclusive to the North, Major Banning."

He regarded her for a moment, then nodded at the roundabout compliment.

"So you would use what you learned at Harvard to put your own father in jail?"

"No, ma'am. Only to stop him from what he's doing and to save him from spending the rest of his years behind bars. I have the greatest of love for my father but unfortunately little respect for his occupation. He gave me the freedom to think for myself, and I will not turn against him by forcing my own values upon him."

Juliet's emotions gave an odd shiver. To stabilize them, she said rather dryly, "Ah, a man of impeccable honor."

"No, ma'am. I have my faults and I struggle with them daily."

"And what might those horrible faults be? Using the wrong glass at dinner?"

He leveled an unblinking gaze, locking hers within it as helpless prisoner. "Nothing so frivolous as that. I allowed my pride to take the lives of those who followed me without question. I let my agenda force others to bend to my will in declaring allegiance to their enemy. I am not without fault, Miz Crowley. Far from it."

Before she could prompt him to say more, they were surrounded by Miles Dougherty and a small party of anxious men, who'd obviously expected to find her broken in some ditch instead of chatting comfortably with the Southern officer.

The look Miles gave her stated he'd have preferred to find her in the ditch.

"Are you all right, Jules?"

"Fine, Miles." She put on a shamed face. "Please forgive my little childish display. I shouldn't have let my vanity cause you such concern."

Miles was immediately all gruff awkwardness. "Don't apologize, Jules. You shouldn't have gone off on your own. You know my first concern is always you."

How she twisted beneath the guilt of that simple statement, because the reverse was not true. "If Major Banning's Rebels can ride as well as he does, I suggest you let them tame the rest of the horses while you escort me back to my father."

Miles hesitated, torn between the want to stay and show up the preening Southerners and the sought-after chance to get Juliet alone. In the end, he made the logical choice.

"Major, I would be obliged if you and your men finished breaking in the mounts. Obviously, you are more suited to the task."

Noble didn't take his compliance without suspicion. It was too quick, too easily given.

His gaze cut between the officer and Juliet, then understood the Northerner's priorities. And he accepted them because to do otherwise would have compromised his own intentions, intentions that did not include courting his commander's daughter, no matter how great the temptation.

But he didn't have to feel pleased about being supplanted by the likes of the stodgy Northerner. His smile was all teeth and no sincerity.

"Why, certainly, Major Dougherty, though

it seems you've taken on the more dangerous chore."

Juliet sat frozen as Noble tipped his hat to her and rode off with the other troopers.

Chore.

Is that how he envisioned her? As a chore to be endured in hope of a later reward—perhaps her father's gratitude? Pride warred with pain, and because she was aware of how closely Miles watched her, she allowed pride to win out.

"Hateful man," she muttered, then bestowed a grudging smile on the dour major. "But he does know how to sit a horse. Shall we go?"

As they fell in side by side, Miles looked relieved and ventured with some chagrin, "I should have known better than to worry about you."

"Oh, Miles, good heavens, you know I can hold my own in the saddle."

"But I wasn't certain you could hold your own equally well with Banning."

It took a moment for his complaint to hit home. "What does *that* mean?"

Not noticing how prickly her manner had become, Miles continued with his self-satisfied findings. "I should have known you were too sensible to fall prey to his slick Southern charm." He cast a quick glance her way to test her reaction. Receiving none, he chuckled to himself. "A man like that is used to having women swooning at his feet. It must be quite a blow to his conceit to have you so immune."

"Yes, I'm sure it would be." Her tone chilled. "If the major was in the least bit interested."

Miles reacted with surprise, then puffed-up pleasure, seeing the field of opportunity opening before him. "Then the man's a bigger fool than I first thought him."

Juliet didn't argue. And the fact that she couldn't gave her no joy.

Because although Major Noble Banning might be immune, she wasn't.

Chapter 8

One of Juliet's greatest pleasures came from coaxing things to grow in the stingy western "soil."

Soil was a misnomer, for whatever good top dirt might be found was quickly blown away, leaving the hard-packed earth behind. Its poor quality and the lack of water created a challenge she could not resist. Each tender green sprout nudging its way through the granite-hard ground was a victory, not to mention a reward. Companies competed for the best garden, but Juliet's had never been outdone. Fresh vegetables augmented bland army fare at her table, and the surplus she sold for a modest price to the fort kitchen. She used that small remuneration to order frivolous female trappings from the East, things she would have been embarrassed to ask her father for. A hat was her latest extravagance. When it would arrive was another mystery.

"Here now, Hortense, get away from those

seeds." She tossed a clump of dirt to send the hen flapping away.

"She'd best be careful or she'll be finding herself in the stew with your vegetables."

The cheerful Irish tones brought a smile of welcome to Juliet's face. "Good morning, Colleen. How are you settling in? Is there anything you need?"

The redhead pursed her lips. "Nothing you can be givin' me. A good swift boot in the missus's behind would do me a world a good." That last was muttered under her breath, so Juliet pretended not to hear. She covered her laugh with the soft clearing of her throat.

"So this is a visit, then?"

"Oh, no, miss. Herself wouldn't cotton to me chatting with someone above me station. She sent me to invite you and your father to a party she be givin' for the officers and their ladies."

"I see." Maisy wasted no time in dividing the post according to social status. But declining wasn't an option. "You can tell Mrs. Bartholomew that my father and I will be happy to attend. And you, Colleen?"

"Me, miss?" She looked startled, then flushed deeply. "Oh, the missus would never allow the likes a me to be smiling at her guests." She lowered her voice confidentially. "She'd be accusing me a trying to find meself a husband."

Juliet hid her smile. Maisy's fears were well justified. One of the hardest things on a frontier post was for a lady to keep a maid. Within a week of arrival, if the maid was at all agreeable, she'd entertain marriage proposals from at least half of the single enlisted men. The girl could do worse than work for Maisy, but if she bided her time she could make a good match. Juliet scrutinized her plump yet pleasing figure and assessed her easy charm.

"And would she be right, Colleen?"

The girl grinned. "If I was to find the right man, miss."

"Well, there's no shortage of men here."

"If that be the case, miss, why is it that you've not found yourself one?" Noting Juliet's alarm and quickly hidden blush, she added, "If you pardon me for my asking."

"I'm still looking for the right one, too, Colleen."

Colleen nodded then added sagely, "'Twould be my guess that there'd be plenty willing to be the right one. Especially two right handsome fellows."

Two? Juliet was about to ask her to clarify her words when another shadow crossed her newly spaded garden plot. She recognized the freckled-faced Southern captain. And she also recognized the way his presence flustered the sassy Irish girl.

"Good morning, Captain Allen. I believe you've met Colleen McDonnal."

The space between the freckles filled in with a flush. "Yes, I have. Hello again, Miss McDonnal. Am I interrupting here?"

"Oh, don't be silly, sir. I was just leaving. Miss Juliet, I'll be tellin' the missus that you and your father will be there."

As the flustered girl turned away, Juliet called, "Colleen? When are we expected?"

A nervous giggle. "Oh! I guess you'll be needin' to know that. Tomorrow night at seven." With another shy glance at George Allen, she skittered away, nearly tripping over the two chickens in her haste.

"A vivacious girl," the captain remarked as he watched her retreat.

"She's very sweet and courageous. She'll do well out here." Juliet peeled off her soiled gloves and stood. "Now, Captain, what is it I can do for you?"

"Noble—that is, Major Banning—mentioned that you had a fine selection of reading material."

"Would you like to borrow something, Captain?"

"If you'd have no objections."

"None at all." She led the gawky officer inside and gestured to her wall of literature. It made her smile to see his jaw drop. "Not what you expected?"

"More than I'd hoped for. May I?"

"Help yourself." Remembering her manners, she asked, "Can I get you some lemonade?"

"That would be lovely, ma'am."

Lemonade was a sorry affair, made with citric acid crystals and water so poor that it had to sit until the mud settled to the bottom. But it was a social ritual and one Juliet clung to in memory of her mother, who loved to entertain graciously no matter the obstacles. George Allen was just as gracious in swallowing the bitter concoction without an obvious grimace.

"What have you found?" Curious, Juliet examined the weighty tome. "Saint Thomas More. You have philosophical tastes, Captain."

"My plan is to continue my work with the church when I return home. I want to be worthy of the task. You look somewhat puzzled, Miss Crowley. You don't think the army is the proper place for religion?"

"I've known quite a few chaplains, but I don't really think religion and the military mix well."

"There's many a troubled soul carrying a carbine, ma'am." His voice dropped off, his sudden melancholy outweighing his years.

"Like Major Banning?"

Allen blinked in surprise, then glanced away. "I cannot betray confidences, ma'am."

"He's confessed to me that he's a sinner, but I have a hard time imagining what his sins might be. He seems to be an admirable leader and possessed of high moral fiber."

Allen jumped upon her praises. "There's the problem, Miss Crowley. Morality and military *do* make a poor combination sometimes. The major's had to make some difficult compromises over the past few years." He fidgeted, uncomfortably aware that he may have said too much already but needing a vent for his own troubled spirit. Juliet was too happy to supply it.

The more she could learn about Noble Banning, the better prepared she would be.

"Like coming here in my father's command? I can't believe that was an easy or a popular choice. More lemonade?"

Gratified by her sympathetic manner, George unbent his resolve. "No, ma'am, it wasn't. He struggles with it along with all the ghosts of the men he's lost." He sighed as if those souls were a nightly burden for him, as well.

"Through no fault of his own," she prompted gently to get him to open up again. She hated to manipulate such a trusting individual, but was also aware of the adage of all being fair in this circumstance.

"No, ma'am. But a good leader always takes responsibility for those in his command. And Noble Banning shoulders the world. He's had to all his life."

"Please sit down, Captain. Did you grow up with the major?" She made her questions relaxed so that he wouldn't be alarmed by her interest. And she was interested in the man and in his past. She told herself it was the smart thing to know as much as possible about the enemy.

"Not really. We grew up in neighboring

counties. I knew of him and his family. Who didn't know Judge Banning?"

"Judge? I thought Noble said his father wasn't involved in the law."

"It's an honorary title, ma'am, having to do with Mr. Banning's influence over folks' lives and such."

"Noble said he was in politics."

"Ummm, yes, I suppose that's true enough. He's a man who likes control, Miss Crowley, and power. And if he can get that through politics, so be it. He's not a man you'd want to cross and breathe of the deed to another soul." He took a sudden breath, then looked ashamed for having spoken ill of another. "But he is Noble's father."

She trod more carefully, not wishing to scare him into silence when his words could prove so valuable. "It must be difficult for Noble to reconcile his pursuit of the law with his father's determination to manipulate it."

"To say the least, ma'am. He would never take an outward stand against his father for what he does. I think going into lawyering is his way of satisfying his conscience."

"And is that why he's after the man who turned his troops in to my father? As if righting that wrong would appease his guilt over his father's misdeeds?"

Allen choked on his lemonade. His gaze flew up, wide and startled. Her font of information abruptly went dry.

After nervously wiping his mouth and pant

leg, he said, "You would have to ask him about that, ma'am." He set down the glass and stood. "Thank you for the drink and for the book. I'd best be going."

Alone with her tart lemonade and bitter thoughts, Juliet asked herself, "What is it you're trying to prove, Noble Banning? That you're not the man your father is? Or are you following in his footsteps?"

Maisy Bartholomew's party was a small, elite gathering in her new abode. Besides Juliet and her father, bachelors Noble, Miles, and George Allen appeared all polished and poised as well as Captain Tom Folley and his wife and Lieutenant Albert Howell. Juliet had never met the dashing mustached blond who'd captured the heart of Miles's giddy sister, Jane, but she liked Albert immediately for his boisterous laugh and warm smile. As each arrived, the room saw a division between North and South with the Crowleys in the middle. While Maisy seemed unperturbed, it didn't please the colonel. His one wish was for all his officers to mesh as a unit, not grind in separate parts. He tried to remedy the situation with a toast as soon as introductions were over.

"To the Fighting Seventeenth, gentlemen."

Just as reluctant glasses began to be raised, Miles added, "To our courageous Union. Long may she stand."

Only half the glasses tipped at that while the

rest dangled in defiance. Juliet was quick to mend the gap for her father's sake.

"To our gracious hostess for inviting us into her home this evening."

That won a unanimous chorus of "Here, here" and goblets emptied to a one. Juliet nodded in receipt of her father's smile of thanks.

Colleen had cleverly fashioned a stylish residence for her mistress out of the few luxuries available. Chair mats of a colorfully woven cloth were reminiscent of the gown Juliet remembered seeing the girl wear during their desert crossing. Curtains were made from the Irish maid's shawl. They were lovely touches, but Juliet wondered sadly over the girl surrendering them for such unappreciated use in a home that was not her own.

The table gleamed with china and crystal that Maisy had apparently been able to rescue from her plantation home. While Juliet and Pauline wore sensible calico, their hostess glowed in fuchsia-colored silk that made them seem drab and sparrowlike in comparison. Never one for affectation, Juliet didn't mind, but being so underdressed obviously embarrassed Pauline Folley, whose scant extra coins went toward keeping her children in shoes, not in personal extravagances.

Maisy had impressed a lowly corporal into presiding at the sideboard, where he stood at stiff attention when not keeping glasses filled and removing dishes at the regal wave of Maisy's hand. Juliet could well imagine her as a queen bee in a bustling hive full of servants catering to her every whim. Perhaps there was some envy at the ease of Maisy's life on her part, for she'd always managed on her own even when her father's rank provided for privileges. She cooked her own meals and cleared her own table with an air of independent pride, because that's how she was taught. Maisy, apparently, was groomed to lift no hand when another could do it for her. Maybe it was shallow to dislike her for such a pampered past, but Juliet couldn't help it, especially as she watched the vain belle lording it over the humble Pauline throughout the evening meal.

Though Juliet was well schooled in the proper use of forks and glasses, she purposely abandoned those lessons in manners so that Pauline wouldn't bear the brunt of Maisy's patronizing tone alone.

Having dined with the Crowleys, Noble observed Juliet's actions with interest. Having seen her impeccable graces, he realized that their absence was to make the less socially adept Pauline feel comfortable. And he admired her for it. In fact, there was little about Juliet that he didn't admire, right down to her saber-sharp tongue and bold opinions. While such a woman wouldn't do as a conservative Kentucky lawyer's wife, she possessed all the qualities he'd dreamed of for an intimate companion. Imagine coming home at night to the fond study of her pleasing features across the table, to the revitalizing challenge of meeting her barbed quips as the day's shadows grew long, to the afterhours luxuries hinted at by her lush lips and galvanizing stare. Imagine...

Growing uncomfortable with the way his thoughts provoked a crowding within his trousers, Noble changed his focus from the colonel's daughter to the man himself. And he found the fellow's steely gaze upon him with an all too keen perceptiveness. Did Crowley know he lusted after the quixotic Juliet? If he did, he probably wouldn't smile indulgently and ask about the horses.

"You should have some fine mounts, Colonel. Definitely your three dollars' worth." They shared a smug moment that Miles couldn't resist interrupting.

"So Major Banning, now that you've tamed the animals, is it your plan to teach us all to ride like raiding Confederates?"

While several breaths were inhaled, Noble took the question in stride with a coolly civil, "I beg your pardon?"

"I'm familiar with the exploits of your John Hunt Morgan, a man you obviously emulate. The colonel believes you can show us how to become the scourge of the plains so no heathen would dare defy us again."

"I would be happy to *show* you, but I can't guarantee that you can be taught."

Miles bristled up at the smooth slur. "What exactly are you saying, sir?"

"I'm saying that the Union's idea of cavalry

is ridiculous. I've seen your men so loaded down with sundries that I could never be sure if they were lifted into the saddle after it was lashed on or if the riders mounted first and had the useless equipment packed in around him like salt in a pork barrel. No wonder your horses are broken down."

"And you have a better way of doing things, I suppose?" Miles challenged. "Better than the Poinsett Tactics used by the dragoon regiments?"

"More practical than what is taught by your drill regulations. I heard it said once of our Southern horsemen: No one ever sees a dead cavalryman."

Miles's glare narrowed. "But that's not true in your case, is it, Major? I understand that you left quite a few of your men behind to be buried by our troops."

Noble went still, a stillness born of dangerous tension and fierce repercussions should Miles be foolish enough to pursue the topic. A man of linear thinking, the career army major never saw the threat. But Crowley did.

"Gentlemen, if you'd give your thanks to our charming hostess for a fine meal, I think it's time we adjourned to the porch for some of my cigars."

All but the two majors were quick to comply, then they, too, rose up like taut combatants readying to move to a different area of confrontation.

When they were gone, Juliet released her

breath. "Goodness, nothing is quite as tiresome as men when they get to talking about battles or politics."

"I thought you enjoyed such discussions, Miss Crowley," came Maisy's arch observation.

"Not at the dinner table, where talk should be of a more refined and congenial nature."

With a stabbing glance at Pauline, Maisy said, "Perhaps such boorish talk is all some of them understand."

"Oh, I doubt that, Mrs. Bartholomew," Juliet said. "War gives men an opportunity to behave badly when they should know better—if they can get away with it. We shouldn't excuse or condone it. After all, if we three ladies don't stick together, all civilizing influence is gone."

Maisy gave her a hoity sniff. "I suppose you're right about that."

Leaping in at the first sign of possible companionship, Pauline said, "Juliet is right. It's only the three of us, so we should get along. At other posts, we women have always stood together, visiting each day to compare notes on cooking, sewing, and the like."

Maisy's attitude cut the other's optimism to the core as she sneered down her nose, "I hardly care to indulge in such plebeian discourses."

"Then perhaps we should form a literary circle to discuss the classics. Certainly, a woman of your stature is well read and socially informed."

Maisy flushed beneath Juliet's smoothly delivered remark, then muttered, "I'm not much for reading."

"Perhaps you should make an effort to cultivate other interests, Mrs. Bartholomew. We have only each other, and it would be a shame for you to feel yourself above the need for camaraderie. Pushing to forward your husband's career is admirable, but I fear you'll find no household of servants to bully to add to your amusement." Juliet rose while Maisy sputtered like a scalding kettle. "Pauline, help me carry these plates to the kitchen. I'm sure Colleen could use a hand in there. Grueling tasks are made so much more pleasant when shared by friends."

Leading a smirking Pauline away from Maisy's table, Juliet marched into the kitchen with her head held high. Just because she'd allowed the mean-spirited Maisy to choose the field of conflict didn't mean Juliet was unfamiliar with the game. She could parry snobbery with the best of them.

Because like her father, she played to win.

The air grew thick and redolent with the smoke of fine tobacco. Differences were momentarily set aside in deference to a good draw and exhalation. As they puffed in silence, the group of officers could almost pass as comrades in arms.

Almost.

Noble watched curiously as Crowley bent to pluck several bristles from a broom left propped against the adobe wall. He snapped them into straws of unequal length, then secreted them in his hand. He extended it to Miles.

"Gentlemen, choose."

Miles picked a straw, then scowled at its shortness. His displeasure deepened as the same opportunity was given to each officer, even the Southerners.

"John, surely you don't mean to include them."

"What are we drawing for?" George asked at last, studying his own stubby reed.

"A duty entrusted only to those closest to me," Crowley answered. "A tradition I've maintained for nearly eighteen years, one that requires the utmost honor and discipline from the select few."

Gazing down at his own long straw, Noble asked, "And exactly what is that privilege?"

Juliet readied for bed, bemused by her father's good humor. She'd asked him to explain himself, but he only smiled, kissed her brow, and wished her a pleasant good evening. His self-satisfied silence annoyed her, because she sensed his amusement was somehow at her expense.

She felt badly about her behavior toward Maisy. It wasn't like her to talk meanly to another, even when that one was so deserving of the set down. She knew it was her obligation to further the spirit of good will. But it was hard to extend an olive branch to Maisy Bartholomew when her strongest urge was to use the branch to switch her pampered behind.

Pauline expressed her need for female companionship. Even with a husband and a brood of her own, she longed to reach out to others of her own sex. Juliet had never had many close friends. Jane Howell was the exception, but one didn't have to work at being friends with Jane. She overwhelmed a body with chatter and good humor. Juliet found such gaiety difficult. More at home with men than with her own gender, she never knew exactly what to say. She could talk about books or gardening, she could complain about the day-to-day running of the post, but the subject she yearned to discuss she didn't know how to broach.

She wanted to ask someone about what it felt like to be in love.

And that was a subject she felt shy of even around the mild Pauline.

If only her mother hadn't passed on before imparting the wisdom of one generation to the next...

She was about to blow out the main room light when a soft knock sounded on the door. To her surprise, Noble Banning stood on the porch, his hat in hand, his features grim.

"Major Banning, it's late," she chided,

drawing her bed gown tighter about her. "My father has already retired."

"This doesn't concern him, ma'am. At least not directly."

In answer to her frown of confusion, he displayed his straw with a flourish and watched her pale.

"I've come to escort you to your bath."

Chapter 9

If he'd suggested scrubbing her back for her, Juliet couldn't have been more shocked.

"What? You?"

He waved the broom straw under her nose, his amusement galling. "Just my luck. I'll wait out here while you get—whatever it is you need."

She slammed the door between them with enough force to knock chinking from the windowsills. Standing in the empty room, her heart a chugging steam engine, Juliet wondered what to do. How could her father have thought such a situation acceptable? She remembered his smothered grin and cursed him low and passionately. She wouldn't have put it past him to have rigged the draw.

It was Noble, then, that he'd chosen for her to wed, not Miles. The idea was absurd. It was impossible. It was... tempting. As tempting as the image of Noble Banning hip deep in a moonlight-drenched pool.

No. She'd tell him no. There was no way she could go through with it.

But a good soaking bath was one of the frontier's rarest luxuries. Spirit of ammonia in a washbowl and a dash of rose water only served for so long, then the body itched for leisurely submersion in water that was clean and pure, for milled soap and a headful of hedonistic suds.

That was the one extravagance the colonel allowed her, her and her mother before her. A monthly bath in a nearby stream, under the cover of night, under the watchdog care of one of his most trusted men. He himself couldn't leave the post, so from the time she was a child, a draw of straws amongst his officers picked an escort who would wait, well armed and ever vigilant so that she could enjoy this single female indulgence.

And now it would be spoiled by a cruel fate that presented Noble with the long straw.

Thinking of the cool water and fragrant soap had her scalp tingling. A vigorous brushing was no substitute for deep-to-the-roots clean.

Why should she allow one arrogant Southerner to ruin her solitary pleasure?

Before she could talk herself out of going, Juliet snatched the blanket from the foot of her bed and gathered up her toiletries in a straw bag. Tugging on boots, she made no effort to change from her nightclothes. Her robe provided ample protection from the brush and from prying eyes, and would give her freedom to sit astride.

She paused to lean inside the door to her father's bedroom. The absence of his gusty snores told her he was still awake, so she whispered fiercely, "Don't think you've been forgiven," before leaving the house and placing herself in the care of the chosen honor guard.

The surprising cool of the late evening faded the burn of humiliation from Juliet's cheeks. It also helped that Noble remained a silent shadow at her side. She wasn't sure she could endure any pithy comments in regard to their situation while vulnerable in her nightwear.

The stream ran less than a half-mile from the fort, a runoff from the Colorado River and the only source of water within a hundred miles. Daily expeditions from the post brought back a limited supply from the tributary, just enough to quench the thirst of man and beast and to provide scant leftovers for necessary washing. Juliet carried four hide skins behind her saddle. Each day she personally fetched the nectar needed for her garden to flourish and her plants to grow, since there was never enough from the Crowleys' allotted ration to spare. First she would see to her own revitalizing, then she would attend her greens.

The gurgle of the stream won nickers of anticipation from their horses as they grew near. Juliet's own eagerness overwhelmed earlier reluctance as she guided her mount through the tangled scrub to the sandy bank of the creek. Noble followed unquestioningly as she continued along the winding edge until she found the spot she sought, a bend where the waters deepened and slowed on the outer curve, where low mesquite trees afforded protection. Eagerly, she slid off her horse and passed Noble the reins along with a warning glare that she'd brook no nonsense from him.

"I shouldn't be more than a few minutes. You can wait with the horses over there." She gestured to the other side of the mesquite thicket. From there he'd have no opportunity to steal a look at her.

"Take your time, Miz Crowley. Enjoy your bath. I'll keep an eye out for hostiles."

The fact that he called her the remote "Miss Crowley" instead of the familiar "Juliet" made it easier for her to relax and even offer him a faint smile.

"I doubt you'll be seeing any hostiles, Major, not this close to our troops. Just make sure that's all you're planning to see." Her brow arched pointedly.

He raised his hand to protest his innocence. "May God strike me blind if I'm lying."

"*I'll* strike you harder than that."

He grinned down at her. "Yes, ma'am. I'll keep my eyes on my duty."

And just for a moment, his gaze canted downward, a slow, thorough caress from head to toe and back, naming her as the duty foremost in his mind. The far from impersonal look made it hard for Juliet to draw a decent breath from the sudden tightening through her chest. She scowled at him.

"Stay over there."

"Yes, ma'am." Then he added in a satin-smooth aside, "Call if you need anything."

Like help reaching my back?

Juliet swallowed down her expectations, the gesture dry and as raw as the smolder in his gaze. Then he nudged his mount ahead, hers trailing behind it, and went to his appointed watch.

Determined to dismiss him from mind, as if such a feat were possible, Juliet let the inviting murmur of the current entice her to the water's edge. After stepping out of her boots, she dipped a toe beneath the glassy surface and gave a delighted shiver. Positively delicious. No more delays. Her robe hanging on a thorny shrub, her blanket folded within an easy stretch, Juliet slipped into the stream.

Paradise.

The sensation of her damp muslin underclothes hugging her skin was next to being naked, wringing a long, low sigh from Juliet as she sank shoulder-deep into the water. With moonlight shining a silvery lavender along the surface and cool eddies swirling about her form beneath it, it took little encouragement for her imagination to suggest the feel of a lover's hands. Or for her seditious heart to put a name to him.

Noble Banning.

With only the nightbird's song to disturb her dreams, Juliet let them wander where her practical mind refused to give them license. To the wickedly handsome face and the pale fire of his stare, a stare that on more than one occasion had devoured her whole. To the memory of a broad, hair-matted chest that incited a feverish wondering as to how this diamond-cool water would look glistening upon it. Wondering how it would feel beneath her palms... how it would feel to taste the sinfully shaped mouth that haunted her nights. To be lost in his kisses, to his touch, to his possession...

The sound of her own wayward moan shocked her back to her senses. Grabbing up the precious bar of French milled soap, she began a hurried scrubbing, willing her overly sensitized skin to cease its quivering. However, the scent of lavender rose about her, a cloud of sensory bliss distracting her from her haste. How wanton and wonderful to feel the bar gliding up wet arms, between the valley of her breasts, over the wisps of muslin clinging to her thighs.

Was Noble watching? She let her hair trail back into the water, feeling the heavy pull of it in the current.

Let him look. Let him dream even as she dreamed of what would never—could never—happen.

* * *

Noble was dreaming all right.

Had she stripped to the skin before sinking into the stream?

The thought of her nude and buoyant figure cast in pearlescent silhouette beneath the stars goaded him almost beyond restraint. The sound of a woman's sighs pulled him from frustration to near frenzy. Carbine clutched in sweat-slicked palms, he prowled the underbrush, almost hoping some luckless critter might appear so he'd have cause to vent his tensions.

Did the woman know she was driving him mad?

Were she other than Juliet Crowley, he would have answered an unqualified yes. But there was a sweet naïveté to Juliet, an unassuming honesty that appealed to him as powerfully as her lushly pouting lips. To have both ... he could picture no greater heaven.

No darker purgatory.

Such thoughts were torture, nothing more. He couldn't act upon them even if she invited him to. Which she wouldn't. Though he'd been receiving enough subtle signals from her to rouse a man from a coma, he suspected she wasn't taunting him purposefully.

Remember your duty, man. Remember your cause. Remember why you brought your men out to this forsaken land a world away from home and hearth and hope.

It was to find a traitor—not to slake his own desires.

If he forsook his obligations now for personal pleasures, how could he return to Pride County and hold up his head? How could he act as if he were any different from his father?

How could he demand sacrifices from others without making a few of his own?

Pride County was full of women. Any one of them would be glad to take whatever he was willing to give.

But it wasn't any one of them he wanted here in this lonesome wilderness where seductive sighs beckoned him into abandoning his pride. At the moment, there was little else left him.

Taking a deep, purifying breath and wishing he had one of the colonel's good cigars, Noble continued his stony pose of sentinel until a sudden shrill cry from behind him brought him crashing toward the stream, heart in his throat.

When he didn't see Juliet in the placid water, frantic thoughts and a tearing guilt collided in his brain. How had he let something happen to her? Then a fine webbing appeared on the stream's surface, and Juliet's head broke through. As she gasped and sputtered, Noble's knees went wobbly in relief.

"Are you all right?"

At the sight of him standing at the water's edge, Juliet ducked back down until her chin bobbed on the current.

"W-what are you doing here? You're not supposed to be here!"

"You cried out. I thought you might need—"

"I slipped on a rock. I don't need . . . you."

Her words failed, then faded.

Their gazes fell unbidden to the lips shaping those anxious words, and the moment stretched out beyond discomfort to a strange sort of inevitability. Knowing duty demanded that he withdraw, Noble continued to linger, fascinated by the provocative way Juliet moistened her mouth in uncalculated nervousness.

She was wearing a filmy something or other. Hints of eyelet lace threaded through with delicate pink ribbon showed at her smooth shoulders. The effect was so startlingly feminine on one as practical as Juliet that it hit him low, like a blow to the solar plexus.

Because he couldn't just stand there sucking wind, he asked, "How's the water?"

"Wonderful." A pause, then a husky, "Come in and see for yourself."

"I don't think that would be a very good idea."

Her eyes grew heavy-lidded, her mouth a teasing pucker. "And why is that, Major? Certainly both you and your clothing could use the wash."

"I'm not disputing that fact. But I'm on duty—"

"Which are you more afraid of, Noble? The Indians or my father?"

He didn't hesitate. "You."

Her blue eyes rounded in surprise, then became all sultry invitation once more. "I'm just a simple girl. What does a sophisticated gallant like yourself have to fear from me?"

"Ah, such words as were spoken by Helen of Troy and Delilah." His gaze followed the movement of the current as it lapped about the curve of her breasts. Oh, to be that unassuming stream...

Her soft laughter played like the rush of water over rough rocks, its low-pitched music undeniably sensual. "Are you afraid I'm a danger to your life—or to your manhood?"

"Both."

That pleased her. "I'll avert my eyes to preserve your chastity—had you any to protect." She splashed at him, the spray darkly dappling his pant legs. "Come in. Consider it an order. Or don't you take orders from women?"

"Those are the ones I enjoy obeying the most."

A slight frown shaped her lips, then she pushed herself away from the creek bottom to ride the current on her back. The sylphlike movement brought her breasts and sweetly rounded thighs above the surface. Wet muslin did nothing to conceal what it was meant to cover.

The blade of desire twisted low in Noble's belly. And he considered her offer for one beat, then two.

"Hell."

It was both oath and prediction. He levered

his feet out of his boots. He draped his uniform shirt over them, then, after one last moment of hesitation, he laid his carbine on the bank and waded in. His worry that he'd gone suddenly insane was quickly washed away by the refreshing sluice of the water.

"I told you it was wonderful," Juliet said as she rolled onto her belly and glided closer. She extended the soap. He took a sniff, then shook his head.

"I'm sure your father likes smelling it on you, but I don't think the same would apply to me."

"I don't think he would mind as much as you think," was her mysterious reply.

"Your father doesn't mind you bathing with men?"

"He likes you." Displeasure tugged at her response, but Noble didn't notice. His thoughts were elsewhere.

"And he's said nothing to Miles when he's returned to the post smelling of lavender?"

Her mood clouded. "Miles never has."

"I'm certain he wouldn't object to playing in the water with you."

"Miles doesn't play, Major. He takes everything very seriously—too seriously."

Now it was Noble's turn to be vague. "And you don't want to be serious with Miles?"

"Not with anyone."

She sent a wave of water at his head, then as he sputtered and cleared his eyes, she swam lithely away. He chuckled but didn't pursue her. This was her game and he'd let her set the rules. He ignored her long enough to rinse his face and hair, wishing for soap that wouldn't leave him smelling like a Saturday night whorehouse to his commander's discerning nose.

But Juliet wasn't to be ignored.

She bobbed up before him, rising like Venus from the water. With her height they stood almost eye to eye. Hers locked into his with a purposeful intensity.

"We'd might as well get this out of the way. I think we've waited long enough, don't you?"

Before he could ask, she made herself very clear. Her palms pressed to his lean cheeks, holding his face between them. Her mouth was on his before he had time to blink. And before he could react, she slipped away. Though she'd said she wasn't serious, there was no playfulness in her stare.

"I had to know," she told him simply, as if explanation was needed.

"You don't know anything yet."

And he reached for her to prove it.

His arm curved around her waist, pulling her toward him through the slight resistance the water made. She made none. Her eyes were closed, her face lifted in anticipation of what he'd teach her.

The lesson was beyond anything she could have wildly imagined.

He tasted of heaven and danger. Alternately soft and persuasive then urgent in his demand, Noble's kiss answered everything in one explosive moment. When his tongue touched to her lips, she opened them for him with an eager abandon, at the same time lassoing him with her arms about his neck to intensify their union.

It was just kissing. It didn't have to be more. Sensations more powerful than anything either had ever experienced engulfed them. She melded to his slick, hard surfaces, erasing the separation between them to learn all she could through the scant barrier of their clothing. What she discovered only made her anxious to find out more. She responded greedily to the plunge of his kisses, gobbling them with uncontrolled urgency as fingers twined and twisted through wet hair.

Finally, shaken, a bit scared yet wildly exhilarated, Juliet let her head fall against his shoulder so that she could grab for breath. For a moment, she was content to ride the labored movement of his chest as her fingers continued to ply among the hair at his nape and stroke along his rough jaw. Then, because she couldn't stand not knowing, she leaned back to study his expression.

He didn't reveal much, and that concerned her. Where she was all trembly and looselimbed, he was yet contained and watching her carefully. She wet her lips, tasting him there and taking strength from it.

"You think this was a mistake?" The gruff

texture of her voice begged him to deny it. He couldn't.

"Maybe." His fingertips circumvented the curve of her cheek. "But I don't know that it's one I can afford to make again."

"Then that would be a shame, but I'd understand it. At least now we know."

Together they were the Fourth of July.

He smiled faintly to relieve her grimness. "I'm afraid I'm going to smell like lavender whether I like it or not."

"Did you like it?" She wasn't referring to the lavender.

His knuckles rubbed beneath her proudly hoisted chin. His husky reply destroyed her.

"Very much." He buffed her soft lips with his thumb. "Too much not to be afraid."

"Of me?" she whispered wonderingly.

"Of myself."

He let her go then and stepped away to wade to the shore. He'd started to climb out, then paused in a moment of sinking dread.

The carbine was gone.

"Juliet."

He had only time to speak her name before another volley of fireworks exploded through his head.

Chapter 10

He breathed in dust and the faint scent of lavender. The salty taste of his own blood came back to him when he dampened parched lips with a scrub of his tongue. His cheek was pressed into hard-packed ground, but when he tried to lift himself up, a host of painful demons clawed through his shoulders and spine and set up a noisy din in his head. It was a moment before the waves of surging sickness eased enough for him to try to think of what had happened. Then he heard her voice close by, her words a shaky whisper.

"Thank God. I thought they'd killed you."

They . . . ?

It reassembled slowly in his dazed brain: the stream, their kisses, the missing carbine—

Indians.

For some agonizing reason he couldn't move so much as a muscle. Every one of them seemed cramped and strained, frozen into immobile screams. He tried to force his eyes open, but what greeted him was darkness, not an answer. Not Juliet's face.

"I was only joking about God striking me blind," he muttered hoarsely.

"There's blood in your eyes."

The matter-of-fact way she said that alarmed him all the more. A pretty grisly statement to make without the slightest inflection.

Where were they and how bad was their situation?

Bad, he guessed from the hollowness of Juliet's tone.

Because he still couldn't see, he tried reaching out with his other senses to learn more about his own position. Even the process of thought set off a roar like cannonfire within his head. Something had struck him. That much he could remember. What he couldn't figure out was why it felt as though his entire weight was resting on his cheekbone. And why the rest of him seemed suspended in some kind of numb limbo where the slightest move sent him straight into hell.

What had they done to him?

And to Juliet?

"Are you all right?"

She answered him with a hushed, "Fine. Stay quiet. Don't let them hear you."

"How many of them are there?"

"Eight. A raiding party."

And their foolish interlude in the stream left

them easy targets. How could he have been so careless with both their lives?

"How long have I been out?"

"Hours. It's almost dawn."

He focused his waning awareness on her disembodied voice because he had to say it, even though it wouldn't make any difference.

"I'm sorry."

Silence.

Then a soft, "Me too."

But not, he guessed correctly, as sorry as they both were going to be.

"Can you get away?"

"No. I'm tied up, too."

Too. He couldn't feel any restraints, and that struck him as odd. "Why didn't they kill us?"

Her pause said they still might. Then she told him, "I think they're taking us to Mexico. We're worth more alive to them as long as we're no trouble."

"Worth more?"

"As slaves. Or worse."

Her voice grew pinched, so he didn't ask her any more. Finally, he said, "I can't feel my hands and feet."

"For now, be glad. You will soon enough."

His head hurt too badly for him to make sense of her cryptic statement. For a time, he let go of the struggle to retain consciousness and simply drifted. But that was too easy to last for long. He woke to the fluttering touch of Juliet's hand against his face. She was speaking to him low and fast and he didn't understand the purpose of what she was saying.

"You have to walk now. You have to. If you fall, they'll drag you. If you can't stand, they'll kill you. No matter how much it hurts, you have to keep up."

He tore his eyelids open through the seal of dried gore. Bright sunlight seared him back into momentary blindness. Then, after a few blinks, shapes began to form: Juliet bending over him, her face grimy and etched with concern, a pair of high-topped moccasins belonging to one of their captors. Juliet was shoved roughly aside. He saw the glitter of a knife blade. There was a moment of weightlessness, then, as he hit the ground, his world exploded into white-hot pain.

His wrists were bound behind him, his ankles, too. During the hours of the night, they'd hung him from a pole running through those bindings like a pig after slaughter, face down, spine bowed backward, his weight dragging on his arm sockets until they'd gone numb. But now with freedom came the awful agony of blood moving back through abused limbs, through joints twisted and muscles nearly torn. And the pain of it came close to stealing away his consciousness.

"Noble. Noble, you have to get up. Try!"

Her urgency stirred him back to awareness. Though every effort brought the need to scream, he bit down hard and inched his knees under him. A rope tether dropped over his head to tighten at his throat. Then his feet were freed. He forced himself to rise up, tottering, close to swooning but focusing on the rope around his neck that led to the back of one of the Indian ponies, the rope that would drag him until he strangled if he couldn't keep up.

As the Indians prepared to break camp, speaking amongst themselves in brief gutturals and ignoring their prisoners, Noble had a moment to assess their circumstances. Not good. Beside him, Juliet was similarly bound, her hands in front instead of behind. Her pallor betrayed her fear, but her gaze was steady and alert. She was wearing just her underclothing, the ribbons and lace making her look all the more vulnerable. Her hair had dried loose about her shoulders in a wild golden tangle. And all Noble could think of was what a prize she'd be in Mexico.

And he knew he had to find a way for them to escape before they got there.

Escape faded from his thoughts and minute-to-minute survival became his only concern as the rope snapped taut, forcing him to stumble forward. His muscles cramped. His bad leg spasmed and threatened to fold under him. But he walked, gritting his teeth and blanking his mind to the razor-sharp discomfort. Because if they killed him, who would save Juliet?

They moved at a leisurely yet relentless pace as the sun continued to rise along with the temperature. Sweat and blood from Noble's head wound blinded him. He was barefooted, an added misery as the rocky ground cut and bruised him. Juliet was lucky enough to be wearing her boots. The ache in his temples massed to a steady throb, drowning out all else. He used the beat of it to measure his footsteps, a cadence that would keep him alive.

Beside him, Juliet kept up with a steely determination. Instead of the neck thong, she was led by a rope to where her wrists were lashed in front of her. She didn't stumble, and his awe of her grew by the hour as his own steps wobbled and weakened. Her face was expressionless, her eyes narrowed in concentration. For once, he thanked God she'd inherited her father's stubbornness.

She would give them no reason to punish her.

He lost track of time. The sky and ground melded into one dark blur as the pull of the rope against the back of his neck propelled him on into that searing oblivion. He couldn't recall ever being so hot. By afternoon, his pores had baked dry and his lips began cracking from lack of moisture. He had no spit left with which to keep them damp. The rasp of his breathing grew as loud as echoing thunder in his head. The edges of his awareness began to ravel as he felt himself fall and keep falling. He never realized just when he hit the hard-packed ground.

* * *

He wasn't going to make it.

Juliet kept a watchful eye on Noble and worried as his steps began to falter. His head wound was ghastly, continuing to bleed and mask half his face in crimson. It could easily have killed him. It might yet. She hadn't thought he'd survive the night, so perhaps she'd underestimated his stamina—at least she hoped so until he collapsed, to be dragged by the noose about his throat.

"Stop! Stop!" She didn't think their captors would heed her cries, but thankfully they did. She stumbled to where Noble lay unmoving and dropped to her knees beside him. She was too scared and exhausted to realize that she was crying.

"Noble, get up. You have to get up." When he didn't move, her tone grew more frantic. "Don't you die and leave me alone with them."

Dust stirred beneath his mouth and nose. His eyes flickered open but his gaze was hot and unfocused. One of the Indians shouted back at them. She was sure he wasn't asking after Noble's welfare.

"Come on. Get up, Major. I'm depending on you. Dammit, don't you let me down."

His toes dug in, inching him up onto his knees. Juliet expelled a tremulous breath and tugged at his arm.

"That's it. Come on."

"I can make it," he mumbled thickly with more confidence than he had strength. She pulled harder, dragging him up with her but unable to support him as he teetered. So she braced him with her words.

"Come on, Major. Look at me. If I can make it, so can you. I told my father you were a soft, spoiled aristocrat. Now, you prove me wrong. Prove me wrong!"

For an instant, the shadow of a smile crossed his chapped lips as he whispered, "Yes, ma'am."

And somehow, he did make it, managing step after tortured step until the Indians felt safe to make camp for the night. He dropped to his knees in the hard sand, too dizzy and disoriented to notice when one of their heathen captors removed the loop from about his neck, then bound his ankles, tethering his wrists to them. Awareness lapped in an irregular tide. He was too grateful that they'd stopped to care what their situation was. Until he got a teasing whiff of lavender.

Juliet.

He had to protect Juliet.

But as it was, she was determined to protect him.

Her touch brushed gently across his brow, a cool breeze wafting through his fevered state. She spoke to the Indians as if speaking to her father's aides.

"I need water. He's not going to be worth anything to you if he dies."

Even if they didn't understand every word,

they took her meaning and apparently had taken no exception to her tone. Perhaps they even admired her for it.

Noble did.

The chill of water upon his face was the shock needed to return him to his senses. Once he'd conquered the brunt of the harsh pain signaling seemingly from every muscle of his body, he was able to observe other things. Their two horses were hobbled alongside the Indian ponies. The raiding party itself was hunkered down at a small fire, apparently confident enough to risk the light to cook several small animals over the coals. The aroma stirred a gnawing rumble in his belly, but he doubted that they'd think of feeding their prisoners any more than they would think of throwing food to camp dogs. While they carried on an animated conversation, only brief glances were cast in their direction. Obviously, they considered him no threat. He worried that if he had to endure another day like this one, they would be right. He wasn't going to get any stronger while in their care.

"My belt buckle."

Juliet paused in her cleansing of his wound and bent closer so that she could hear his raspy whisper.

"Undo it."

"What?"

There was just enough maidenly shock in her voice to make him chide, "Don't worry. I won't think any less of you for fumbling with my trousers. There's a blade hidden in the buckle."

When she remained unmoving for a long moment, Noble canted a look up at her. Her expression was cautious, gauging him and their situation should she obey.

"I'm going to get us out of here," he told her, not caring how impossible such a claim might seem at the moment.

She offered a flickering smile and an unquestioning, "I'm ready any time you are."

God, what a woman. No hesitation. No doubts. Just quick acceptance and total belief.

She bent over him, pretending to flutter and fuss, using her body as a shield while reaching purposefully for his buckle. She felt along the raised lettering. CSA. Standard issue except for fancy ornamentation on either end. She focused there, letting her fingertips guide her as she located and carefully released the small blade from its copper sheath.

"I have it."

"Put it in my hands, then wait."

She didn't press for more details. She slipped the blade into his palm while her fingers caressed his. Then she backed away, giving him room to work at the ropes as she kept an eye on their captors and waited for his signal.

And waited.

The fire died down to white ash. The members of the raiding party sought their blankets, leaving one brave to guard the horses and their prisoners. Noble remained slumped over his knees, unmoving, as the hours ticked by.

Had he lost consciousness? Juliet studied him covertly, seeking any clue that he'd managed to free himself. Finding none.

Finally, she relaxed her vigil and allowed her weary eyes to close. She'd given Noble too much credit. He was just a man, after all, trying to rise above impossible odds. She'd let her own admiration for him imbue him with the superhuman strength it would require for him to overcome injury and exhaustion to effect a dramatic escape. Because she wanted—no, *needed*—to believe he could.

Now she would have to accept the facts. She forced down her hopes with a hard swallow. Chances were they'd be in Mexico tomorrow. And beyond that, she didn't want to speculate.

"Call the guard over."

Noble's hissed whisper shocked her back into full readiness. Her breath came faster as anticipation rose. She didn't look at him to see for herself that he was prepared. It was time to trust.

"*Puede usted ayudarme por favor?*" She called out quietly for help so as not to disturb those slumbering. The guard took a step nearer, his every movement conveying wariness. Most Apaches knew passable Spanish, so she phrased her request awkwardly in that language. "*Me duele aquí. La muñeca.* My ropes are too tight. Can you loosen them?"

She lifted her bound hands, feigning an expression of helplessness and distress. It wasn't that hard to look frightened.

Lulled out of his caution, the brave approached, his rifle cradled easily within his forearms. Juliet lifted her arms higher, continuing to hold his attention as he reached out to tug at the ropes. She almost yelled as the Indian suddenly fell across her, driven by Noble's lunge. She scrambled out of the way as the freed Noble smashed the man's head into the stony ground until he ceased moving.

"Get to the horses. Quick and quiet."

She was already moving. Staying low to the ground, where the shadows were thickest, she could hear the rustle of Noble following. She went directly to the big gray stallion, easing up so as not to startle it into giving them away. It snorted in alarm but was easily calmed by the stroke of her palm upon its nose as she untied its crude hackamore. At the same time, Noble sliced through the hobbles. He made a cradle with his hands and boosted her aboard.

A shout came from the camp.

With no time to free another mount, Noble leaped up behind Juliet, using the braided halter rope to jerk the animal around, then kicked it into an anxious gallop.

There was no time to feel afraid.

Juliet bent low over the horse's neck, grabbing handfuls of its whipping mane, as they plunged wildly through the darkness. Whoops from the pursuing raiding party split the night air, growing ever closer. Noble's form engulfed hers, his arms and powerful thighs holding her to the animal's bare back, his body making a barrier between her and their enemies. She hung on tight as the stallion raced over the rugged terrain under Noble's relentless goading. Until they came to the edge of a ravine that broke away and fell straight down into total darkness.

Noble wheeled the horse about in a tight circle, assessing their chances of eluding the Indians by heading either to the right or left. He saw only one means of escape and took it without hesitation.

"Hang on."

Her scream caught in her throat as Noble urged their mount down the crumbling side of the ravine. To keep her seat, Juliet lay back flat along Noble's chest, and he against the animal's scrabbling haunches. Loose dirt and rock slid all around them, careening ahead toward whatever waited at the bottom. They heard splashes; then they were in the water.

The creek wasn't deep but it was fast-moving. It took the gray a moment to gather its footing, then they were surging upstream away from the awed and angry Apache, who lined the lip of the ravine, none willing to follow their reckless descent into what should have been certain death.

Chapter 11

Though the immediate threat had ended, Noble continued to push on throughout the night. Only when the searing peach hues of daybreak streaked the horizon did he rein in from the mile-gobbling canter to a jouncing lope, guiding them to the crumbling walls of an abandoned mission. There they could find shade and concealing shelter while the horse had a chance to blow. And only when they stopped within the roofless structure did Juliet risk speaking.

"I've never seen such daring on horseback," she began breathlessly. "Noble, I—"

She twisted just in time to catch him in a headlong plunge toward the ground. Gripping the animal's sweat-slicked sides with her knees for balance, she managed to swing him down in a more gentle descent, then quickly dismounted.

"Take care of the horse," he mumbled as she started to bend over him. A true cavalryman.

By the time she'd finished rubbing down the animal with a ruffled flounce torn from the hem of her drawers, Noble had managed to drag himself to one of the adobe walls. He slumped against it, his eyes closed, hand kneading his cramping thigh. Juliet paused before approaching him, stunned and dismayed by how worn and ravaged he appeared—not at all the dynamic hero who'd whisked her from under the Apache's very noses in a desperate bid for freedom.

"That was some piece of riding." She knelt down in front of him, pitching her voice in a conversational tone.

"Dangerous times call for reckless measures."

"And I for one am glad you were willing to take them. I have no real desire to see Mexico just now."

His eyes opened slowly, gaze fixing upon her face with difficulty. "Do you think they're still following us?"

"I don't know. We probably shouldn't stay here for very long. It's a hard day's ride to the fort if we want to make it by dark."

He nodded, then grimaced at the pain that movement caused. Worriedly, Juliet touched the back of her hand to his brow. His skin was fever-scorched. He scowled at her concern.

"I'll be fine."

Her silence stated her opinion. Seeing it was useless to argue, Noble shut his eyes once more, determined to make the most of their brief rest.

Wondering what she could do to relieve some of the discomfort she saw in the pinch of his features, Juliet studied his head wound. A nasty gash that no longer bled. Again she noticed his preoccupation with his leg.

"Are you hurt?"

"You'll have to be a bit more specific. I hurt all over."

She touched his knuckles. His hand paused in its restless massage.

"It's nothing. I took a bullet when your father captured me and my men. It grieves me some when I overtax it. The past few days have done some mighty serious overtaxing. It just aches a bit."

Most likely an incredible understatement, but she let it pass, because there was nothing she could do for his leg. Her attention shifted to his bare feet. There she found the source of his fever. The soles were raw from the forced trek the day before. Several sores had begun to fester.

"Let me have your knife."

He slid a suspicious look at her, alerted by her tone. "Why?"

"You've got thorns embedded in your feet. If I don't get them out, you'll get blood poisoning."

She didn't need to elaborate. He'd been in a war where more lives were lost to putrefaction of the flesh than the actual wounds themselves. Wordlessly, he passed her the blade. She braced his foot upon her thigh, and because talking was better than screaming, he asked, "What kind of Indians were those?"

"Apache. Mescalero."

"I thought Kit Carson rounded them all up and stuck them on that reservation—I can't recall the name."

"Bosque Redondo. He did. You know your frontier facts, Major."

"Carson's a fellow Kentuckian. I thought it wise to find out what I could when your father offered to relocate us out here."

"It's always wise to learn all you can about your enemy." She probed for the first thorn, steeling herself against the hurried sounds of his breathing.

"Are you—are you sure they were Apache?"

She didn't look up as she answered matter-of-factly, "I know a great deal about the Apache. I learned most of it watching them murder my mother when I was a girl." She lifted out the thorn and tossed it away.

While his breathing regulated itself once more, Noble observed her curiously. What a marvel she was when he compared her past experiences to her composure during their captivity. He'd have thought that having faced such horror at a young age, she would have been terrified beyond rational thought by the idea of being imprisoned by the Indians. But her calm, clear thinking was one of the reasons they'd been able to escape.

"She must have been some kind of woman." Like her daughter, was what he meant.

"She was."

"Tell me about her."

"She was strong." Juliet said that as if it said it all. "She grew up in Ohio. Her father believed in improving the status of women, and saw she had the finest education he could afford. She went to the Huron Academy in Milan and then a female seminary in Hudson and planned to become a teacher—until she met my father." Her smile took a wistful turn. "Then she had only one student, me, and she taught me that knowledge and love were everything. We were on the way to join my father at what would later become Fort Davis in Texas. Our party was attacked. My mother shielded me with her own body so that they would think I'd been killed as well. I was nine."

He wanted to express his regret, but she'd begun probing his foot, and the words got locked behind the gritting of his teeth. When he was able to breathe normally again, she quickly turned the topic.

"Tell me about Kentucky. How long has it been since you've been home?"

"Three years."

"I hear it's lovely country."

"God's country. Green and growing. At least that's how I left it." He clenched his teeth, sucking air noisily between them. "I don't know what I'll find when I go back."

"To practice law?"

Unable to speak with his jaw locked against the pain, he nodded jerkily.

"Then let's make sure you survive this to go home." She withdrew another wicked barb.

"I'm in your hands."

"Ah, if only that were true." Her grip tightened, conveying more warning than her casual tone. "This one's deep."

He endured in silence, then asked, "Do you still consider me soft and spoiled?"

"No."

He wished she would look up so that he could read more meaning into that single barely whispered word. "So," he prompted, "how do you feel about me now?" *Look up, Juliet.*

But she wouldn't. Nor would she satisfy his need for an answer.

"I fear I've given away more than I should already. There. That one's done." No tender sympathies, apologies, or anguished observations, only a gentle caress along the back of his foot. That, too, gave away plenty.

"You have an angel's touch, Juliet."

She did glance up then, her gaze startled, flustered. Then she scowled. "And you have a devil's tongue, Major. Keep it from making improper suggestions, if you will."

"I could put it to better uses—ow!"

She steadied his foot and her jittery nerves. "It's best not to agitate a woman holding a knife, sir, especially when it's your flesh she's carving."

"It's not my flesh you've been carving on lately."

He could see he'd shocked her. A wonderful flush spread from her ears across her cheeks. Crouched at his feet in her underclothes, with her hair unbound in riotous golden glory, she made a tantalizing sight.

"Juliet—"

"Don't." She ducked her head. "Don't say anymore."

"Why?"

"Don't say things you'll wish you hadn't said later."

His tone lowered to a husky rumble. "And what if I don't regret them?"

She stared up at him, her eyes wide with fright and anger and, he thought, with remorse. "Then I will."

"I'm sorry," he told her softly. "I didn't mean to scare you."

Her laugh was brittle. "Scare me? We've just escaped with our lives from Apaches. What could you possibly do that would scare me now?"

But he had scared her. Badly. Her previously steady hands shook slightly as she cut into the next infected puncture. Noble winced, considering the pain a small price for having pushed her onto the defensive. If she had no regrets for having kissed him at the stream, what then had worked her up into such a ferment of emotion?—the fact that she didn't have regrets or the wish that she did?

"I think that's all of them," she said gruffly. "We should go now."

"I'm ready."

Juliet stood, then gazed down at him dispassionately. "You've impressed me mightily, Major Banning, and I've seen too much to be easily impressed."

He quirked a smile up at her. "If that's the best compliment I can wring from you, I'll take it."

"You are arrogant enough, sir. You don't need my compliments."

"No, I don't. I much prefer your honesty."

Somehow, that rattled her all the more—and continued to fluster her throughout the day as they rode on toward Fort Blair. She handled the reins while Noble sat silently behind her, his arms making a loose circle about her waist. Over the course of the afternoon, he began to sag more and more against her until his head finally came to rest upon her shoulder. She welcomed his heavy weight, willing to support him in this small way. In any way.

It was nearing twilight when she said, "Noble, wake up. We're there."

When he didn't stir, her worries leaped up again. She goaded the last bit of strength from their played-out horse, urging it across the parade ground straight to the infirmary. She didn't acknowledge any of the commotion their passing caused until the post's surgeon

Robert Penny was reaching up for Noble.

"What happened to the two of you? The whole fort's on alert."

She hadn't given a thought to how they might look until that very moment: she in her undergarments, Noble out of uniform, both of them dirty and riding double. But looks weren't what concerned her.

"We were captured by a raiding party. He's lost a lot of blood and has been running a fever." She slid off the pony to follow Penny as he carried the unconscious Noble inside. Without hesitation, she knelt at the bedside, giving Penny a brief, grateful glance when he draped a blanket about her shoulders to cover her near nakedness. Weak with weariness and worry, she remained a quiet sentinel while the doctor conducted a quick examination.

"Some rest should do the trick," he pronounced at last. He placed an empathetic hand on her shoulder as her breath gushed out in relief. "Dehydration, blood loss, both curable ills. Did you tend his feet? Smart thinking. Probably saved them for him." He turned her away from her anxious study of the still figure to scold, "Now, you be smart and take care of yourself. There's nothing more you can do here."

"He saved my life," she murmured. Tears welled up in her eyes. She was too tired to combat them. "He has to be all right."

"He will be. Go home."

Running an unsteady hand through her

hair, she began to think beyond her concern for Noble. "My father, do you know where he is?"

"He led a patrol out yesterday to search for you and the major."

A reprieve. Time for her to think of what she'd tell him.

Once home, she sat in his rocker, bundled in the blanket, as minutes ticked toward dawn. Though she was exhausted in body, her mind refused to let her rest as she imagined her father's fear driving him across the desert while she sat safely at home. Wishing for his return became a desire to forestall their meeting when she heard his unit arrive without fanfare at first light. She heard the rattle of his saber as he ran toward their house.

Gazing into her father's features as they slowly altered from relief to suspicion, she knew her explanations would never be enough.

"Are you all right, daughter?" He was covered with two days' dust and the evidence of a hard ride. In his hands, he held the robe she'd discarded at the stream.

"Yes, I'm—"

"The major?"

"An Apache raiding party surprised us. He's in the infirmary."

"I'll want a report when he's well enough to give it." His unswerving glare said he'd demand more than that.

"Of course. Papa—"

"Get some sleep." His curt words said clearly that whatever she would say, he wasn't yet ready to hear. He wheeled around and announced, "I'm going to check on the major's progress."

She rose up out of the chair. "I'll go with you."

His stare slashed back to her. "Not like that. Make yourself presentable."

Clutching the edges of the blanket, she blinked back the sting of pain his words provoked and nodded. He drew a fierce breath, then calmed enough to say in a tight voice, "I'll wait here for you. It would look better for us to make this visit together."

She washed up hastily, fighting to drag her comb through hair tangled beyond taming, then slipping on a simple calico gown. Her fatigued thoughts tumbled over what conclusions her father must have come to, but knowing him to be a fair man, she didn't fear he'd act upon angry impulse. He'd first find out the facts. Then the two of them would feel the backlash of his distress.

He was more than an upset parent. He was the post commander with the power of supreme justice in his hands.

The fact that Noble appeared at their door before they could go to him spoke well on his behalf. Wearing a fresh uniform and white bandaging at his brow, he looked haggard but no less determined to see to his duty.

Crowley's expression was struck from stone

as he said, "Come in, Major." No offer of a drink or a smoke. Strictly business. Or strictly personal. Either boded ill.

Noble's gaze flickered briefly to the corner chair Juliet slipped into to sit pale and silent. In her simply cut calico dress, her wayward hair restrained in a ribbon, she looked almost like a chastened schoolgirl. Her expression was similarly restrained; she met his smile of encouragement with an impassive nod.

"Your report, Major."

"There were eight hostiles, sir. Mescalero Apache. I believe their intention was to take us south of the border to be sold into slavery."

Crowley paced, listening distractedly to Noble's factual rendering that made little of his heroics and much of Juliet's. Suddenly, he paused, his back to his junior officer.

"And what were your intentions?"

"Excuse me, sir?"

Crowley whirled toward him, using the momentum to put staggering force behind his cold demand. "What were your intentions toward my daughter that left you open to attack? Dammit, man, I entrusted you with the only thing I hold higher than my honor. I thought you understood that nothing—*nothing*—was more important than her safety. You have failed me and you have failed her, and I've a mind to have you shot for dereliction of duty."

"I would deserve it, sir."

Colonel Crowley glared at the younger man,

trying to find a chink of self-interest in his flat claim. Finding none, he gave a snort of disgust and turned away, fearing the other would see his grudging admiration.

Juliet took advantage of the pause to say, "It was the major's cunning and superior horsemanship that earned our freedom from the Apache."

Crowley refused to be impressed. "And was it his poor judgment that led to your capture in the first place?"

"Papa," she beseeched quietly, "it was not the major's fault, it was mine. No harm was done."

He stared at her, the anxiety and sorrow he'd suffered over the past days etched clearly in his features. "No harm? Is that how you summarize the conclusions drawn by a detail of men sent to retrieve you when they arrived at the riverbed to find only your clothing and the major's dress shirt and boots laid out ever so neatly on the bank?"

Noble spoke up then with a formal civility. "Sir, if your daughter's honor has been compromised by my actions, be assured that I will do the right thing."

Juliet sat bolt upright, too shocked to react to what was coming.

Crowley glared through him. "If you'd done the *right* thing, we wouldn't be having this conversation." Then he unbent slightly. "So you are willing to repair the damage done by wedding my daughter."

"If that's what it takes, sir."

Juliet's disbelieving gaze flew between the two of them. It was a joke, of course, a test on her father's part to gauge the depth of Noble's sincerity. Surely no more than that. Surely her father would accept the gesture for what it was, a token offer, and dismiss the whole affair.

But that wasn't her father's intention.

"I suppose that would be a satisfactory solution to this unfortunate matter."

That's when Juliet lost all patience and surged from her chair.

"Satisfactory? To whom?"

"Hush, girl. This does not concern you."

"Doesn't concern me? I beg your pardon—who then does it concern?"

"This is a matter of honor between men."

Her stare focused on Noble in amazement. He stood at stiff attention, willing to shoulder this unnecessary punishment without complaint or betraying emotion. Without any emotion at all.

And that's what stabbed to the heart. After what they'd endured, after all they'd shared, how could he let her father push them into an arrangement so bereft of feeling? Or think that she'd be a party to it?

She'd always dreamed of receiving a proposal of marriage. And this was not how she'd pictured the moment. Distress quivered through her response.

"Oh? Then if this does not concern me, it's

the two of you who'll share the marriage bed?"

Her bold reply took her father aback. "Juliet, your behavior is unacceptable."

She turned on him, fighting back angry tears. "What is unacceptable is your belief that I would willingly wed a man who considers having me for a wife preferable only to a firing squad." She drew a fractured breath and faced Noble in all her shredded dignity. "Thank you, Major Banning, but that sacrifice will not be necessary."

"Jules—"

"Nothing happened between the major and me that requires hasty nuptials. I will not crawl into wedlock as if I've done something sinful."

"No one is saying—"

"Isn't that exactly what you're saying, Papa?"

He met her challenging stare for as long as he could, then shamefacedly turned away. "Of course not, my dear."

Stepping between them, she demanded, "Then dismiss Major Banning. I'm exhausted and need to sleep. I'm eager to put this whole event behind me."

"Major Banning, you may go. I thank you for bringing my daughter back safely."

"Just doing my duty, sir."

That crisp rejoinder slashed Juliet almost as sharply as his icy stare. She made her tone cool to deflect the hurt. "I appreciate your rescuing me, Major Banning, but my virtue does not require your heroic efforts."

His gaze narrowed. In a soft aside for their hearing alone, he asked, "Is it the situation you found so intolerable, or was it my offer?"

She never missed a beat. "Both, sir."

"Then forgive me for attempting to rescue that which was never in jeopardy." He turned from her to give his commanding officer a brisk salute. "Good night, sir."

"Good morning, Major."

When he was gone, Crowley sighed and shook his head at his daughter. "You've ruined things this time, Jules."

"What? What do you mean, ruined things?"

"He would have married you, you know."

She swallowed down the massive lump of missed opportunity to mutter, "Yes, I know. But I couldn't let you railroad him for something he's not guilty of."

"I never thought him guilty."

"You—you knew he was innocent of any wrongdoing? Then why were you going to accept his offer?"

"Because he would have made you an excellent husband, Jules. He has no plans to remain in the army, and I was hoping that when he went, you would go with him."

She stared at him, aghast. "But Papa, why?" Tears of confusion glimmered in her eyes.

"I lost my wife because she insisted upon following the drum. I just yesterday realized I could lose you as well. And I couldn't bear to lose you, Jules." His voice broke, and he started to turn away. That's when Juliet caught him about the neck in a fierce embrace.

"Oh, Papa, you're not going to lose me. Not to the Apache. Not to Noble Banning. I promised Mama I'd look after you and I've no plans to break that promise. Ever."

John Crowley held his daughter to him, loving her so much that he was furious with her for foiling his attempt to see her happy. A young woman didn't find happiness keeping house for her father. She found it with a husband. And he'd found that man for Juliet, whether she was ready to accept the choice or not.

And he hoped he wouldn't have to resort to the threat of a firing squad to get them to the altar.

How dare she throw his proposal back in his face as if it were an insult!

Noble headed for his quarters, too angry to limp. The pain in his feet was nothing compared to the raw state of his pride. It was pride. What else could it be? Why else would he react to her rebuff with such surprise and indignation?

With such a sense of loss.

He'd only meant to do what was proper. The gentlemanly thing. That's how he'd been raised. These crazy Northern women didn't have the social acumen to realize that. What kind of man would he have been if he hadn't volunteered to shield her honor from loose talk?

Well, if Miss Juliet Crowley considered herself above the stain of gossip, who was he to try to save her name?

She'd made it very clear, hadn't she, that she had no interest in anything serious.

Well, that suited him just fine. Just fine. The last thing he needed was to return to Pride County dragging an opinionated free spirit like Juliet as his bride. The very last thing...

Damn her, she could have at least said thank-you.

It was then that Miles Dougherty had the bad timing to step into his path to grab his shirtfront and sneer, "How dare you put your hands on her, you—"

Noble filled in the rest of his nasty supposition with the row of his knuckles.

He stood over Dougherty, too angry to seek self-control. "How dare you, sir, suggest that the lady would allow me that kind of liberty or that I would take it. And if I find that you are treating her as any less than the lady she is by repeating your filthy innuendos, I will do the honorable thing and carve your heart out."

At least here was a man who understood honor. Miles paled, and though still plainly furious, stammered, "I never meant to suggest that Juliet was anything less than a lady."

"Didn't you?"

Noble stepped over him and continued to

his quarters. Once inside, he leaned back against the door and wondered who'd angered him more—Miles for insinuating what hadn't happened or himself for wishing it had.

Chapter 12

Juliet!

Noble sat up, breathing hard, his gaze darting about for signs of danger.

But it was the impatient blare of the bugle that jerked him from slumber, not the Apache war cries that undulated through his dream.

He exhaled slowly and eased back onto his bed. It seemed like only minutes ago that he'd laid his head down and closed his eyes. The temptation to pull his pillow over his head was mighty, but he resisted. He couldn't hide from the day forever.

Or from Juliet.

Movements as slow as those of an ancient, he eased from bed and dressed for duty, indulging in a full chorus of moans and groans because there was no one to hear him. Tugging on his boots gave him a long moment's pause as leather met the throbbing soles of his feet. But the thought of coffee, harsh and black, was enough to coax him into taking the first few baby steps that eventually became a gingerly wobble.

If Juliet could see him now, she'd find nothing to impress her.

That thought stiffened his spine. Heaven forbid that the perfect Miss Crowley find him lacking as a man. She'd made no bones about how she felt he'd fare as a husband.

The morning air was already hot enough to steam the crease from his trousers. He'd joined in the grumbling exodus leading to the mess hall when he heard his name called.

"Banning."

The lack of rank or civility in that address brought him about with a frown to see Miles Dougherty. The sight of the major's swollen upper lip almost made him smile.

"The colonel wants to see you and your senior officers. Right now."

Something in the hard edge of that command alerted Noble. Whatever was on the colonel's mind that would take precedence over coffee wasn't something he was going to like. He grabbed onto a private, bidding him locate Bartholomew and Allen, then started for the colonel's quarters at a less than enthusiastic amble.

Miles held the door open for him. The man's grim demeanor again warned of trouble to come. Crowley was pacing in front of the wood stove, his hands working fiercely at his sides.

"Where are your officers, Major?"

"On their way, sir. Might I ask what this is about?" Had he decided on a firing squad after all?

"You've no idea?" He studied Noble with a penetrating glare.

"None, sir."

"We'll wait until the others arrive. At ease, Major. Jules, some coffee, please."

Noble wasn't prepared for the odd lurch in his emotions when Juliet entered the room. It was almost as if he'd been anticipating her appearance, and now that she'd arrived, he was inexplicably content, an unsettling notion he dismissed as fatigue.

"Coffee, Major?"

"Yes. Black, thank you."

He took the cup from her, noticing that she purposely avoided eye contact, not only with him but with Miles as well. He'd expected her awkwardness but sensed that this was something bigger. Her tension increased his anxiety one hundredfold. Juliet often mirrored her father's moods, and if she was this tightly wound, something terrible must have occurred while he slept. He could do nothing but wait and wonder as he sipped her strong brew appreciatively.

His captain and lieutenant arrived, and Crowley wasted no time cutting right to it.

"Four of your enlisted men disappeared between lights out and reveille with fresh mounts and all they could carry. What do you know about this?"

Noble received the news like a rifle blast to the gut. Deserted! After they'd given him their word that they would stand fast and serve well!

"Who are these men, Colonel?"

"Bright, Colvin, Worth, and Rogers."

He knew them, each one of them. Family men, honorable men, not the types to sneak out in the night.

Noble looked to his two seconds and demanded, "Do you know anything about this?"

Both answered with negatives, but Bartholomew was a bit slower in his reply. Noble looked from them to his impatient commander.

"What are your orders, sir?"

"I want them found and returned."

"To what end, sir?"

"Whatever I decide. They left this post with three hundred dollars of army provisions apiece. They are costing me the time and manpower to hunt them down. Right now, I'd say they'll be dragging around twenty-five-pound balls for the remainder of their service. That should slow them down some in future."

Noble said nothing. Desertion couldn't be excused under any circumstances, and the penalty for such an act was always severe. He guessed he should be thankful the price wasn't execution.

"I'll mount a detail, sir, and have them back by nightfall."

"I'd expect nothing less, Major."

"And lest you be tempted to join them," Miles interjected coolly, "I'll pick the men you'll be leading."

Noble looked to the colonel in protest, but what trust Crowley might have felt before was strained by the events of the past few days. Noble, and now his men, had failed to carry out their sworn duties. Crowley couldn't be blamed for his lack of faith.

Noble snapped off a salute. He risked a glance at Juliet, but from her remote expression he could read no clues of what she was thinking.

The minute he and his junior officers left the building, Noble turned on them in a cold fury.

"What do you know?"

George Allen was clearly in the dark, but Bartholomew's gaze dropped away.

"Don? Did they come to you first? Did you know what they meant to do? Tell me!"

His gaze darted up, filled with fiery righteousness. "Yes, I knew and I applauded them for it. If it hadn't been for Maisy, I'd probably have joined them."

"Why didn't you tell me?"

"Tell you? And what would you have done? Trotted right in there to your little toy-soldier colonel and informed on them, that's what." His fierceness took Noble aback. "You've lost sight of who we are and who they are. We're not like them, Noble. They're still our enemies. They're still killing our friends and family back home."

"I gave my word—"

"Good for you. And I'm sure you'll keep it come hell or high water. Well, some of us just aren't as honor-bent as you are. Some of us just want to get home. Some of us are wondering what the hell we're doing out here letting these Yankees push us around." He took a breath and glared at his superior. "So what are you going to do? Bring me up on charges?"

Noble swallowed back his first answer, then said stiffly, "I'm going to go find those fools before the Indians do. And God help you if I'm too late."

The small detail left the fort with little fanfare, its purpose a grim one. Noble led the way with Tom Folley at his right hand. Pauline stood tall and dry-eyed next to Juliet on the porch, waving her handkerchief gaily until her husband was out of sight. Then she sagged against Juliet, shaking with sobs. Putting a fortifying arm about her, Juliet shooed away the children, sending them to scatter feed to the chickens, a job they coveted.

To Pauline she said gently, "Come inside with me awhile. I've been wanting to get that recipe for those sourdough biscuits my father raves over. Do you think you could help me beat up a batch?" At the other's teary nod, Juliet gave her a hug. "Wonderful. I'll put on some tea."

But as they crossed the threshold, Juliet's

gaze went to the dust cloud growing ever smaller, her own heart twisting anxiously.

Don't you dare get yourself killed, Noble Banning.

Then a more somber thought occurred to her.

Keep your word and come back.

They moved hard and fast. The heat soared, but the lack of air movement had preserved the trail they now followed—a trail left by men Noble had a difficult time calling traitors.

How could they have been so stupid? Why hadn't they come to him instead of Bartholomew? He would have given sound counsel, not the fervid rhetoric the captain had most likely filled them with, fiery words that could well be sending them all to their death.

By midday, they had picked up more tracks, these crossing and recrossing those made by the fleeing Confederates, tracks of unshod horses moving in single file to disguise their number.

Apaches.

Even though he urged the patrol to a greater pace, Noble knew with a sick certainty that they'd never make it to the men in time.

But nothing could have prepared them for what they found. Not the ravages of war. Not seeing men blown to pieces by mortar shells. Nothing was as indescribably brutal as the sight of four poor souls who'd been staked spread-eagled in the broiling sun to be leisurely skinned alive.

Several men fled the ranks to heave up their scant noon meal. Noble sat unflinching, a cold weight of horror and guilt settling low in his gut.

"Cut them free and wrap them for transport."

His men hesitated to obey the emotionless order, unwilling to approach what was left of their friends, now unrecognizable as human beings.

Wordlessly, Noble dismounted and drew his own knife. He hobbled to the first of the four and bent to cut the rawhide bindings. He didn't try to avert his eyes but instead studied the carnage with a dispassionate care.

This was Indian fighting.

He'd killed these men by bringing them west, and this was a memory he'd carry with him for the rest of his life.

The patrol made good time returning to the fort. They saw no sign of the enemy, though several nervous enlisted men swore they'd noticed flanking shadows skimming the horizon. None of them drew an easy breath until within the compound. They were too haunted by what they'd seen to ever feel safe again.

"Take them to the infirmary and have Lieutenant Allen meet me there," Noble called as he dismounted outside the Crowleys' home. By the time he'd forced his game leg to support him, he turned to see the colonel and his daughter waiting in the deep shade to hear his report, a report that tore the heart from him to deliver.

"They must have been ambushed sometime early this morning." He didn't elaborate on their condition. What words could adequately convey it? "I know they are considered deserters, but they served me well in the war. I hope you'll allow them to be buried with dignity, because they sure as hell didn't die with any."

"As you wish, Major. See to it."

Noble gave a half-hearted salute and led his horse across the parade ground. Both man and mount were slowed by exhaustion.

And in the shadows of the porch, Juliet blinked her tears away.

George Allen stood in the midst of the covered bodies praying for their souls. Noble waited in the doorway, listening to the words that should have given some comfort but didn't. All he could think of was how much these men must have suffered before going to that better place George spoke of.

The chaplain paused in his final benediction when he saw Noble, waving him inside as he continued. Noble joined him for the concluding amen.

"Maybe you can give the poor fools some peace in heaven, because they sure endured a hell on earth."

George knew him too well not to comment

on his words. "And you? Are you finding any peace with this?"

Noble walked away from the four draped figures, moving to stand by the window, where the fading daylight still refused a cooling breeze.

"Colvin's wife was expecting their first child right after New Year's. He wanted to see that baby more than he wanted to take his next breath. Worth, he was planning to marry his second cousin as soon as he got home. We used to tease him about how few branches were on his family tree. Rogers was a dirt farmer with six kids to feed and clothe and see raised properly. Bright was just a kid. A kid. They just wanted to get back to the things they loved. No harm in that, no wrong. I told 'em it was the right thing to do, coming out here. I told 'em it was the best way to get home to their loved ones safe and sound. Why didn't they listen? They stopped believing in me, George, and they died. For what?"

"For what was important to each of them, Noble."

"I promised to take care of them and they promised to follow me. Who broke their promise first, George? Answer me that. Am I to blame for the four of them lying there like that, with nothing left that their families could identify?" His words fractured, and he waited, hoping George could find some miraculous means to erase his sense of responsibility.

"If you're looking for someone to blame, blame me."

Noble turned, surprised by that fierce claim. Apparently just as startled, George continued hurriedly, "Blame Donald for encouraging them. Blame Jeff Davis and Abe Lincoln for pulling the country apart and us from our homes. Blame those ignorant heathens. Blame the heat for slowing them down and making them careless. Blame the stars, the moon. But it won't make you feel any better. Only time can do that. And only God can forgive any of us."

Amazingly, Noble chuckled. "Do you want to know what's the very worst about this, George? The very worst?"

"What, Noble?"

"When I heard they were gone, I didn't sympathize with them for caving in to the need to go home. I didn't despise them for being weak. I didn't even think of the danger they'd be in. You know what I felt, George? I was angry with them for making me look bad. Can you believe it? I was furious with them because they made me look like a liar. If Crowley planned to slap a twenty-five-pound ball on one ankle, I was going to chain a twenty-five-pounder to the other. What kind of a leader does that make me? One who values his pride over the welfare of his men."

George looked beyond them, then placed a consoling hand on his friend's shoulder. "It makes you human and too tired to think straight. You have been through enough of an ordeal. Go get some rest. I'll do what needs to be done here and write letters to their families." He paused, then added thickly, "It's the least I can do."

Too weary to argue, Noble nodded and turned toward the door, startled to see Juliet posed within that open frame and even more surprised by the tender empathy in her expression. He didn't need that now. He didn't want absolution or soothing sympathy. He wanted someone to understand the heinous wrong he'd done and why he needed to be punished for it, not Juliet's melting gaze and tear-moistened cheeks.

He meant to push by her without a word, but that wasn't her plan.

The instant he was within reach, she put her arms about him, tightening them when she felt him balk. She was stronger than he'd suspected, strong enough to embrace his shame and guilt without condemnation. He'd always been the strong one, the one to carry everyone else's doubts and fears and woes. He'd never turned to another human being to ask for relief from that burden. But Juliet held him, offering ease, and for once in his life, he relented, surrendering his resolve with a shaky exhalation and letting her guide his head to her capable shoulder.

She didn't say anything. He couldn't have borne words just then. All would have rung as empty as his soul. In her silence he found support. From her gentle toughness he drew courage and comfort. But only for a moment. And when he straightened, she stepped back to let him go.

In that gesture, with her show of quiet wisdom, Juliet earned a place in his heart forever.

After he'd gone, Juliet turned to the somber chaplain.

"Is there anything I can do?"

"Pray for them and their families." He glanced at each covered shape in turn, his own features twisting in unvoiced sorrow. He swallowed hard, then added, "That's all any of us can do right now."

It didn't seem enough when there was so much pain weighing down their commanding officer.

"You knew these men, Captain. Why did they run?" Suddenly, she had to know. "To get back to the fighting in the East?"

"No, ma'am. These men saw only one thing worth fighting for and that was their homes, their families. That's where they were going. Home."

She studied the shrouded shapes, thinking wistfully of a place one would risk death to return to. She'd never known such a place. She'd never had anywhere she could call home.

"I wish there were some way we could have them buried in familiar soil." She sighed heavily. "Do what you can to ease their way, Captain."

"And you need to do what you can to ease the major's conscience."

Juliet couldn't meet the man's eyes. There was too much intuitive knowledge there ready to see right behind her facade. "He doesn't need me for that."

"He needs someone, ma'am, someone to make him understand that he's not to blame." Allen's voice trailed off in anguish. "He's not to blame."

Chapter 13

Juliet had only two Christmases to her memory that were white and snowy. Those had been during her stay in Ohio, while her father was campaigning with the Union Army. She hadn't seen anything to celebrate on those occasions, and she found herself wondering what this year would bring.

It brought a surprise none had suspected.

"Riders coming!"

A shout from the guard house brought the curious out to greet the new arrivals, who came in a column of twos. Juliet stood on their porch with the colonel watching the dusty unit file by.

"I didn't know we were expecting new recruits."

Crowley shook his head. "I didn't know, either."

"I hope they have some fresh supplies with them."

"I hope they brought me some cigars."

The army ambulance swayed to a halt in front of them. The door opened, giving them a view of frothy petticoats as its single occupant scrambled to exit. A head of curly brown hair beneath an enormous hat emerged, and Juliet gave a squeal of surprise and delight.

"Jane!"

Jane Howell tumbled down into her embrace, laughing, hugging, and crying happy tears. "Oh, Juliet, how wonderful to see you again! Merry Christmas! I know I'm a few days early but I couldn't delay the surprise any longer. Say you're surprised."

"Surprised? You're the last person I expected to see. Drat your husband for keeping such a secret."

Jane leaned back, her big brown eyes lit with merriment. "He doesn't know."

"He doesn't know? You mean you came all this way without telling him?"

"I simply couldn't stand another holiday to go by without him. Having a father-in-law who's a senator gives a girl a certain amount of influence when she wants to have her way." Dimples danced mischievously.

"Jane! Oh, my God! Jane, is that you?"

Albert Howell broke into a run, barely giving Juliet time to step out of the way so that he could sweep his wife up in his arms. The sight of their reunion woke a twinge of reluctant envy within Juliet's breast. Never had she had such an emotional welcome. Oh, to have a man waiting to shower one with such a display of devotion! She had to glance away.

"Merry Christmas, darling," Jane cried.

"The merriest ever now that you're here, you minx. How did you manage—no, never mind."

"You're not mad, are you?" Jane leaned back to beseech him with a melting gaze.

"No, of course not, silly creature. How could I possibly be angry?"

Juliet chuckled at the clever manipulation. Angry? The man was most likely livid that he'd had no forewarning so as to be able to prepare for an incoming wife. But Jane was so dear, so eager to please that one simply could not stay irritated with her. One could only get caught up in her enthusiasm.

"Now we shall have to put together a Christmas ball, just like the one we had in Texas, Juliet. I've brought all the trimmings. It will be great fun. Now, where is that brother of mine?"

Miles's usually dour features split into a grin as he spun his sister about. "Jane, you scamp. Why didn't you let us know you were coming?"

"What, and have you boys worrying over me the whole time? You know how I like surprises." She winked at Juliet.

She also knew both men would have done everything possible to prevent her trip. But now that she was here, what could they do but welcome her? And Juliet, for one, was thrilled to embrace the sunshine her best friend brought with her.

Later that day, as the two of them sat together in the shaded twilight, watching a detail strike the colors, Juliet was grateful for the empathetic company.

"So, tell me, how did you end up with a company of Southern boys?"

Juliet chuckled. Her friend asked no easy questions. "My father captured their unit and was so impressed by their horsemanship that he had them paroled from Point Lookout and brought out here to serve under him."

"And you sleep nights?"

"Not very well." When she hesitated, Jane gave her a shrewd glance.

"Tell me everything."

"Just after we arrived, someone shot at my father." She tried to make the statement nonchalant, but the catch in her voice betrayed her anxiety.

"Oh, darling, how awful! So that's why you've been so jumpy. One of the Rebs?"

"I don't know." She rubbed at her temples, wishing she could ease the constant throb of worry. "I can't imagine why anyone else would have a reason." She couldn't look at Jane. Noble's suspicion came back to her, pointing the finger at another man. Because she didn't believe his insinuation for a moment, she wouldn't trouble her friend with it. She sighed. "Father's trying to pretend nothing happened, and their leader swears it wasn't one of his men."

"Their leader? Oh, you mean that positively gorgeous major? It seems he would have more reason than anyone."

"More than you know," Juliet murmured.

"What does Miles think?"

"Of Major Banning?" She made an unkind noise. "He thinks he's a treasonous dog who's looking for the first opportunity to kill us all in our sleep."

"Delightful. Do you believe that, too?"

"Of Major Banning? No. He's many things, but I can't name murderer as one of them. Miles can't see beyond the color of his uniform."

"And is he perhaps just a tad jealous?"

"Well, Major Banning does outrank him."

"I wasn't speaking of rank, dear." Jane smiled at Juliet's confusion. "Oh, come now, that Southern boy positively sizzles when he sets his eyes upon you."

Juliet gaped at her. Color flooded her cheeks. Jane laughed at her naïveté.

"Well, if you haven't noticed, Miles certainly has. And I couldn't be more pleased. My brother needs something to light a fire under him. And I plan to add kindling."

"Jane, I really don't think you should meddle—"

"Why not? What else is there to do out here?" She fanned herself lazily, her mouth pursing in speculation.

"Noble Banning is not in the least bit interested in me, and I think it unfair of you to taunt your brother with what is not true." If her matchmaking friend ever got wind of Noble's impetuous offer, she'd never hear the end of it. But there was no reason to mention that, either, when there was nothing motivating his proposal other than duty—a fact that gave her no pleasure at all and heartache best not discussed. Being humiliated in front of her father was certainly nothing she cared to rehash.

"Oh, Juliet, you have no womanly wiles at all. How else do you plan to get Miles to propose?"

Startled from her train of thought regarding another man, Juliet stared at her. "Who said I wanted Miles to propose?"

Juliet's comment shocked Jane. The other woman stared at her, aghast. "You don't want to marry Miles? Juliet, he dotes on you."

"He's a good man, a fine soldier—"

"But—"

Juliet sighed. "I don't know, Jane. I don't know anything about love or courtship."

"And my oaf of a brother knows even less. You certainly aren't going to learn anything reading those dusty old books and fetching your papa's slippers. I can see how desperately I'm needed here." She patted her friend's knee confidently. "Leave everything to me, dear."

"Jane," Juliet warned her uneasily.

But her gaze was already far away, focused

on the schemes her mind was busy hatching.

And that gave Juliet another reason for worry. It was one thing to dodge her father's battering-ram attempts to force her toward the altar and quite another to sidestep Jane's more subtle plotting. If she wasn't careful, she could find herself saying "I do" with Miles before she knew what she'd agreed to.

Trouble started when Jane invited her to her new home to help her plan a dinner party for that evening.

"What do you think?"

When Jane lifted the evening gown for Juliet's inspection, it was like the sun rising. Pale gold silk overlaid with row upon row of bronze lace dazzled her eyes. Her lips formed a silent O.

"I had it made by Worth. I ordered it ages ago," Jane told her, holding the sumptuous creation up to her shoulders, then fitting it to her waist with the wrap of one arm.

"It's beautiful," Juliet whispered. She'd never had the occasion or desire to own elaborate clothing, but now, thinking of how she'd compare in her serviceable calico with Jane in this golden dream and Maisy Bartholomew in her flashy frills, she wished for just one impractical gown that would make her feel their feminine equal.

But what would a woman with no wiles need with such a dress when there was no one she had to impress?

"Yes, it is lovely," Jane agreed, holding the

gown away from her to examine it critically. "Unfortunately, the clothier must have thought I was a good six inches taller and of a sunny complexion. When I put it on, it positively washes me away." Then she smiled and placed the wide scoop of the lace-tiered neckline against Juliet. "But on you it would glow."

"Surely you're not suggesting—"

"No, I'm not suggesting at all. I hate to see my husband's good coin go to waste. Please say you'll take it, so I won't feel so guilty having it packed away in my trunk."

Juliet caressed the stiff silk of the bodice reverently. "I've never had anything so fine. Are you sure?"

"Absolutely. And it's high time you gave the single fellows of this post a glimpse of your full female potential. Not that there's a thing wrong with you just as you are," she was quick to assure her.

But Juliet was too entranced to take offense.

"Try it on."

Juliet needed no urging. She shucked off her commonplace plaid and shimmied into the embrace of silk and lace. As she stared in surprise at her reflection in Jane's cheval glass, her friend chattered happily.

"I'll heat up some slate pencils to curl your hair, and with a dab of cornstarch to take the shine off your nose, poor Miles won't know what hit him."

Miles . . . Juliet wasn't thinking of Miles at

all. She gazed at the figure in the mirror, wondering where the gawky girl had gone. The sleek golden sophisticate looking back at her wouldn't shame an up-and-coming Kentucky lawyer in front of his highfalutin' friends.

Tonight she would make him see that Juliet Crowley wasn't a burden any man had to bear.

Her father's reaction gave Juliet all the encouragement she needed.

"Jules," he murmured in awe. "Seeing you like that makes me think of the first time I met your mother."

As his tears welled up, Juliet stepped forward into his embrace to scold, "Now, Papa, don't get all misty. It's just a dress."

"It's more than the dress. It's the woman in it. She would be so proud, Juliet. So proud."

Emotions crowding up in her throat, she took his proffered arm and let him guide her toward the true testing ground.

Chairs scraped loudly as all the men in Albert Howell's main room surged to their feet. And it wasn't because a superior officer had entered the room. They were staring at her with an amazement so apparent that it would have been insulting had Juliet not been rendered so suddenly shy by all the attention. Jane and Pauline beamed in approval. Behind them, Maisy glowered. The sight of her envy restored Juliet's confidence.

"Please, gentlemen, do be seated," she murmured in a husky purr. "There's no need to stand on formality."

"I hate to disagree with a lady," Noble answered, lifting her gloved hand in his, "but I think in this case there is every need."

While he touched his lips to the back of her hand in a show of Southern gallantry, Miles simmered hotly beside him, wishing he'd thought to pay the compliment first.

Throughout the meal, Juliet followed Jane's lead, making flirtatious small talk punctuated by fluttering lashes and playful gestures. Feminine wiles, Jane called it. Games was a better description to Juliet. She had no talent for games, either for playing them or for watching them, but Jane continued to coax her on. The behavior felt awkward, as if she were wearing someone else's personality as well as someone else's clothes, but the men responded to it. All except Noble.

He leaned back in his chair, his close-lipped smile polite, his pale eyes remote in their study of her. Wondering why she was unable to win him over as easily as the others, she turned her attention to Miles, who flattered her efforts with his eagerness and fumbling charm. Instead of boosting her morale, his attentiveness shamed her for the insincerity of her own ploys, reducing the evening from one of pleasurable conquest to a headachy regret. As soon as politely proper, she excused herself from the table and Miles's ardor to slip out the back door, seeking the humbling indifference of the vast western sky.

"Makes you feel insignificant, doesn't it?"

She turned in alarm to find Noble had followed her out into the night.

"I'm not interested in company, Major."

"Ahhh, too overpowered by all that fawning attention inside? A lovely lady like yourself should be used to that."

She looked back at the heavens, gruff in her embarrassment. "Well, I'm not. And I don't like pretending for the entertainment of others. I feel ashamed of myself for trying to be something I'm not."

She started at the sudden brush of his fingertips rounding her cheek, guiding her face back to him. In the darkness, his eyes held a piercing luminescence.

"You don't need to pretend, Juliet. You don't need to be other than who you are."

"And what am I, Major?" There was no coquetry in her question, just a frank curiosity. He smiled.

"You are unique."

She gave a cynical laugh and jerked away. "Oh, a girl loves to hear things like that. Unique could cover anything from walleyed to daft in the attic."

His chuckle was wooingly warm, making her recall Jane's observation about his interest in her. But kissing a woman who nearly threw herself at his head and claiming a personal interest were two very different things. She wasn't sure where between those two poles Noble Banning stood.

"You have lovely eyes and a fine mind and an unflagging honesty that quite amazes me."

She glared at him to cover the way his praise made her feel all jumpy inside. His words came so easily. He'd probably said phrases along the same lines to any number of goggle-eyed females to make them feel special—even when they weren't. It was part of his charm, part of the politician side of him inherited from his father. Tell them what they want to hear but not what you really think.

"Were you such a fan of honesty, you wouldn't have made that ridiculous proposal just to placate my father."

His gaze grew shuttered. "Ridiculous?"

Feeling the frost in his tone, she corrected herself, "Well, not ridiculous but certainly insincere."

"Just what kind of offer would you consider as sincere, Miz Crowley? One from a man who sees you more as a convenience than as an individual? As a means to further his career? One who would share your bed but not your interests? Is that what you're looking for when you toy with Miles Dougherty?"

She winced at his accuracy yet was moved to speak up in her own defense. "I'm not toying with Miles. How dare you suggest that! He and I are old friends, just as I am with Jane."

"I don't think it's friendship he has in mind, Juliet. Open your eyes."

She faced him angrily to demand, "And what is it you have in mind, Major Banning? Something less honorable? Or is it all of the above? Or are you only interested in me as a tool for your revenge?"

His stare went ice-cold. "Why would you think that?"

"I'm not such a fool as not to guess how much it would hurt my father if you were to—to break my heart just to spite him for what he's done to you and your men."

"I never thought you a fool," he corrected in a dangerously low rumble. "Not until now."

His hands shot out to circle her upper arms, to yank her up against him. Her gasp was quickly muffled by the grinding crush of his mouth over hers. She issued a soft mewling sound somewhere between protest and surrender, then parted her lips to encourage a more intense union.

This was the truth she wanted to hear.

His purpose altered immediately from harsh conquest to the sweet ravishment of her will. She had no desire to fight him or the yearning he stirred within her. For the moment, it was just the two of them alone beneath the infinite southwestern sky, unfettered by opinion or doubt or confusions while in the thrall of their nakedly honest desires.

Juliet met him kiss for kiss. Her palms prowled the rough wool of his uniform jacket, seeking a way inside to feel his body's heat and strength, wishing recklessly that she could peel it from his shoulders right there in the Howells' backyard. Wishing they had more time to explore what exploded between them each time their lips met. Wishing she knew how to interpret their kisses, to know if it was more than just the passion of the moment or somehow significant of the way he felt about her. Wishing the sound of her father's laughter wasn't quite so loud, so near, reminding her of where they were.

But not reminding her soon enough.

The creak of the door forced them to break off the kiss, but they were still very much in each other's arms when faced with Jane's impassive stare. For a moment, she stood there, pale and stunned beyond reaction. Then when she did speak, her voice was toneless.

"Major Banning, the colonel was wondering what became of you. Will you go in, or shall I—invent something?"

"I'll go in, thank you, ma'am." His hands fell away from Juliet as his brief stare conveyed his regrets and reluctance. He went inside without another word.

Mortified, Juliet waited for some sign of what her friend was feeling. Surely she must have been shocked and betrayed. But her words gave nothing away.

"And here I thought you needed my advice on romance. Silly me."

"Jane," Juliet cried softly.

But the other woman returned inside without listening to her explanation.

Chapter 14

Eyes gritty from lack of sleep, Juliet knocked upon her friend's door in the morning. Jane's greeting was unusually cool, grinding Juliet's sense of shame deeper.

"I was wondering if you still wanted my help to prepare for the party tonight."

There was a long silence. At any moment, Juliet expected her friend to chase her from her doorstep with angry recriminations. She'd deserve them for her disloyalty.

"Whom else would I ask?" Jane replied flatly. "That Carolina cow? Really, if I'd had to listen to her say, 'Well, my Donald' one more time, I would have strangled her where she sat."

Juliet smiled anxiously. "She is quite overbearing, isn't she?"

"An understatement. I know one of the duties of a military wife is to further her husband's career at every opportunity, but to have the man's obvious superiority rammed down my throat with each swallow is quite intolerable. And the poor captain looked ready to die of embarrassment. Why doesn't he take her aside for a good talking to?"

"I don't think Maisy is a very good listener."

"Well, if she hates it here so much, I'd be happy to get her started on the walk back to her precious plantation home."

Juliet chuckled at her friend's typical sarcasm and felt the void between them that much more keenly. What would she do without Jane Howell as her companion? She couldn't let the breach widen any farther.

"Jane, about last night—I took advantage of your kindness and led you on regarding my feelings for your brother. I'm sorry. And I feel so awful."

Jane sighed, then appeared chagrined. "Dear Juliet, please forgive *me* for acting so foolishly. It's just that I'd so hoped you and Miles..." She let the rest dangle meaningfully.

"Believe me," Juliet told her truthfully, "it would have been so much easier if it had happened that way."

Jane smiled wistfully. "But it didn't, did it? And I can't blame you for that." She opened her arms, and Juliet stepped into them with a grateful sob. After a long emotional moment, Jane's question shocked Juliet from her tears.

"Are you in love with him?"

Sniffing, she leaned back. "With whom?"

"With your pretty Southern boy?"

"I—I don't know," she stammered unhappily. "I don't want to be."

"Sometimes we have little choice in matters of the heart. Come inside. I must finish a special repast for my escort. They're due to leave midmorning, and I just feel that no one should be denied a touch of Christmas spirit."

And that's why everyone loved Jane, Juliet thought with a smile. She would consider the lowliest soldier with compassion and treat him like a king. "What can I do to help?"

"Put on your sunniest smile and that apron and help me serve up these flapjacks. I made the preserves myself. Don't look at me like that. I *did!* I'm not totally without domestic skills. And when we're finished, I'll help you sort out that question of whether or not it's love."

Juliet wasn't sure whether she felt relief or reluctance.

The troop marched out right after the guard mount. Jane waved and called to each man by name, even shedding a few tears, as if she'd formed a personal friendship with every individual. Knowing Jane, she probably had. Then she turned to Juliet, all business.

"Let's start making ribbon bows while you tell me everything."

Juliet told every detail, no matter how personal. Every feeling, no matter how confused. She spoke of her fear that Noble was leading her on to get closer to her father or to exact some cruel revenge. She admitted that a part of her didn't care if that was the case. That's how far gone she was when it came to the Kentucky major. When she ran out of words, she looked to Jane, hoping the other could make some logical suggestion to solve her dilemma.

"Goodness," was all Jane said. So Juliet was forced to draw the answers out of her.

"How could I be in love with a man I can't trust?" she cried, pausing in the middle of tying her fancy loops of red. "He's told me his plans, and I know there's no place in them for me. He wants a local girl with money and influence to aid in his career. He wants a Maisy Bartholomew, not a Juliet Crowley, who's followed the drum so long, she doesn't know any other kind of life."

"But you can learn, Juliet. If you love him, you can learn. And besides, what man would want a Maisy when he could have a Juliet?"

Thinking she was only being kind, Juliet knotted the fluffy bow and gave a stubborn scowl. "But I like my life the way it is."

Jane said nothing. She knew that was a lie. She knew Juliet wanted nothing more desperately than a permanent home, with neighbors who would holler over the fence and children who could play in the yard without fear of an Indian raid. She knew because Juliet had told her all that during a soul-baring moment one long winter night in Texas.

Jane examined their overflowing basket of

cheerful bows and grinned. "It's almost lunch time. Let's see if we can coax a few of those handsome boys into helping us string our streamers and hang our bows."

The minute Jane, in her dainty half boots and peeping petticoats, climbed up onto a chair in the mess hall, she was surrounded by troopers offering to lend a hand. Within the hour, the walls were decorated with flags and holiday wreaths and the ceilings draped with colored tissue, bows, and strategically placed boughs of mistletoe. Tables and chairs were pushed aside so that canvas could be stretched tightly over the wetted-down dirt floor. An area was set aside for the post's musicians, who would play sprightly reels and nostalgic waltzes. Chairs lined one wall next to the food and beverage tables, so that ladies could rest their feet between dances. With a limited number of females, no jig or galop would find a lady without a line of eager partners.

As the afternoon wore on, Juliet found herself swept up in the excitement. She loved military balls—the dancing, the music, the formality, and the fun. This year was different. Previously, only her father's opinion mattered. But on this night, whether she liked the notion or not, she wanted to bewitch Noble Banning the way he'd dazzled her. To what end she hadn't quite decided.

She wore the gold gown again, simply because it was the most flattering thing she owned and the most suitable for the occasion. Instead of the chignon she'd worn the night before, she let her hair flow loosely about her shoulders, spun with random curls and clipped up on one side by a sprig of holly Jane had nurtured all the way from Washington. After the shabby way she'd treated both Miles and Noble, they probably would refuse her a second look.

When she emerged from her room, she came to a startled stop as both Miles and Noble surged to their feet. Both were impeccably garbed in freshly creased uniforms and stood stiff as their starched collars: Miles capable and confident and so dear to her, Noble sleek, elegant and so staggering in his appeal that it was all she could do to look away from the smoldering self-assurance in his gaze.

Behind them, her father wore a cat-at-the-cream smile of self-congratulation.

"Jules, your escorts are here."

Recovering from her shock and aware of the look of hostile competition the two men exchanged, Juliet chose the diplomatic route.

"Oh, my. I am so flattered, really I am, but I've already promised the first dance to the most handsome and eligible man I know."

While they blinked, perplexed, she skirted them to take up her father's arm. "I'm ready, Papa," she cooed with feigned innocence. He patted her hand in approval.

"Gentlemen, you may fall in if you like," Crowley instructed them as he led his daughter proudly across the torchlit parade ground toward the inviting noise of the mess hall.

The moment they entered, there was a unison thunder as every man came to immediate attention. Never was Juliet's pride in her father so acute as in these formal shows of respect.

"At ease, men, and a happy Christmas to you all."

"Thank you, sir," came the returning good wishes.

"I have it on good authority that through the generosity of Mrs. Howell, we have at our disposal some very fine champagne. Enjoy it—in moderation—gentlemen. Please carry on."

The music started up, a surprisingly well-tuned assortment of instruments plucking out the melancholy strains of "Lorena" as the colonel and his daughter swept out onto the floor for the first dance. The married couples followed, and the other men indulged in some good-natured pushing as they jockeyed for opportunities to cut in. Juliet enjoyed the moment, but her father spoiled it with his amused observation.

"Which of your impatient suitors will you grace with the next turn about the floor?" Crowley teased as he observed his daughter's distraction. Both Miles and Noble stood on the fringe of the jubilant company, their eyes on her and each other, tension arcing between them. Whichever she chose, the happy mood of the evening would be broken.

"I think George Allen."

He laughed. "What an excellent choice to insure no ill feelings. And if you weren't being so cautious?"

"I would continue to dance with you."

A deeper chuckle rumbled from him as he spun her around and left her in the chaplain's capable hands.

George Allen was a fine dancer. He moved her about the floor with graceful twirls, making the appropriate conversation. But he seemed distracted.

"George, is there someone you'd rather be dancing with?" Juliet asked.

He looked to her with a fiery blush. "Yes, ma'am. I mean, no, ma'am."

She glanced over to where Colleen was serving up the champagne, her smiles intoxicating the men more than the drink. "No offense taken, Captain. But you might want to get in line before the rest of her evening is spoken for."

"Yes, ma'am. Thank you, ma'am."

"Juliet."

"Yes, ma'am. Juliet."

She smiled as he scrambled over to the refreshment table as soon as he could do so without insulting her. As he spoke hurriedly to the servant girl, Colleen blushed happily, then cast an uneasy eye toward Maisy Bartholomew. But bless him, George refused to relent until Colleen shyly offered her hand so that he could lead her out for the next dance.

Across the floor, Maisy took notice, her features mottling unattractively. Hoping to avert disaster and preserve a well-deserved moment between two well-deserving people, Juliet moved to intercept the indignant woman.

"Mrs. Bartholomew, I must compliment you upon that exceptional choice of color. What is it called?"

Maisy frowned at being interrupted in her intentions but was too vain to let the flattery pass. "Chartreuse. My Donald had it dyed especially for me in Charlotte. Back before the war, you could obtain such extravagances. Now, if you'll excuse me, I simply must go speak to that slattern of a maid. How dare she think to humiliate me by fraternizing with those above her station."

"Maisy, please." Juliet laid a staying hand on her arm and offered her most long-suffering smile. "Don't embarrass Captain Allen by pointing out his lack of social graces. As a man of the cloth, he sees all as equals. I'm sure he is unaware that he's chosen his partner unwisely, and poor Colleen is probably just trying to spare his feelings. Let them share a dance. Surely no harm will be done. It is Christmas, after all."

Maisy huffed, trying to reinflate the sail of her indignation without success. "Perhaps you're right, Miss Crowley. Even in this godforsaken place, there's room for charity."

If there was, Maisy Bartholomew would be the last person to recognize it. But just to be on the safe side, Juliet continued the conversation. "How have you been? We've had so little time to chat of late."

Juliet knew Maisy's cordiality was because she feared being rude to the commander's daughter, rather than from any interest in talking with her.

"I long for home," Maisy said. "What kind of place is this where only the centipedes, scorpions, tarantulas, and snakes seem to thrive?" She sighed mightily.

Juliet regarded her with the arch of one brow. "Yes, they do, don't they?"

"I begged Donald to let me return today, accompanied by those men, but he would not agree. He said I could no longer stay in our plantation alone. Said it was too dangerous. More dangerous than this place? Hah, I hardly think so, especially after what happened to those poor boys who deserted. But I wish I had the courage to try what they did."

"You'll adjust and you'll realize how foolish such a wish sounds. Stay with your husband, Mrs. Bartholomew. I'm sure he knows what's best."

"For himself," she shrilled, drawing several glances. "He never thinks of me or what I might want. He has no idea how despondent I've become since coming here, with only that Irish hussy to tend my needs. Why a woman—"

The dance came to an end, and Colleen returned to the drink table. Juliet had no need to prolong the torture of Maisy's company.

"Please excuse me. Mrs. Howell is waving to me."

Maisy harrumphed to think the wishes of a junior officer's wife should supplant her own, but she didn't quite dare correct the colonel's daughter in matters of etiquette.

"I thought you looked as though you needed rescuing," Jane intimated naughtily when Juliet joined her. "What a harridan. No wonder her poor husband is chasing the champagne down with straight whiskey. I'd need a good bracer, too, if I had to spend a lifetime listening to that whining."

Juliet glanced toward the far corner, where a group of the Southerners had gathered with Donald Bartholomew in their midst. A brown bottle was passed discreetly among them while their laughter grew increasingly loud. Not a good situation. Thinking she should bring it quietly to her father's attention or perhaps to Noble's, she was about to turn when Miles appeared at her elbow.

"I believe this is our dance, Jules." He smiled and bowed, and she knew at once from Jane's apologetic smile that her friend had arranged to corral her for her brother. But Juliet couldn't decline, for the sake of their long friendship. She allowed him to wheel her out onto the dance floor like a coveted prize captured.

And across the room, Noble Banning ground his teeth upon his irritation.

He had no claim on Juliet Crowley. He had no actual right to feel the jealousy gnawing through him. She wasn't his business, even though she'd made herself his extreme pleasure in the brief, yet passionate, interludes they'd shared. He watched her move in time to Dougherty's steps, and in the recesses of his imagination, he saw her moving with him to quite a different, more intimate dance.

He shook off those thoughts and downed another glass of champagne, then stared at the glass moodily. Maybe it was the bubbly wine turning his mind against itself. Or perhaps it was his loneliness. Hearing the music, watching the couples whirling about the floor conjured up memories increasingly hard to suppress. He didn't want to look back at a world that might no longer exist. Back upon the faces of friends who might no longer be living.

But when he closed his eyes, the stuffy mess hall became the soaring ceilings of Glendower Glade, the post musicians transformed into the skilled orchestra brought down from Louisville at an exorbitant expense for one night of entertainment. Instead of uniforms, the men wore polished evening wear, and women, the most beautiful women in the world, twirled about in abundance in swirls of lace and silk.

And he could picture his childhood friends with a clarity that hurt. Mede Wardell shooting him looks of embarrassed panic, pleading for rescue from the onslaught of attention from three lovely marriage-minded belles. Tyler Fairfax at his wicked best, charming the pantalets off the bevy of giggly beauties hanging on his every drawled-out word while he gulped down his daddy's bourbon. Tyler's sister, Starla, conquering every man in sight with her sultry Creole sensuality while making shameless eyes at him. Patrice Sinclair, all Southern grace and sophistication, and her somber brother Deacon scaring off potential suitors with a single quelling glare. Jonah Glendower, the perfect host, the consummate gentleman. And Reeve Garrett, his best friend, lingering on the fringes of acceptability, regarding all with a cynical eye and a careless indifference that Noble had always admired.

But Jonah was dead. He didn't know about the others. He couldn't bear to speculate, for even considering that they wouldn't be there when he was finally able to return to Pride made a mockery of all his dreams—dreams that seemed so far away from this place of arid heat and violent death, where grim duty wiped out all hopes of romance.

All that left him with was day-by-day survival until he could restore the honor of his troop by uncovering the name of their betrayer—even if it meant manipulating the heart of the woman he was dangerously close to falling in love with.

That fact required another drink. And still it wouldn't go down smoothly.

"You look as if you're having a wonderful time."

Noble gave George Allen a thin smile. "Oh, yes. Just wonderful."

George nodded his red head toward the dancers. "Why don't you just cut in? Dougherty might object, but I don't think the lady would."

Noble shook his head. "I'm not out here to enjoy myself, George."

Taking his meaning immediately, George took a step back and frowned in concern. He glanced about to see if they'd be overheard, then for once was outspoken in his criticism. "Still obsessed with your holy crusade?"

"Don't mock me, George."

"It wasn't meant as mockery. Don't you see the danger of what you're doing?" Hearing a lecture coming on, Noble started to turn away, but the young reverend gripped his arm. "You're placing yourself above everyone else in this single-minded quest. You're making judgments that aren't yours to make."

"I'm doing what I have to do, George. We've had this conversation before."

"And we'll have it again until I can persuade you to let it go. You can't move forward until you can let go of the past." That last was almost a plea.

"I'm not going anywhere until we leave here. So what else is there for me to do?"

George sighed in frustration. He looked angry and agitated and even annoyed by Noble's persistence, a sign of how far Noble had fallen off his pedestal in the younger man's eyes. "Has it ever occurred to you that the man you seek might already be dead?"

Noble stared at the chaplain, an eerie stillness settling over him. Then, in a tight voice, he said, "Crowley would have told me."

George's gaze asked who was being naive now. "You're wrong there. If he'd told you from the start that this turncoat you're after was already dead, you wouldn't have agreed so quickly to come out here. The man's not stupid."

"But I am. Is that what you're saying, George? That I'm on a fool's errand?"

Conjuring a mighty patience, he placed a hand on Noble's shoulder. "That's for your heart and mind to tell you. Listen to them, Noble. Don't be led astray by your pride. It's a road that can come to no good end." Again the beseeching tone, making Noble feel ashamed for so straining the chaplain's compassion. He knew George was worried over the state of his soul. But George was a man of conscience, and he one of conviction. On this matter they could not agree. As if realizing that, George left him alone, but Noble was sure he hadn't heard the last of his argument.

If only he could put it aside . . .

He watched Juliet turn in Dougherty's arms, a golden Athena who could be his if he were to surrender his goals.

If he could forget his honor.

It was too hard to yearn for what he could not have. Lost in the silent study of his empty glass, he was beset by George's words. Was he following a dead end at the urging of his pride? Pride that had more than once blocked sounder judgment.

What kind of justice was he pursuing? The righteous course toward the truth? Or an easy means to absolve himself of a damning guilt?

Because if there was no one else to blame for his men having died, he could only blame himself. How could he live with that? With knowing his arrogance, his blind confidence in his own cleverness, as Crowley had put it, had led to the death of eighteen men in the field and eleven more at the prison and four out in the desert. He didn't want the weight of those souls resting upon his shoulders.

Was that why he'd narrowed his focus to one dedicated point, to finding the betrayer, to seeing justice done? Because someone had to pay the price for his vanity. Someone had to atone for breaking the trust he had in his men. He'd ridden with them, eaten out of tin cans and worse with them, had listened to them talk of their wives, their mothers, their sweethearts, their sisters, and never once, never once, had he guessed that one of them would stick a knife into the back of their whole unit and ruthlessly twist it.

How had he been so gullible? Why hadn't he seen the treachery where it lay, dark and deceiving and ready to strike? Hadn't he learned his lesson? Hadn't he discovered that the most benign surface often covered the foulest undercurrents?

He'd been just a boy, a lad of perhaps twelve, too young to see his father as anything less than perfect. He'd listened outside his father's door, something that was forbidden, but he so loved to hear the judge's silken orations, as caught up by his charm as any man who'd ever done business with him. He recognized the voice of the other man, a rye grower, but what confused him was the man's panic and outrage.

"But you promised you'd pay top dollar for my crop," he was saying. "You backed me when I refused to sell to that bandit Fairfax at the intolerable price he offered. You said you'd take the grain off my hands and see I got a fair price, so I waited, like you said, so that Fairfax would think he had the last laugh. But now it's too late to sell my goods anywhere else. All the other harvests are in and sold and mine's surplus. Are you telling me now that you don't mean to keep your word?"

"Now Mr. Potter, did I ever say I was in the commodities business? Did you ever know me to buy and sell grain at any price?"

"N-no—"

"Then why did you listen to me, a man with no experience, just because you thought you'd squeeze out an extra dollar or two?"

"But you said—"

"I said Fairfax's price was unfair and that I

would have offered one much higher, had I been in the business, sir. Had I been in the business. But we both know I'm not. What we have here is a misunderstanding—"

"What I have is a crop I can't sell!"

"Well, now, Potter, I'd wager that if you went back to Cole Fairfax and asked him real polite-like, he'd take that rye off your hands. He's the only one I know of who can afford to buy more than he actually needs."

"B-but he'll only give me half of his original offer."

Suddenly, the judge's tone lost all its congeniality to cut right to the bone. "Then you should have set aside your greed and said yes to it in the first place, shouldn't you? And that's exactly what you'll do next year, isn't it?"

"You was in on this scheme with Fairfax the whole time! The two of you worked this whole thing out just to get my crop for next to nothing. You cheats!"

"Now, Mr. Potter, is that a nice way to speak of them who've tried to help you?"

Noble stood on the other side of the door, sick to the heart and soul at what he'd just learned about his father. The truth. The truth that had been whispered but he'd refused to heed before. His father was a crook, a liar, a cheat, a schemer who sold his honor and his word to the highest bidder.

And inside the room, he heard his father's deep chuckle. "Do you hear that sound, Mr.

Potter? Do you know what it is? Do you? It's Cole Fairfax having the last laugh at your expense."

That was the night Noble vowed to himself that his word would matter more than his life, that his honor would never be compromised by greed or self-interest.

And that he'd never again be taken in by deceit or have his heart broken by betrayal.

So to what lengths would he go to now to see that the man who'd fractured his trust on the battlefield was made to pay the price for it? A price he'd never been able to extract from the master of lies.

His father.

Unable to answer that most important question, he sought solace in another glass of champagne.

Chapter 15

One minute he was standing off alone, nursing a glass of champagne, and the next time Juliet had a chance to look, Noble Banning was gone.

Trying to smile at what Miles was saying and appear to be listening, Juliet covertly scanned the mess hall for a glimpse of the Confederate major. But he'd left without ever asking her for a dance. So much for a perfect end to what might have been a perfect evening.

As the last few strains of music faded away, Juliet stepped back from her dance partner with a polite murmur of thanks. She was about to turn away when Miles caught her arm.

"Take some punch with me, Jules."

Not caring for the authoritative tone, she dropped a meaningful gaze to the hand upon her elbow. "I am not thirsty, Miles. Thank you."

"Then we'll talk. I seem to be having no luck in getting you alone lately, so this will have to do. Let's go outside."

"I don't want to talk now, Miles. This is a party, a celebration."

"Then let's give them something to really celebrate." He leaned toward her, his features somber, his gaze compelling, his mouth set and unsmiling.

She took his meaning with a sudden shock of dread. He meant to ask her to marry him.

She'd never known just how opposed she was to the thought of that union until this instant. Everything inside her cried, "No!" and urged her to break away before he had the opportunity to speak, to hurt and embarrass them both.

"Miles, I need to get some air. I simply cannot think straight at the moment, and you deserve my full attention. We'll speak later, I promise. Oh, look, Jane needs a partner for the next quadrille and that dreary Private Morris has cornered her. Be a dear brother and rescue her."

Miles hesitated, sensing her evasion yet not clever enough to find a way to circumvent it. But his scowl told Juliet clearly that he was far from discouraged. He sketched a bow and uttered a prophetic, "Until later then," which pealed like doom, before going to his sister's aid.

Juliet slipped out into the deep-starred night and drew a reviving breath of air. Had Jane known of her brother's plan? Had she encouraged it well knowing how seriously Juliet's affections were tied up in another? An unsuitable other. Was her friend trying to keep her from committing a grievous folly by throwing another option in her path?

She couldn't avoid the issue forever. Miles would have to be answered, and that answer would hurt him and possibly destroy their friendship. There was no way to escape that other than to accept his proposal. And how could she do that when she knew well that she didn't love him? She loved someone else—someone she recognized by the unbending silhouette he presented at the far end of the porch.

So he hadn't left the festivities after all.

Juliet hesitated. Dare she approach him with so much uncertainty hanging between them? Would she just be setting herself up for rejection or another round of his kiss-and-don't-tell games?

Fortune favors the bold, she'd always said.

"Makes you feel insignificant, doesn't it?"

She saw him smile as she repeated his words of the other night.

"I find myself in sore need of humbling," was his cryptic reply.

Juliet stood at his elbow as if it had been her intention all along to admire the heavens. "In many ways, this is preferable to the crush inside. One can't own one's own thoughts amid such revelry."

He slid a curious glance her way. "And what's on your mind this evening that requires open sky and quiet company?"

"The future."

"Ahhh," was his only comment.

"Don't you wonder what will happen, what fate has in store? Or have you got your course sunk as deep as fence posts in your Kentucky soil?"

"I'd thought so," he mused. Then he laughed at his own reflections. "I've always prided myself on my focus. I've known exactly what I wanted since I was a boy. It's only lately that I've begun to question those goals."

"And why is that?"

He was silent for a long moment, then answered with a disappointing evasion. "Many reasons."

Now wasn't the time for reluctance. Attacks that were swift and merciless were the ones that succeeded. Her father had taught her that.

"Am *I* one of those reasons, Noble?"

He could have devastated her with a word or a chastening look. Instead, he stared straight into her eyes and said the unexpected. "Yes."

She didn't know what to say once she had that truth.

When he looked back at the stars without offering further explanation, Juliet was forced into a reckless advance. "And is that good or bad?"

He chuckled at her directness. "Isn't it

enough just knowing that you've managed to throw me off course?"

"No."

"I didn't think it would be." He angled himself slightly so that he faced her. "Do you need it explained in words or would a display suffice?"

"Whichever you'd feel most comfort with."

Her brash confidence faltered at the light brush of his fingertips along her cheek. She found her breath suspended as he leaned down. Closing her eyes, she lifted her face invitingly, then was chagrined when he didn't kiss her. Instead, his mouth traced a warm line along the slope of her bared shoulder. She shivered all the way to her toes. Her hand rose of its own accord, coming to rest upon the back of his bowed head, trembling there in indecision. Should she pull him closer or push him away? Jane would advise her to be coy. But that wasn't in her nature. She didn't want to play games, she wanted . . . more.

She wanted Noble Banning.

Her fingers threaded through his black hair, clutching restlessly, answering the question of her willingness without words. The breath shuddered from her as his mouth swept up the arched column of her throat, pausing to taste her hurried pulse, then again to tug at her earlobe. Her fingers tightened in his hair as heat scalded through her body in a long, undulating wave. By the time he moved to her mouth, she was as far past reason as the distant stars.

They feasted from each other's lips with abandon, as if the sweetness found there was the cure for their every loneliness. Juliet was gasping by the time Noble lifted his head only far enough to breathe, then to say, "This is a mighty wide-open place for such a personal conversation."

Giddy with anticipation, she whispered, "The infirmary is empty."

He started toward it in an almost angry stride. Juliet had to run to catch up to him. He didn't pause or slow, even when she took hold of his arm and trotted anxiously at his side toward whatever a fickle fate had in store.

The fort hospital was dark, empty, as Juliet had known it would be. They slipped in at the side door. Medicinal odors and the bite of pure alcohol were quickly replaced by the rugged scent of wool and clean-shaven man as Noble turned her into his arms and shut the door with his boot heel. Juliet began thinking nervously of the cots lining the opposite side of the room. Would Noble take her there upon one of them? Excitement battled with inexperience. Perhaps she should insist they return to the party...

Then he kissed her and she stopped thinking altogether.

If there was persuasion in the shifting pressure of his mouth, the movement of his palms upon her bare shoulders was wild encouragement. His skin was rough and warm, the friction intentionally seducing. Her will pooled like hot wax. She savored his kisses and encouraged him with teasing nibbles and some very serious suction to his lower lip and tongue. His hands shifted lower, curving about the shape of her breasts while his thumbs rode the rapid rise and fall of creamy flesh swelling above the lacy neckline of her gown. When he lowered his head to trail damp kisses over that same soft territory, her bones seemed to go to liquid.

When his name moaned from her in helpless wonder, he paused, then straightened, his icy hot stare probing hers.

He'd never been so eager and anxious to have a woman. Staring down into her flushed face, into eyes so inviting and at the same time vulnerable, he knew it was more than just the wanting. The wanting was a powerful force in itself, a constant throbbing reminder of how she'd looked in damp lace and linen as she teased him into the water—of how she'd tasted during that initial exploration—of how the scent of lavender aroused him into a painful hurry. But it was more than the wanting. It was the having, the holding, the right to claim her as his own, to put her forever out of Miles Dougherty's reach. It wasn't competitive male drive goading him to stake that claim. It was an odd twist of possessive need that scared and surprised him, because he was powerless to resist.

But Juliet had rejected him bluntly, bruisingly. Dare he risk more than a moment of passion? Could he settle for that and no more? Staring down into her star-kissed eyes, the answer made him tremble.

"Juliet, are you sure this is how you want this to happen? Without commitment or ties of any kind?"

"Yes," she told him fiercely, not wanting to be distracted from the raw pleasures, not wanting her practical sense to overcome her sensory self to begin asking those same questions.

Was she ready to take this irreversible step with this man she couldn't marry?

To drive away those doubts, she clasped his handsome face between the press of her palms, kissing him with open-mouthed fervor. It took him a moment to respond, almost as if her answer wasn't what he wanted to hear. And then he swept her up and away with an aggressive assault on her senses.

He bent briefly to catch the bottom of her voluminous skirts, reaching up underneath them with a dexterity she didn't possess to release the tapes holding her hoops in place. They collapsed as easily as her inhibitions. Without the steel circles to hold him at bay, Noble leaned into her, pushing her back against the wall, letting her feel his weight and strength and heat. And his urgency. His breathing sounded harsh and fast in the surrounding darkness, her own playing fast and light against it. He kissed her hard, then deep, then with a searing sweetness that shook loose the last of her moral resistance. When he started to ruck up her skirt, she helped him, her own efforts much less efficient.

Mindless with the need he'd created, Juliet made no protest as he bared her legs and scooped his palms beneath her naked bottom to lift her off the floor. Instinctively, she wound both arms and legs about him. His mouth slanted across hers, his tongue plunging so deep that she nearly swooned with untested desire. Then with one piercing move, he was hard and fast inside her.

Juliet gasped against his mouth as her mind registered the splintering pain, but almost as quickly her body realized a new, intensely private pleasure: the pleasure of having him a part of her, streaking her inner walls with fire and shivery delight, a sense of oneness that went beyond any simple words.

And just as he began to move, awakening her to sensations her female self was crafted to enjoy, a different sound intruded, one that gradually surpassed their labored breathing to become . . .

Footsteps.

The door to the main infirmary flew open, and the heavy steps of at least a half-dozen booted men pounded across the floorboards.

"Lay him down there," came an anxious voice, drowning out Juliet's soft cry in the adjoining room as Noble pulled himself from her. Her feet hit the floor with a jarring thud of reality as he bent to yank up her hoops and reattached them without a word.

The commotion in the examination room increased.

"How the hell did this happen? Press that here. We've got to get this bleeding stopped. Hurry. Does anyone know where his daughter is?"

Juliet's cry of realization was muffled by the clamp of Noble's hand. *Her father.* It was her father they'd borne in senseless and bleeding.

Wide, frightened eyes glittered in the darkness as she looked up at Noble. He motioned for her to be silent and removed his hand.

"Shhh. Easy. We've got to get out of here," he whispered close to her ear. She swallowed jerkily and nodded, blond hair brushing his lips. "Follow me out the side door, straighten yourself up, then come in the front. I'll go to the mess hall to see if I can find out what happened. All right? Juliet, are you all right?"

She closed her eyes, trying to get a grip on the panic, the fear. The shame. Finally, she nodded. Noble stepped back, gripping her arm to guide her out the side door. Once in the deep night shadows, he pulled her tightly to him for a brief, bracing hug of support, then he was gone, leaving her on wobbly legs, her face tear-streaked, her gown hopelessly rumpled. Leaving her alone to discover what horrible thing had befallen her father while she indulged in a passionate frenzy.

How could she explain where she was when she should have been watching her father's back for the attack she knew to be coming?

How could she ever begin to forgive herself for not being there when she was needed?

To John Crowley the evening was perfect. He hadn't failed to notice that both his daughter and Noble Banning were missing from the festivities. The significance of those absences gratified him. He figured he'd have a son-in-law long before it came time to release the Confederates-cum-Federals at the war's end. Losing his Juliet to Banning would be a small price to pay for her safety.

So he drank champagne and intercepted Dougherty with small talk to keep him from an inopportune search. And he frowned as he watched the Southerners grow more obnoxious in the absence of their leader. He didn't trust Bartholomew for a minute. The man was as mutinous as he was proud. It took no great imagination to guess what the batch of them were discussing in the corner as they shot sullen looks his way. Banning was a man of his word. Bartholomew . . . He wasn't sure, and when he wasn't sure, he was cautious.

"Should I put a cork in the champagne, Colonel, before some of the men get out of line?" Miles glared across the room, his meaning clear.

"Subtly, Miles. Subtly. And keep the men separated. No sense in causing a commotion.

This is supposed to be a festive occasion, and I'd dislike seeing it turn into a brawl."

"Perhaps you should have Juliet speak to the Reb captain's wife, then. She seems to be causing the most trouble."

It was true. Maisy had pulled her husband away from the others and was lashing him with her caustic tongue. Ordinarily, Crowley would have ignored it, with a gentleman's disdain for getting involved in private matters, and let the captain handle it himself. But in his cups, in front of his grinning men, Donald Bartholomew forgot himself. He gripped Maisy by the arm, the cruelty of the gesture clear in her pained expression. With a few harsh words, he pushed her away from him, then turned his back, reaching for another drink from his companions.

Maisy stood, stunned then furious. Drawing back her shoulders in a posture of dignity, she left the gathering, head held high. After staying a few minutes to reestablish his superiority, Bartholomew excused himself from his drinking companions and slipped out after her—to make apologies or to seek retribution?

"Miles, would you mind keeping a judicious eye on those two. I would hate to learn that the captain grew churlish, if you know what I mean."

"I'll keep a discreet distance, sir."

With Bartholomew gone and the champagne ebbing dry, the tensions eased within the room and the men turned toward dancing instead of drinking, waiting for their chances with the vivacious Jane, the modest Pauline, or the pert Colleen.

Content to leave the situation alone, Crowley stepped outside, planning to enjoy a leisurely smoke before seeking out his daughter. Though anxious for a son-in-law, he was a father first and unwilling to give the major too much leeway where his daughter's virtue was concerned.

Of course, if he came upon them in a compromising circumstance, no amount of objection from Juliet would keep her from standing before a Bible the following day this time. He knew his daughter wasn't as opposed to the man as she was to the match. Once he got her over the idea of setting up her own house, he didn't think she'd mind his choice of housemate. No matter how great his haste to have her safely wed and producing grandchildren away from the dangers of the West, he would never force his will upon her. It would be her choice, of course. But he wasn't above helping her make it.

Banning was a good man. Smart, ambitious, strong-minded, just what his willful daughter needed. She'd never tire of him and regret her choice. Though that might not have mattered to many fathers, it mattered greatly to him. He'd had far too few years with a wonderful woman who'd been a constant delight and challenge. He wanted no less for Juliet.

He lit his cigar and inhaled deeply, letting

the smoke out upon an appreciative sigh. The parade ground was still, no sign of the Bartholomews or Miles. The musicians played a jolly holiday tune inside. Time to go find Juliet.

But as soon as he walked the length of the porch, stepping into the darker shadows, a prickle of warning stirred at the back of his neck. And his first thought was of Juliet's cautionings. He started to turn.

Pain scissored along his ribs. The shock of it kept him from striking out at the coward who attacked from behind. Instead, he stumbled off the edge of the boardwalk, dropping hard to his hands and knees in a whirl of agony, waiting for his assailant to jump down and finish him. No attack came. A weakening blackness swirled up around him. Seconds or minutes later, he heard a shout of alarm. Then nothing until he opened his eyes to see his daughter's face above him. Miles Dougherty stood behind her.

"Papa? Oh, thank God." She kneaded his hand in anguished spasms, unaware of the strength of her grip. "I was so afraid..." The rest trailed off, but her features said it plain. She was terrified and worried—and something more. Something else shadowed her tear-brightened gaze, but he was too weak to analyze it.

He patted her clutching hand with his free one, then tried to pry her fingers loose before she cut off his circulation. "I'm fine, Jules. Just a scratch. Isn't that right, Doctor?"

Robert Penny, the post surgeon, failed to concur. "You've lost a lot of blood, Colonel. I wouldn't brush this off so lightly. Plan on staying in this bed for the next few days." He held up his hand to ward off protest. "Just to be on the safe side. You don't want your daughter to worry, do you?" He winked at Juliet, and she seemed to relax a bit.

She leaned closer to ask, "Papa, who did this to you? Did you see?"

He shook his head in aggravation. "The sneaking bastard came up behind me—pardon my language, dear."

"My language will be stronger than that unless we discover who attacked you and soon."

Strength ebbing, Crowley's eyes began to sag shut. It was a struggle to focus on what needed to be done. "Banning, he's in charge. Miles, you support him. And see Juliet safely to our quarters. Don't argue, girl. You can do me no good here. I'm in fine hands. Take her home, Miles."

"Yes, sir." He took Juliet's elbow and lifted her away from the bedside of the now unconscious man. Juliet didn't fight him.

Once outside, she paused to draw a breath, trying to control a fresh bout of weeping. Beside her, Miles was a study in outrage. Her heart warmed toward him until he spoke.

"Damn that Banning. Putting him in charge. It was probably his blade that laid the colonel low. Let's see if he can account for his whereabouts."

Juliet stared at him, shocked and dismayed. His anger wasn't over her father's injury; it was at having his authority usurped by Noble. Her cold tone reflected her disappointment in him.

"The major was with me."

Miles's jaw unhinged slightly, then snapped shut, his teeth grinding together. Through them he said, "You and... Banning?" Saying nothing more but meaning everything.

"Yes," she told him with a proud tip of her head that dared him to make something of it. "I don't need you to show me to my quarters. I know the way. Perhaps you should be helping Major Banning in his attempt to find out the truth instead of making slanderous accusations."

"Jules—"

But she wasn't interested in hearing anymore he had to say. She started across the drill ground, not looking toward the mess hall, where the music had stopped and confusion now reigned. It took all her energy just to focus her tear-skewed vision on where she was going.

Then a cry came from the man on watch.

"Riders coming in fast. It looks like the boys from H Troop."

The soldiers who'd ridden escort for Jane Howell. What would they be returning for?

Dashing the back of her hand across her

eyes, Juliet stood firm as the disorganized group of riders poured into the confines of the fort. It took only a moment to realize the cause of their haste.

The first man she saw was slumped over his mount's neck, an Apache arrow jutting from his shoulder.

Chapter 16

Juliet had no idea what time of day it was when she wobbled out of the infirmary. Every bed and most of the floor inside was covered with wounded. She and Colleen had been at the doctor's side for hours, assisting him however they could, bandaging limbs and brows, measuring out doses of morphine, holding basins to receive bloody arrow tips and misshapen bits of lead that the doctor carved out of the injured.

Juliet's back ached from constant bending to wipe fevered foreheads and dip out water. Fatigue burned her eyes. Her soul was weary from holding in her emotions while men screamed in agony. Finally, when Jane arrived to relieve her, Dr. Penny had steered her to the door with orders not to return until she'd had at least eight hours of sleep.

She lingered just long enough to check on her father's progress. He was still unconscious, but his color was good and he seemed to be resting easy. She hoped her own rest would be as undisturbed, but knew that was unlikely.

"Juliet?"

Her system registered the shock of hearing his voice, but she didn't stop. The last person she wanted to see was Noble Banning. Her heart was too raw, her mind too blunted by exhaustion for a confrontation that would stir up the guilt she held inside. She heard the rattle of his saber as he jogged to catch up.

"How's your father?"

Instead of answering, she demanded, "Who tried to kill him?"

"I don't know that yet. But I'll find out."

"Good. Talk to me when you know." She tried to alter course away from him, but tired legs wouldn't support the sudden movement. She stumbled, and his arm provided an immediate bolster. She attempted to pull free, her emotions rising in a panicky crescendo, but he wouldn't release her.

"Let go. Please."

"I'll see you to your door."

"No. I'm fine."

"You're not fine, Juliet. Let me help you."

"I don't want your help. I want you to leave me alone. Just leave me alone." She swiped at her eyes in angry embarrassment, too upset to recognize that without his guidance, she would have been wandering blindly.

"Juliet, what's wrong? Is it your father?"

His concern only made things worse. Nearly choking on her grief and guilt, she cried in a low anguished voice, "It's your fault, don't you see? It's our fault. If we hadn't been— If I'd been where I belonged instead of with— He could have been killed, Noble. He could have died."

Understanding dawned with that wretched confession. By that time, they'd reached the shelter of her porch. Noble stopped her outside the door and forced her to look at him. She had no knack for pretense. Everything she felt was etched starkly into her pale features. And Noble didn't like what he saw—the condemnation, the awful self-blame.

"Juliet, darlin', you had nothing to do with what happened to your father. Nothing." He cupped her damp cheek with his palm, brushing away the tears with a gentle rub of his thumb. "And it had nothing at all to do with us. I won't let you believe that."

But her tragic eyes said she did and she would go on believing it until he could prove otherwise. That would have to wait. For the moment, she was as fragile as dandelion fluff. The slightest wind would have scattered her in indiscriminate directions. He pushed open the door and angled her inside.

"We can talk about this later. Right now, I'm going to put you to bed." He saw her wild objection and added firmly, "Alone."

She still had on the golden dress, but it was clear she'd never be able to wear it again. The delicate lace was splattered with blood, the silk darkly stained with medicines and perspiration. Noble turned her and worked down the fastenings. The ruined gown followed her collapsed hoops to the floor. She stepped out of them and started for her bedroom without a backward glance. After a moment's hesitation, he picked up her clothes and followed.

She'd curled up on her narrow bed like a vulnerable child and was squinting against the bright glare of the sinking sun that flooded in through her window. Noble drew the curtains to seal the room in a more sedate dimness, then looked back to her. A mistake. The sight tore through him with a ruthless savagery, daring him to deny he felt nothing for this brave and extraordinary woman.

He hesitated to act, uncertain of what he could do to make her rest any better. Did she still blame their passion for her father's present situation? If she did, what else could he say to dissuade her? That he was sorry? He wasn't. That it wouldn't happen again? He hoped it would. He knew it would unless she used this awful event to create a wall between them. The best thing, he decided, the only thing he could do for her now was to find out who'd done the deed. He knew about guilt and he understood blame, and he wouldn't allow Juliet to carry the crushing responsibility for what had happened tonight.

He was readying to leave when she called out to him softly.

"Don't go."

She didn't name a reason, but he could read

it in her expressive face. She was frightened and lost and couldn't bear to be alone with her worries. That he could handle.

Slowly, he unbuckled his saber and sidearm and laid them across her chair. His uniform jacket covered them. He stretched out on her maiden's bed, and the moment he put out his arm, she was snuggled close, despite the heat. And on the weight of a single sigh, she was asleep.

Taps had already sounded, and there was no place Noble needed to be. Shifting Juliet into a more comfortable position, he purposely blocked all thoughts of passion from his mind to concentrate on her father.

He mulled over what various revelers had told him during questioning, using the pieces like a puzzle to make a whole picture of what had immediately preceded and followed the attack. The only people everyone could agree were missing from the room at that time, himself and Juliet excepted, were Miles Dougherty and Donald Bartholomew.

Donald was an arrogant troublemaker, but was he a killer? How could Crowley's death advance his schemes?

And Miles, what would be his reasoning? Unless he'd thought to frame his rival in order to return to the colonel's—and Juliet's—good graces. But that idea was so far-fetched.

Was he missing someone with a grudge and a dagger?

The heavy heat of the early evening made it

difficult to focus. Soon he was dozing in a contented lethargy with Juliet's arm curled about his neck and her knee nudged across his thigh. A pleasant way to seek out a temporary slumber. A perfect way.

He knew exactly when she awoke. Her palm stiffened against his shoulder and her breath caught. He kept his eyes shut, his breathing regular, and waited to see what she would do.

Slowly, she exhaled, her slender body relaxing along the long line of his own. Her palm pushed in a circular pattern over his bared shin, then moved upward so that her fingertips could brush along his neck. There was no point in pretending to be asleep after that.

"Feeling better?"

She gave a slight start, then nodded. Her voice was low and rough with sleep. The sound sent an odd quiver through him. "Thank you for staying."

"My pleasure."

He touched her hair and felt a ripple of warming desire flow through him. Her head tilted back so that she could look into his eyes. Hers were softened by an artlessly exposed yearning. She waited for him to say something tender, something that would ease the sting of guilt from what had begun between them. What had he expected? She wasn't a clever debutante who used her body and charms to win what she wanted. What had happened between them earlier that evening had been an honest offering, her first. She needed him to tell her she'd done nothing wrong, that he thought no less of her and that she should think no less of herself.

But considering her earlier words, perhaps now wasn't the best time to invite emotion into play. She was still so vulnerable, so confused by sorrow.

"I'd better go."

She was silent for a long moment, contemplating his offer, then said, "You don't have to if you don't want to." A pause, then a more fragile, "Do you want to?"

"No."

He heard her swallow. She still hadn't looked away from him. Her fingers were making maddening little forays around his ear and down his stubbled jawline. She was thinking about what she'd say next, so he stayed silent and waited.

"I'm sorry for what I said earlier—that you were to blame. I was upset. I know that's not true now."

"I'll forgive you only if you forgive yourself."

Silence then, "Deal."

The subtle beauty painted by the half light took his breath away. Her smile was small, heartbreakingly pure. Something broke loose inside him then, a truth he'd tried to suppress and deny but could no longer. God, he was in love with this impossibly headstrong woman who'd first spurned his attempt to protect her virtue then surrendered it to him without pause. He was crazy about her.

And the instant her big blue eyes lowered to the shape of his mouth, he knew he wasn't leaving her bed any time soon.

They met in the middle for a light reacquainting of their lips. A soft brush, a tentative parry of tongues followed by a long, leisurely exploration that lasted to the limit of their breath. They parted to study each other within the parameters of this oddly quiet mood. Desire was there, yes, but it was muted by a stronger need to connect on another, more intimate level.

Never had Juliet felt more sure of herself and at the same time so dangerously out of control. She touched her fingertips to Noble's mouth, learning its shape, and charted the rough bristle of his late-day beard along one lean cheek. Dropping to the buttons of his red woolen undershirt, whose color had long since faded to dark pink, she released those fastenings so that she could thread her fingers through the mat of black hair she found so fascinating.

"Take this off," she told him with the gruffness of an order.

"Yes, ma'am." He sat up and pulled the undergarment over his head. As he did so, her hands glided over the hard muscles of his back and shoulders. She sat up, too, pressing a hot kiss at the nape of his neck. He turned to take her in his arms, but instead, she rode him down to the mattress, straddling his hips with her long legs. Their kiss was more fervent, quickly becoming serious business. After tasting the back of his throat until a restless groan rattled through him, Juliet sat back on her heels, her lips pouty, her expression half shy, half sassy. This wasn't the fragile girl of moments ago but rather a woman just beginning to feel her power and strength—a mesmerizing transformation impossible to ignore.

He unfastened the front of her corset cover. His hands were unsteady. He'd never had that happened before. He was shaking all the way down to his boots, as if this was the first time he'd crossed this intimate ground. It was the first time with Juliet. And that made it new. He bared her breasts and just stared for a moment, as if enchanted by their firm roundness, by the slow pucker of arousal that drew their pink tips up into hard coral buds. He thought now was the time he should say something tender, but his mouth was suddenly too dry for words, so he lifted his head to wet first at one supple breast, then at the other, sucking, tugging, laving until she cried out, her fingers clenching in his hair, drawing him closer as her back arched in unexpected delight.

Encircling her lithe form, he rolled her down to the mattress, kissing his way back up to her eager mouth. There was nothing playful about the aggressive exchange of plunging tongues and labored breath. Noble reached down to shuck off her drawers. His palms rubbed over the smooth flesh of her thighs and taut bottom until her legs shifted restlessly, until she pulled at his Union-issue trousers and commanded, "Take these off, too."

He was quick to oblige her, toeing off his boots, peeling down his breeches, long johns, and socks in one impatient motion. Then he turned back to her, and for a moment, time stopped as he took in the sight of Juliet laid out all golden and willing, part wanton, part innocent, all desirable. His heart shuddered within his chest. Then she reached up for him, breaking the spell, allowing him to settle between the spread of her knees, onto the yielding curves of her body, then so deeply inside her that he felt all at once lost then welcomed home.

And he began to move.

With her eyes closed and Noble Banning her only awareness, sensation enslaved her: the scent of him, hot and male, the harsh burr of his chest hair abrading her nipples, the sound of his breathing—an erotic melody the likes of which she'd never heard before. And the power of him moving within her. Relentless. Demanding. Coaxing her to the edge of sanity and beyond. He swallowed up her wild cry of surprise and discovery with a fierce kiss, riding out her completing pleasure spasms, then expending his own in a seemingly endless surge. Then the silence after the storm: their breath sharing a waltz, their heartbeats a gradually slowing march. A moment of perfect harmony. But only a moment.

"I should go," Noble said, not moving.

"Yes," she agreed, not releasing him.

"I can't stay." His head burrowed into her hair.

"I know." Her fingers combed through his.

"I have to be back in my quarters before reveille." He eased from her upon a reluctant sigh.

She scooted over to give him room to settle in beside her. "I'll make sure you're awake."

But she didn't. She slept hard and deep, stirring only briefly at the feel of his lips brushing hers as he whispered a predawn good-bye. And when the bugle finally broke her slumber, she woke to her solitary bed and to what might have been a dream. Except for the leather-bound volume lying open beside her. Shakespeare, opened to the balcony scene in *Romeo and Juliet*.

Defy thy father, and refuse thy name. Was that what he was asking of her? Or she of him?

all this is but a dream, Too flattering-sweet to be substantial.

She closed the book and held it to her breast, wondering what interpretation to make of the message he'd left her.

Chapter 17

"**P**apa, what are you doing up? Get back to bed!"

John Crowley appeared sheepish at his daughter's edict but refused to obey it. He continued to fasten his uniform jacket. "Now, Jules, I have a command to run. I can't lie around just because of a scratch."

"A scratch? That scratch could have killed you."

"Could have, but didn't." He touched her cheek to ease the expression of worry. "I'm fine. And my place is in plain sight of my troops if I'm going to hold them together. I don't need to tell you of the rumbling already circulating—that the Southerners plotted this assassination attempt."

"No, you don't." But her concern didn't lessen.

He smiled. "That's a good girl. A smart girl. I can't afford to have suspicion run wild. The men will look to me for guidance, and if I show them strength, we'll get through this. If I show them doubts, chaos will reign."

She nodded, hating to agree but knowing he was right. "Be warned, I will not let you overtax yourself. My eye will be on you every minute." Then she glanced away, suffering a pang of regret. She'd failed in that vow once before, but never again. Never again.

His features softened. "I would expect no less from you, my dear." He took her arm and allowed her to escort him out into the bright morning sunlight where the troops were gathered in the central square for inspection. The lines came to attention immediately, and Juliet faded back so that her father could step forward without assistance.

"At ease, men. I would like to commend my senior staff for maintaining order during my brief incapacitation and to assure you all that I am fine and fit for command. I would have my officers report to my quarters as soon as the companies are dismissed. Carry on."

There was no trace of weakness from his ordeal as the colonel strode across the parade ground. And Juliet found herself studying the faces first of the officers, then of the enlisted men to see if any betrayed disappointment. What she saw was a grudging respect, but no hint of a killer.

She'd made coffee and was bringing it in to the men gathered around her dining table when she got the first unpleasant indication of her father's plans. He wasn't discussing the search for an attempted murderer.

He was discussing blatant suicide.

"The Mescalero have gone beyond boldness with their attack on H Company. It's time we made a show of force to scare the heathens back to Bosque Redondo. What I plan is a massive sweep of the area. There are several homesteaders I want collected and brought in to the safety of our post, because the first move the Apache will make is one of retribution against the civilians. Major Banning, you will lead your company out first thing in the morning."

Juliet's knees weakened. She slid the tray quickly to the tabletop lest she spill its contents with the sudden shaking of her hands.

Noble leading the attack upon the Apache.

She was careful not to look up as she poured out the coffee and added the appropriate sugar and milk to suit each man. While distributing the cups, she glanced up to meet Noble's gaze, his cool and unblinking, hers bright with welling fears. His smile was small, a reassurance masquerading as thanks. She couldn't respond without betraying too much.

"Colonel, are you sure Banning is the right man for this detail?" Miles couched his objection as a question, but no one was fooled. Miles made his concerns clear. He didn't think Noble could be trusted to lead a group of men, mostly Southerners, without supervision.

"Yes, Major Dougherty, Major Banning is exactly the man I want in charge."

"But, sir—"

"You've had your say, Miles. Any more will be considered argumentative."

"Yes, sir," he grumbled, casting a hostile glare at his rival.

"Do you have any questions, comments, Major Banning?"

"No, sir. Not at this time. I'll see that my men are prepared and properly rationed."

Crowley nodded and the matter was settled—except in Juliet's heart.

Carefully, Juliet measured out a rationed amount of water onto each of her newly sprouted vegetables. Despite her daily fussing, the additives she put in the soil, the canvas she'd erected to shade the tender seedlings during the scalding heat of midday, and the precious water, the plants failed to prosper. The delicate shoots lay flat upon the unyielding soil, their leaves wilted and underdeveloped. Checking each one for signs of infestation, Juliet blinked her tears away.

Her mind could no longer deny what her heart had embraced. What she felt for Noble Banning went beyond desire. She admired his quick mind. She respected his sense of honor. She delighted in simply looking at him. She went deliciously weak at the mere thought of his touch. But what had her trembling with distress and close to crying was the thought of never spending time with him again, be it in argument or intimate agreement.

She was in love and she didn't like it, because of the pain it was sure to bring her.

Unwise—an understatement. She held no illusions. To the handsome Kentuckian she was most likely a diversion, someone with whom to amuse himself at an isolated frontier post until restored to the preferred pickings in his home state. She was the means to an end he'd made no secret of pursuing with more than just a vengeance.

What to do? The first time her emotions were engaged with a man, the man was totally unsuitable. She would have laughed at the irony if she hadn't feared falling into hysteria. Noble was everything she'd ever dreamed of, and the last man to make those dreams come true.

And for a moment, as she spaded the infertile ground, she chastened herself for letting pride get in the way of her father's obtaining Noble as her husband. She should have damned the reasons and accepted the offer. Then at least she'd have had the right to enjoy these final moments with him as his wife instead of being forced to accept a token smile across a crowded table. It wasn't fair.

A man's shadow crossed her garden plot. Wiping her eyes as if blotting the perspiration from her brow, Juliet glanced up to see the object of her yearnings silhouetted against the sun.

"Is there any hope of me sampling your produce when I return?"

She didn't dare read more into his soft-spoken words. Prodding a limp bean sprout, she said, "It doesn't look like it. I'm afraid the environment is too harsh for such tender things to flourish."

"You might be surprised," was his cryptic reply. He extended two volumes. "I wanted to return your books before I left. I enjoyed reading them, symbolism and all. Perhaps you could select several others for me to start when I get back." He spoke as though there was no chance of him not returning. Juliet knew better. She couldn't meet his steady gaze.

"You seem to be fond of Shakespeare."

"I've read all of his sonnets and most of his plays."

"And have you any particular quotes?"

"One comes to mind of late. 'With love's light wings did I o'erperch these walls; For stony limits cannot hold love out, And what love can do, that dares love attempt; Therefore thy kinsmen are no stop to me.'"

"A pretty sentiment," she told him, daring at last to look up again. The aura of light surrounding his form was blinding. "One you're carrying back to some sweetheart in Kentucky?"

"I've no one waiting for me there with romance on their mind."

Then who inspired him to think of words of love? His fair Juliet? Her heart beat faster with wanting to believe that, but her features pulled themselves into a frown of doubt. It was one thing to act the fool in private and quite another to lay bare her thoughts and prove herself one. In all likelihood Noble was speaking rhetorically or simply teasing her. She didn't respond well to either in view of what they'd shared. Though she vowed not to want commitment or to demand permanence, in her heart she mourned that loss.

Because she couldn't speak of the tender worries that plagued her, she sought another course of conversation.

"I've known campaigns to last for six months. Are you sure you wouldn't rather take a book with you?"

"Our motto is Travel light and return in a hurry."

Her smile was a trifle cynical. "And was that the philosophy you carried into the war?"

He chuckled at her wry observation and put down his hand to her. Placing her dirty one in his, she allowed him to lift her to her feet. Instead of releasing her, he continued to hold her hand within his.

"I won't have your cunning father out there as my enemy. Nor will I have one of my own to betray our strategies. I have every intention of coming back with my shield and not *on* it."

"So that you can continue your quest for retribution, or so that you can live long enough to go home to practice law?"

"Both."

"And if this traitor you seek is already dead? What will you have to drive you from day to day, Major Banning, if not thoughts of revenge?"

He didn't answer for a long moment, and when he did, she wished he hadn't.

"And what if this man I seek tried to kill your father to keep him from telling me his identity? You might try to discover that truth for me. It seems to be in the best interests of both of us now."

Juliet paled. She hadn't thought of that, but it made complete sense, an awful amount of sense. What better reason to kill her father than to silence him forever?

"I'll take care of my father," she said at last. "You'll have your hands full with the Apache." She glanced down regretfully at the drooping plants. "I've done all I can do here. If you'll excuse me, Major."

She started to turn away, but he still retained her hand, halting the motion. In a voice low and persuasive, he said, "I want to see you again before I leave."

"Of course you will," she replied nervously. "At noontime and dinner."

"Alone."

That clarification left her breathless.

"I—I don't know if I can." She didn't know if she should.

He let go of her hand and said with a maddening lack of emotion, "Let me know what you decide."

* * *

She spent all day trying to come up with a solution.

It was no great mystery why he wanted to see her alone. That she wasn't opposed to the notion of sending him off satisfied should have alarmed her. She didn't have loose morals. But she was practical. Did she want to pass up on the opportunity to be with him for what might be the last time? Did it matter if he spoke words of love and commitment or if he spoke of nothing at all? There was no question of what her heart wanted. It was persuading her mind to go along that gave her pause. He'd be leaving the fort with more than just a token of her esteem. He'd be riding out with her heart pinned next to the chevrons on his sleeve. And there was the chance of him leaving her with more than just pleasant memories.

She was momentarily distracted from her choice by the arrival of a freight wagon. The burly drivers claimed to have seen no trace of hostiles and were anxious to be on their way. One of the parcels they delivered was Juliet's mail-order hat. Grateful to have something to lift her spirits, she carried it to the shade of her porch and tore open the paper.

The minute she lifted it from the box, her mood plummeted. She'd ordered a modest bonnet to provide practical shade and a few feminine frills. What she'd received for her twenty dollars and an additional twenty for shipping was a huge, gaudy affair made up of satin bows and bobbing plumes, all in an eye-blinkingly brilliant shade of purple.

Lavender. She stared at the hat, her eyes misting over in dismay. Certainly she'd told the milliner that she wanted a pale lavender, a subdued hue to match one of her nicer calicos. But this grand monstrosity was too outlandish for anything less than the opera and certainly not appropriate for the mess hall.

"Oh, my," gasped Maisy Bartholomew as she peered over Juliet's shoulder. "Is that someone's idea of a sad joke?" Her own amusement was clear in her sarcastic tone.

Having to admit her disappointment for Maisy's entertainment suddenly stuck in Juliet's craw. She set her jaw and forced a delighted smile and she plopped the creation atop her blond head. "Gracious, no. Poor dear, you must have been sadly out of touch with fashion out there in the wilds of the Carolinas. Why, this is all the rage in Paris. Jane ordered it for me from Washington. All the senators' wives were wearing them."

Maisy squinted. "Really?"

"Oh, yes."

Hating to admit that she was behind on the current French fashions, Maisy viewed the atrocity more favorably. "It does have a certain *joie de vivre*." Then her smile took a crafty turn. "Such a shame that color looks so poorly on you."

Juliet gasped as if that news distressed her.

"Oh, dear. Do you think so?" She hurried inside to peer into the mirror to see that the hat sat upon her head like a Spanish galleon under full sail—purple sails. She pretended to be distraught. "Oh, Maisy, I fear you're right. This shade does nothing for my hair. What am I going to do? I paid an absolute fortune for it, and my father will be so upset to think I threw my money away."

Maisy grew positively sly. "Perhaps I can help. I know it's not nearly what it must have cost you, but I would give you thirty dollars, just to save you the embarrassment."

Juliet's brows rose. "I couldn't let you do that. That's too much to spend just to be kind."

"Forty."

"Oh, I really can't—"

"Fifty. I insist. Think nothing of it. I've got more hats than I need, but I suppose I could use one more. Donald won't mind."

Juliet gave her a blameless look framed in purple. "Well, if you're certain."

Maisy practically snatched the feathers from her head, then preened before the mirror, congratulating herself on the fashion coup. Juliet watched her, thinking something about pride going before a fall.

But when the ladies promenaded before the dinner hour and Maisy appeared in bold purple plumage, the amazing sight brought everyone to a gawking standstill.

Jane, the soul of discretion, took Maisy aside

to whisper sympathetically, "Thank heavens I caught you before anyone saw you."

"Whatever do you mean?"

"Oh, dear, that hat, I simply could not forgive myself if I let you wear that to the shame of your husband."

Maisy blinked at her in owlish disbelief. "But it's all the style."

"*Last* year's style. Heavens, no one in the East would be caught dead—I mean, it's just too, too much. Perhaps if you removed the feathers and most of the bows and dyed it a more appealing shade. Lavender, perhaps. Yes, that would be lovely. Don't despair. It's not a total loss."

Maisy turned a malevolent glare upon Juliet to see if she was laughing at her expense. But Juliet appeared honestly ashamed enough to murmur, "As you've told me, Maisy, and often, I have no sense of sophistication. I should never have thought to advise you on fashion. I'd be happy to return the money—"

"There's no need for that," Maisy snapped, hanging onto her pride with a fierce smile. "Excuse me while I go change."

As soon as the self-inflated female was gone, Jane looked to her friend with new admiration. "Juliet, tell me you were somehow behind that awful hat."

Juliet felt no real joy in admitting it. True, the woman had practically begged to be humiliated, but dishing it out sat heavily upon her conscience.

Then Jane changed the subject abruptly. "Albert is riding out with Major Banning in the morning."

Juliet was immediately all concern. "Oh, Jane, I didn't know."

The frivolous Jane Howell took a deep, bracing breath to display the fortitude of a soldier's bride. "I'll send him off with a smile and cry for him every night until he comes home. And you?"

"Me? My father isn't going."

"I wasn't referring to your father."

Seeing no reason to lie to her best friend, Juliet admitted, "I'll most likely shed my share of tears, too."

"We'll have each other for company tomorrow, but tonight I plan to enjoy my husband while I still have him. What are your plans, Juliet?"

The gentle prodding caused her to mutter, "I haven't decided."

As Noble Banning strode the length of the parade ground in full dress, Juliet's gaze followed in helpless longing. Jane put an arm about her shoulder.

"You'd better decide fast, darling."

Noble had washed up and was in the process of bundling extra clothing, a blanket and a rubber sheet to ward off the chill from damp ground, his rations, 150 rounds, half a pup tent, extra shoes for his horse, fifteen pounds of grain, a short-barreled carbine, and his rifle into a pack that he'd strap behind his saddle, where his armaments would be within easy reach. His mind should have been on the details of moving fifty men across the desert floor in search of a dangerously elusive enemy.

But he couldn't steer it away from the equally elusive lover he couldn't manage to lure across the parade ground for one final good-bye.

He wasn't a fool. He'd gone into battle too many times not to know there were even odds that he wouldn't come back. He'd gained an entirely new respect for the Apaches' fighting ability after stumbling behind their horses. It wasn't a position he wanted to be in again. Nor did he want to come back to Crowley admitting to failure.

It wasn't the amount of time he'd be living out of a saddle that bothered him. It was the amount of time Miles Dougherty would have to charm Juliet in his absence. There was little he could do to keep her out of Miles's arms from a hundred miles away.

He threw his pack into a corner and wondered if he was being overly optimistic to think he might actually be able to sleep tonight.

A tap on his back door broke into his broodings. And when he opened it, all was forgotten.

"Juliet! Did you bring me a book after all?"

She stood in heavy shadow, her pale hair

concealed under a colorful Navajo shawl. When she stepped across the threshold, she let it fall away. And when her arms encircled his neck to pull his head down, tomorrow's worries fell away just as easily.

She kissed him as if there was no tomorrow. She could be right about that, he knew. Her mouth was hot, aggressive, devouring, stating her decision for her. No explanations, no words, no promises were needed. He closed the door and snuffed the single candle between his fingers. It sizzled, just as they sizzled in the sudden darkness.

Juliet kissed him again and again, afraid that if she spoke a single word, all her fears and feelings would come pouring out in an unforgivable torrent. That's not how she wanted to send him off—with a memory of her tears and clutching panic. Better he have something more pleasant to hold onto, something to encourage him to come home in a hurry—something like the image of her warm and waiting.

There was a moment's chill as the night air met her newly bared skin, then Noble's hands were there to stir the heat up again. Having anticipated, having hoped how their meeting would culminate, she wore nothing beneath her gown but a splash of lavender water. Within minutes of laying her down on his bed, he had her moaning his name in restless abandon. Then he was joining her in those hot throes of pleasure, twisting, twining together on his tousled sheets, giving, taking, not caring about what would come with the dawn—only how they would spend this night together in search of mutual delights.

In the aftermath of their first discovery, Juliet sprawled in sated lethargy, with no ambition to move a muscle except to smile when Noble came up on his elbow beside her.

"You've a look that says you've been well satisfied."

She chuckled and drew her fingertip through the black furring on his chest. "And in your vanity, you claim all the credit, do you?"

She arched and sighed as his mouth moved upon her left breast, willing to give credit where it was due, until he lifted himself up to say, "I can't claim more than my fair share, darlin'. And you've done more than half toward exhausting me."

"I've done my very best," she purred.

"If you'd like to do more to convince me of it, go right ahead."

Her mood grew serious. "I'd like to convince you to come back safely."

His gaze probed hers intensely. "That's my plan. I've too much to do to have it otherwise."

Juliet looked away. Of course, his plans. His vengeance. His law practice. His carefully regimented life that could never include her. Suddenly, it was too difficult to pretend those thoughts didn't devastate her.

"I have to go."

Her quiet claim won an instant objection. "Right now?" The idea seemed somehow abhorrent to Noble. He rolled onto her sleek figure, pinning her between his forearms and knees. "What can I do to persuade you to stay?"

"You can't—"

"Maybe this." He nuzzled her neck, the hot brush of his breath exciting a shiver.

"Noble—"

"Or this." He moved against her, letting her feel the power of his renewed interest pushing into her softer flesh.

"I can't—" But her protest was weakening.

"How about this?"

His mouth claimed hers in a will-sapping exchange that continued to deepen until he felt her fingers press into his shoulders, until her legs shifted, knees lifting to accommodate him. He sank into the tight heat of her body, losing himself almost at once as she breathed his name in welcome and wonder. With a force of concentration that caused him to tremble, he held himself still, savoring the sensations until he could control the pace of their pleasuring, until slow, shuddering waves of completion took them both in perfect harmony.

And this time when she said she had to leave, Noble let her go, watching from the warm tangle of his covers, where the scent of lavender clung, as she swiftly, soundlessly dressed. Her quick farewell kiss twisted sweetly to his soul, then she slipped out into the night, abandoning him to a restless slumber.

Juliet hurried through the shadows toward the single light she'd left burning. She hugged herself, holding in the feel of him, the memory of him for as long as possible, but knowing it wouldn't last for long. She wouldn't think about watching him ride out in the morning or of the long, fretful days that would follow. Instead, she would gather the moment about her to insulate her fragile heart from those inevitable sorrows.

Lost in those golden reminiscences, she slipped inside her adobe home to the sudden shock of discovery.

"Where have you been, Juliet?"

Chapter 18

She drew up with a gasp, then exhaled when she recognized her father's silhouette by the stove and smelled his pungent pipe tobacco. Had he been waiting there for her, fully aware of where she'd gone and why? She tried a desperate bluff, not so much to protect her virtue as to keep the glow of the intimate night with Noble to herself in privacy.

"I—I went for a walk."

His silent doubting was worse than the meanest accusation. Guilt assailed her, wringing out a version of the truth without him having to say another word.

"I went to see Noble Banning."

"And?"

"And what? We talked."

"About—?"

She needed to distract him from the obvious direction of his thoughts. "About what happened to you. About who might want to see you dead."

The Rebel

He stared at her, astounded, and, she thought, a little disappointed. "You went to see the man at close to midnight to discuss your father?"

"I'm worried about you. Noble thinks—"

"What does the honorable Major Banning think?"

"He thinks it could be the same person who betrayed his troops."

"He's wrong." Again he closed down tight about that declaration, allowing no other interpretations.

Juliet frowned. He sounded so certain. What if he were wrong? That alone was worth pushing the point. "It makes sense, Papa. If the man fears you'll expose him, he might be trying to silence you forever."

"No."

"How can you be so sure? Who is this man you're trying to protect? Why would you value his safety over your own? I don't understand."

"I don't expect you to, child."

"I'm not a child. And I'm afraid for you."

"I know you're not a child, Jules. So I'll say this straight out. If I were to give Banning the information he wants, what do you think the odds would be of him heading due east all the way to Kentucky without ever once looking back? What would keep him here?"

"His word." How strange for her to use the same argument she'd once dismissed.

"His word," Crowley repeated. "Yes, perhaps you're right. But a man makes plenty of vows, daughter—to his family, to his home, to his country, to his conscience. Where do you think Major Banning's vow to me would fall in there amongst the *others*?"

She couldn't answer. She didn't know. She was afraid to guess.

The bowl of her father's pipe flared bright with his deep inhalation. "It's not as though I fault him. In his place, forced into submission by his enemy, I would feel no great allegiance either. His sense of personal justice is all that holds him here, Juliet—unless you can name another conviction which he holds to as strongly."

Her? Would he stay for her? Juliet stood silent, mulling over that question, forcing herself to be brutally honest in her answer.

No. No. He wouldn't place her in front of any of those things.

"I'm very tired, Father. I'm going to bed."

"Jules?"

The tender snag in his voice held her.

"I don't say these things to hurt you."

She gave him a wan smile. "I know, Papa. Good night."

It wasn't her father's words that hurt like a cruelly wielded saber. It was the truth.

The post band played "The Girl I Left Behind Me," a gay yet sentimental song that had all the ladies' eyes misting as the men of Company B prepared to ride out, perhaps for the last time. Noble Banning, with Albert Howell and Tom Folley flanking him, led the line of mounted men past the gathering. Without a pause, he presented his saber in a formal salute to his commander while his gaze was fixed upon that man's daughter. Juliet couldn't offer him a smile. Her jaw was too tight from withholding her tears. Instead she just nodded, and his quick wink said it was enough.

And as the column of fours became an indiscriminate cloud of dust that could be seen from horizon to horizon, Juliet heard Miles's quiet words of encouragement.

"Don't fret. He'll be fine."

Of course he was speaking to his sister about her husband's welfare, but Juliet clung to the sentiment. It was the only way to keep the awful anguish at bay.

At the close of the first day out, they came across the spot where Company H had been ambushed. The ground was bristling with arrows. The company's dead still lay where they'd fallen, mutilated in Apache fashion so that they would be maimed in the hereafter. Grimly, Noble ordered the remains buried. For the next few days, they'd be moving fast, and he couldn't spare the men to return the bodies to the fort. He said a few words over the fresh-spaded dirt, then was perplexed when Howell used branches and rocks to disguise the graves.

"So they can rest undisturbed," his lieutenant told him.

Thinking about that kept Noble awake most of the night.

Thinking about Juliet kept him up the rest of it.

They were mounted and moving before daybreak, intent upon reaching the first of three homesteads before noon. Their haste proved unnecessary.

The Bowdens had been dead at least a day.

"Bury them," Noble ordered, trying to shut out the sight of the butchered woman.

One of the privates emerged from the still-smoldering house with a child's dress in one hand. His expression was filled with tragic confusion. "They had two little ones."

"Are they inside?" Noble asked, dreading the answer.

The private shook his head.

"Spread out, men. I want them found and properly buried with their folks."

"Major, there's no need," Howell told him. "Most likely the savages took the children to raise as their own."

Noble stared at the tiny calico dress, his insides clenching in anguish. His voice was soft and conclusive. "We'll find them and bring them back with us."

Howell looked at him sadly, not saying anything.

"I said we'll find them."

"Yes, sir."

The Fenton place they reached midafternoon. It was a small ranch that had just managed to subsist. Now it was smoking rubble. They were only hours late. The wood was still burning. This time, the children hadn't been spared.

Again Noble ordered burial and spoke the words, which didn't come quite so easily.

"How far to the Stacy ranch?"

"About two hours."

"Two hours," he echoed. So much could happen in two hours. "Mount up. We'll double-time—"

"Major, the men and horses are nearly spent."

"And that last family is probably out there fighting for their lives."

"That family is probably already dead. We should conserve out energies to save ourselves. Sir."

Noble stared straight through him. "Lieutenant, can you guarantee me without a doubt that those people are dead, that we can be of absolutely no use to them?"

Howell hesitated. "No, sir. I can't."

"Then mount up. Dammit, I want to bring someone back alive with us."

The glare of flames hugged the horizon. Within ten minutes, the sound of gunfire reached them.

"Bugler," Noble shouted over the thunder of hoofbeats. "Let them know we're coming."

Against the blare of the horn, the troop swept down upon the besieged homestead, carbines drawn, eager to vent their horrified anger over what they'd already left in the hard New Mexico ground that day. Apache scattered as soon as they saw that they were outnumbered. Company B swarmed into the yard, to a man praying they were in time to effect a rescue.

The barrel of a rifle protruded from one of the shuttered windows. With the roof ablaze, it was only a matter of minutes before the entire structure caved in.

"Hello in the house. This is Major Noble Banning, United States Army, out of Fort Blair. You're safe under our protection. Show yourself."

A long moment passed in which the roof joists creaked and tiles began to fall inward. Finally, the front door flew open and a woman of about fifty years staggered out, choking on smoke, but still with the presence of mind to keep her rifle trained upon them.

"Mrs. Stacy, you can put down your weapon. You've nothing more to fear."

The barrel drooped. "My husband, he's inside."

"Is he wounded?"

She shook her head, gulping for air and courage. "He's dead, but I want him buried properly."

"Anyone else?"

Again the head-shake.

"Sergeant, fetch Mr. Stacy."

Another burial, more words he hoped would bring comfort to those sent on their way, because they left none for those who remained. Anne Stacy stood dry-eyed at the grave site, her home now rubble, her only possession the empty Spencer rifle.

"Ma'am, I don't mean to intrude on your grief, but we need to get to safer surroundings so we can set up camp for the night."

Calm dark eyes lifted to his. "I'm ready, Major. I've said my good-byes."

Noble nodded, respectful of the woman's quiet fortitude but anxious to put some miles between them and the glowing timbers that pointed out their location like a beacon in the night.

They made camp under the stars a half-hour later, silently rushing through tending the animals and pitching tents. After a cold supper, they gave their safety over to the sentries and slept hard until daybreak, too exhausted for even Anne Stacy's soft weeping to disturb them.

Moving out with the dawn, Noble considered what his scouts told him. The Apache were heading west, back toward Fort Blair. Needing to get Mrs. Stacy to the safety of the fort, he was willing to follow their trail, grateful not to have to divide his number to provide the widow with an escort. That didn't lessen his concern.

"Albert, will they attack Fort Blair?"

"It's unlikely, sir. They prefer to pick off the weak and the easily dominated. But if they set their minds to it, they could attack the fatigue details and keep them from bringing water to the post."

"How many would you guess we're dealing with?"

"Hard to say, Major Banning. Three can do as much damage as three dozen."

"When we're close to the fort, we'll send a detail in with Mrs. Stacy. The rest of us are going to track down our murderous friends. And we're going to rescue those children."

Howell sighed, obviously thinking his plan without merit. But he said, "Yes, sir."

However, his doubts weren't shared by the majority of the men who'd gone into battle at Noble's back. And seeing that unswerving confidence, the mood spread through the remaining troops like a bolstering contagion.

Observing his men—*his men*—Noble saw a single unit bound by grim circumstance into a whole, one no longer divided by geography or accent. They were soldiers, joined by respect for their leaders and by their hatred and fear of a common enemy—just as Crowley had predicted they would be. Too bad it took the sacrifice of two families to bring about that change.

They were within twenty miles of the fort when one of the scouts raced up on a lathered mount.

"I've spotted the hostiles, Major. About fifteen of them heading fast for Bright's Canyon. It's a box canyon, sir. We can trap them inside, but once they get up into those hills, we'll never catch them."

Thinking of those two captive children, Noble didn't hesitate. "Sergeant Dell, take a detail and get Mrs. Stacy to Fort Blair. The rest of you men, we've got some renegades to run to ground."

A unified whoop of agreement filled the air. Not quite a Rebel yell, but close enough.

The trail was fresh, better than a dozen riders on unshod ponies, carelessly dashing for the concealing rocks of Bright's Canyon. Determined to catch them while he still had the advantage of numbers, Noble led an all-out charge through the mouth of the canyon. Up ahead he could see the dust from the Apaches' horses. He called for his men to draw arms, the roar of battle in his blood.

It should have been a simple assault. The Indians had abandoned their horses at the back wall of the canyon and were running for the cover of the rocks. Flank them, call for surrender, and cut them down if they failed to comply. Simple. Except that the fifteen Apaches weren't running away. They were purposely leading Noble and his troops—straight into a trap.

The troops realized it just seconds after it was sprung. Gunfire and arrows rained down on them from the rocks above, where the main body of Apaches had lain in wait for the decoy group to lead the soldiers in. Shocked and startled, Noble called for a retreat. Again too late, for the mouth of the canyon was already closed by hostile sharpshooters picking off every man and horse that came within range.

Caught in the open, the troops circled in a natural depression, dismounting and trying to hang onto their horses as the Apaches fired down upon them.

Tom Folley was one of the first to fall, an arrow piercing his throat. Albert Howell crumpled beside him, blood blossoming high on his chest. The rest of the troop crouched to make smaller targets, dragging their horses down to provide a shield, but also rendering escape impossible. Noble pulled Howell behind one of the downed horses and bared the wound in his shoulder. It bled fiercely but not fatally. Howell placed his hand over the wadding Noble had made to stanch the flow, pressing hard and grimacing. His pain-filled gaze fixed upon his field commander.

"What the hell are we going to do, Major?"

Noble glanced from Howell to the high surrounding cliffs from where the Indians pinned them effectively to the ground. His mind worked frantically for a solution.

"We've got to get help from the fort. It'll take someone who's half centaur to ride through those bastards."

"I know a man like that," Howell said with a grim smile.

"Who?"

"You, sir."

Noble recoiled from the idea, then shook his head. "I can't abandon my command."

"If we don't get word to the fort, you won't have a command. Noble, you're the best chance we have of getting a man through. I'll hold down our position until you bring Crowley back with reinforcements."

He hesitated and in that brief moment, another man fell, mortally wounded. There was no glossing over their situation. They were all going to be dead if something wasn't done and soon. Noble gave Howell his ammunition box.

"Keep 'em alive for me, Albert."

"Yes, sir. Good luck to you."

Noble wasted no time once the decision was made. He broke from cover, dashing across bullet-chewed ground to where one of the Indian horses stood. He could make better time without extra weight. He vaulted onto the animal's bare back and grabbed up the rope bridle, kicking back his heels as he did. The horse lunged forward with him leaning low.

The Apache must have expected the troops to try an escape, for they were on him in an instant, first with a rain of arrows, then with a mounted attack. He wasted no time trying to place a shot. His goal was to get out of the canyon alive.

Once he made it into the clear, Noble glanced back to see three braves in pursuit.

Only then did he fire off a couple of rounds, knowing them to be out of range. Still, it made the Indians think twice about closing the distance.

Without regard to man or mount, he drove his horse down into rocky washouts and up crumbling banks on the other side. In the mad scramble across open ground, he remembered all the times he'd raced to glory on a hard-packed Kentucky dirt track for the fun and sport of it. This time he was gambling not with his pocket money but with other men's lives. They were counting on him, and time was his enemy—time and distance and his three pursuers.

He bent low over the animal's neck, urging it to greater speed. He tried to keep his mind on the single objective of survival, but a great cloud of blame hung over him.

How could he have been so stupid? How could he have led his men right into that shooting gallery?

It wasn't his military skill that would save them now. It was his horsemanship.

But even the best rider in the world could do nothing once his horse's foot went down into a prairie-dog hole. With a scream and the crack of its fetlock bone, the Indian pony went down, casting Noble over its head to slam into the dirt and roll into darkness.

Chapter 19

Waiting was hell.

Juliet had watched her father leave on perilous marches countless times during her growing-up years, but somehow this was different. The way she missed Noble was different.

Instead of just loneliness and worry to cope with, a deep gnawing ache settled inside and refused to be soothed. No matter how much time she spent at the infirmary, nursing the invalid men of H Troop, no matter how many volumes she read until her eyes no longer focused, no matter how many witty conversations she had with Jane, the fear of losing Noble failed to ebb, because he'd ridden away without telling her how he felt about her.

Jane and Pauline had history with their husbands and futures upon their return. She had nothing but stolen moments, as fleeting as they were unsubstantial. She had pieces of his past and no guarantee that there would be more than that if—not when—he came back. Though she'd sworn not to need it, she craved that sense of permanence, the stability of a ring upon her finger, a shared cupboard of clothing, the right to cherish his personal belongings. She wanted to bear his children.

Having never allowed herself to consider what she'd missed in her nomadic life, fearing that longing for something her father couldn't give her equated to disloyalty, Juliet was surprised by how deeply she desired ... more. The house, the family, the sense of community that didn't revolve around a bugle call. A man who wore lace-up shoes and suspenders and didn't risk meeting death each time he left the yard. These were no longer vague wishes. It was what she wanted with Noble Banning.

She was tired of sacrifice, tired of being afraid and brave and silent in her suffering. And because she felt all these things churning inside her, sitting across from her father at dinner was too torturing to endure.

"If you'd excuse me, Papa, I promised to take some fresh milk over to Pauline for the children."

He studied her expression, and for an anxious second, she was sure he could see right through her to the treachery of her heart, to the fact that if Noble Banning asked her in the next moment to desert with him to Kentucky, she would be packed and gone in an instant, without thought or remorse. But of course, he wouldn't. And her father had no way of guessing at her treachery.

He smiled. "Enjoy your visit, daughter."

How could she enjoy it?

Juliet measured out a pail of milk from the cooling jug hanging close to the ceiling, her emotions in turmoil. How could she enjoy a meeting with Pauline, well knowing the talk would revolve around Tom and the life they shared. She had no such experience to relay, no tender times, no fond recall, no routine to miss, no empty sheets to mourn. She didn't even have the freedom to discuss the sentiments she was feeling, because they didn't belong to her and Noble the way they belonged to a man and wife.

She was about to step out the back door when she collided with George Allen. After they'd steadied the pail of milk between them, she smiled and said, "Good evening, Captain. My father is just finishing his meal. I'd be happy to set you a place if you'd care to join him."

"No. No, thank you, ma'am. Actually it was you I came to see."

"Me?" She set down the pail, noting the pallor on the young man's face that had his freckles standing out like a rash of measles. "What can I do for you, Captain?"

Despite his awkward shifting, there was a seriousness about George Allen that alerted her. "This is a delicate matter, ma'am, one I promised I would not involve you in."

"Promised whom?"

"Colleen—that is, Miss McDonnal."

Juliet was suddenly all concern. "Is something wrong with Colleen?"

"More than she'll admit, at least to me. I thought you being another lady, perhaps she would confide the cause of what I've witnessed and she denies."

"What exactly have you seen?"

At her taut command, the chaplain relaxed, seeming to realize that he'd done the right thing in coming to her. "Bruises, ma'am. More each day. On her arms and legs and now on her face."

Juliet summed it up in a word. "Maisy."

"I fear the woman is beating her. This morning, she could hardly walk or lift so much as a broom without—" He broke off, clearly distressed by the evidence of abuse.

Refusing to vent her fury in front of him, Juliet merely placed a hand upon his arm. "Thank you, George. I'll take care of it."

He sighed in relief. "Yes, ma'am. I was hoping you would. I could only arrive at one other solution for freeing her from that household, a last resort if you wouldn't help."

His embarrassment made Juliet smile. "George, I hardly think Colleen would see a proposal from you as a last resort."

His ruddy face stilled. His expression grew somber. "I'm not worthy of her."

"You are a good man, George Allen."

He shook his head sadly, his features tragic.

"Being a man of God does not excuse him from sin."

Wondering what sin the devout young man could have committed, she said gently, "It's no sin to want to protect those who are weaker or to love them."

He looked uncomfortable, as if there was more he needed to say, but he didn't speak. Nor did he deny what Juliet plainly saw. He was in love with the Irish servant girl.

She smiled reassuringly. "I'll do what I can, George."

"Thank you, ma'am."

Juliet quickly delivered the milk to Pauline, then cut her visit there short to confront Maisy Bartholomew. Her anger grew with each step. How dared the woman think she could abuse another with impunity? She could think of no greater abomination and cursed the Southern slave-owning mentality that allowed one human being to treat another like property. Then she caught and corrected herself. Not everyone was like that. Noble would never condone such a thing. Neither had George. It was a single mean-spirited female who saw her own comforts as superior to another's.

And Juliet meant to correct that thinking at once.

Juliet paused outside the Bartholomews' door, breathing deeply to control the urge to take a horsewhip to the woman. As she stood there, forming a diplomatic argument, she heard a different, louder argument coming from inside.

Maisy and her husband were fighting.

Or rather Donald Bartholomew was on the receiving end of his wife's cruel rantings.

"Coward! You useless coward! How many times must I ask you, *beg* you, to let me go home? And you do nothing."

"Maisy, what do you think I can do?" His voice was weary, long-suffering.

"Something, *anything*, to get me out of here. This heat, this filth, it's making me go mad. I cannot stand it. I have to get away."

"If you'd left with that troop the other day, you would have come back sporting an Apache arrow. Or not at all."

"Maybe I'd be better off. Maybe I'd rather be dead than trapped here in this hell."

"Maisy, my darling, no. You don't know what you're saying."

His dismay was plain. He didn't think she said the words just for shock value. And hearing them, neither did Juliet. She'd known women to lose control completely in the frontier isolation. She'd thought Maisy too full of herself to break down to that level, but perhaps she was wrong.

"Yes, I do. I know exactly what I'm saying." That sounded more like Maisy—selfish, shrill, and blaming others for her discomforts. "I've been saying it all along. Damn you, Donald, for bringing me to this place. I'd rather you were still in prison. Then at least I'd still have my things and my friends around me."

There was a shocked silence. Juliet was about to withdraw, embarrassed and alarmed by what she'd overheard. But she'd promised George and she owed it to Colleen. She knocked.

Maisy jerked open the door. Her face was flushed, her eyes red-rimmed. There was a moment's panic as she wondered how much Juliet had heard.

"Good evening, Captain, Mrs. Bartholomew," Juliet began cheerfully. "I've come to beg a favor of you." She paused. "Have I come at a bad time?"

Maisy immediately composed herself. "Not at all. Please come in."

Not wishing to linger any longer than she had to, Juliet got right to the point. "I've come to borrow Colleen's services—just temporarily."

"What?" Maisy all but roared. Her eyes narrowed in fierce suspicion. Juliet guessed she was wondering if ranking out applied to domestic help, too.

"My father needs special care while he recovers from his injury. I've been helping at the infirmary and haven't been there for him as I should be. I was wondering if I could impose on you to allow Colleen to stay with us, just until my father is better."

"But what am I to do in the meantime?"

"I would have an enlisted man appointed to serve as a striker for you. I realize this is a tremendous favor to ask and no soldier could perform Colleen's duties as well as she, but my father feels uncomfortable asking personal favors from one of his men, so you see the difficulty of my position. I would be *greatly* in your debt."

Maisy weighed the benefit of that debt, but it was her husband who answered.

"If Colleen has no objections, I'll send her over with her belongings tonight."

He knew. Juliet stared at him in surprise. Donald Bartholomew might be a conceited agitator, but he was aware of his wife's cruelty and was willing to do something about it. Juliet smiled at him, but he looked away as if ashamed of what he'd allowed to go on within his own home.

Maisy gaped at her husband, her features flushing darkly. Juliet saw that as her cue to cut in.

"Oh, I am so relieved. How can I thank you for your unselfish generosity?" She sucked a breath, gritted her teeth, and embraced Maisy with a vigorous squeeze.

After that, what could the woman say?

Racing home to advise her father as to why he suddenly needed a nursemaid, Juliet hoped she'd covered everything. Knowing the colonel would never interfere in the domestic problems of his officers unless they affected his duty, she told him that Colleen was going to be helping her with her workload. Though surprised, since Juliet had never asked for a maid, he nodded, saying she was certainly entitled to it. She procured a tiny room for the Irish girl to call her own, and when showing her to it, found herself on the receiving end of Colleen's tears.

"Oh, I'm ever so grateful to you, Miss Crowley," the girl sobbed against her shoulder. "It was George—I mean Captain Allen—who told you, wasn't it?"

"Now, Colleen, don't be angry with him."

"Angry? Saints be praised! I don't know if I could have stood up to another day of that woman's bullying without taking a stick to her meself."

Juliet chuckled at the girl's courage and at the same time felt guilty for not noticing her troubles earlier. "Now you won't have to. And until we think of something, you won't have to do anything you don't want to. You won't have to go back to working for Mrs. Bartholomew if I can help it."

"But I'm to take care of your da."

"Heavens, don't let him hear you say that. He sees himself as completely independent of anyone's care. We'll help each other, how's that?"

"That sounds fine, ma'am."

"Juliet. That's my name, Colleen."

"Thank you, Juliet." Her brow puckered worriedly. "Mrs. Bartholomew, she can't do anything to me now, can she?"

"I'll make sure she doesn't. Why did she hit you?" That, she still couldn't understand.

"Just mad, I guess."

"At you? For what? I can't believe you did anything to deserve it."

"Mad at the world."

That summed up Maisy Bartholomew in an unpleasant nutshell. And her nasty disposition had a ripple effect through Fort Blair. As officer of the day, Donald Bartholomew rained down punishment upon the head of any Union soldier who happened to cross his path the following morning while he gave his own Southern troops preferential treatment. Noble wouldn't have allowed it if he were on the post. But he wasn't, and the captain took full advantage, much to Miles's irritation. Juliet and her father hadn't finished their coffee before the irrate major was at the door demanding that something be done.

"Is he out of line with his edicts, Major?" Crowley asked. He was short-tempered himself because of his enforced inactivity while he healed and in no mood for pettiness within the ranks.

"Not exactly, sir."

"Then what is your complaint?" His narrowed eyes should have cautioned Miles, but the junior officer was caught up in his own sense of indignation.

"He's inciting the men to mutinous thoughts."

"Has it gone beyond thoughts to actions?"

"Just grumbling in the ranks."

"This is the army, Major. The men grumble

about everything from the lack of variety in their diet to the itching caused by too much soap left in their laundry. Do you expect me to bring the cook and the laundresses up on disciplinary charges, too?"

Miles flushed but went on doggedly despite Juliet's look of warning. "Hard tack and soap scum are not the same as provocation to riot. Something has to be done. The Rebs need to be taken firmly in hand—not ignored as if they were naughty children. If I were in charge—"

"But you're not, Major Dougherty, are you? That's your main point of contention, isn't it?"

Miles clamped his mouth shut a moment too late. His superior continued with a frosty disdain, "Last time I looked I was still wearing silver eagles. This is my post, those are my men, and I will deal with both any way I see fit. As for being soft on the Southerners, as you so oftentimes complain, I treat them with no less dignity than I do those under your command. It isn't favoritism, it's equality. And if you can't handle that fact, Major Dougherty, then perhaps it's time to do something about you."

Realizing he'd gone too far, Miles swallowed down his pride. "I did not mean to question your authority, sir."

"Didn't you?"

Suddenly, Juliet remembered Noble's suspicion. She'd dismissed his doubts as impossible, but now she was forced to reconsider.

Was Miles resentful enough of her father's position to wish him out of the way permanently? A week ago, she would have laughed off the suggestion. But now, with her father sitting next to her, his side stitched together like a ragged seam, she couldn't afford to casually eliminate any possibility. Therefore, Miles Dougherty, her best friend's brother, had to be taken seriously as her father's possible attacker.

The thought made her ill. It would have been so much easier to transfer all the doubts, all her suspicions onto Donald Bartholomew. But she no longer had the luxury of tunnel vision. She couldn't let her personal affections influence her better judgment.

"If there's nothing else, Miles, I'd like to finish my coffee in peace."

Miles regarded the older man through slitted eyes. He snapped to crisp attention. "No, sir. That about covers it all."

"You're dismissed. I don't expect to have you back here carrying tales unless you can substantiate them. Is that understood?"

"Yes, sir." And for the first time, Juliet picked up an insubordinate cadence in both tone and attitude.

Had she misread Miles Dougherty all this time? Could he present a danger both to her father and to her? Hating the notion but unable to ignore it, she made herself follow Miles outside.

"That's no way to endear yourself to the colonel."

He turned to her, now clearly angry. "I'm sick of trying to endear myself to him. My record should speak for itself."

"And it does, Miles."

"I'll never advance my position stuck in second slot behind that damned—begging your pardon—Reb."

Her tone cool instead of commiserating, Juliet said, "If it's advancement you want, perhaps you should look to a transfer."

He blinked at her, totally surprised by both the suggestion and her lack of support. His jaw firmed into a granite line. "It's not easy getting a transfer out here in the West. You know that, Jules. Besides, there are ways to be promoted other than abandoning the place you worked so hard to secure."

The words sounded ominous to Juliet. Frowning, she was about to ask if he was making a threat when a commotion distracted them. A small group of Company B, escorting an exhausted older woman, had entered the fort.

"Report, sergeant."

The weary soldier presented Miles with a salute then burst into a telling of the previous day's events. All the homesteaders dead but one. Juliet swayed at the news. Two children captured. She closed her eyes against the horror those facts conjured up . But duty called her from her own wish to weep.

"Mrs. Stacy, you must be ready to drop. Let me offer the hospitality of my home."

With a grateful nod, the woman allowed Juliet to lead her into the colonel's quarters. The sergeant and Miles came behind them on their way to make a grim report to her father.

Juliet digested the news with a sinking sense of fear. Noble and the rest of the company were in pursuit of the Apache band, chasing them into Bright's Canyon.

Did Noble have enough experience to realize he could be riding straight into a wily Indian trap?

The three Apache braves approached the fallen man cautiously. He lay sprawled and motionless in the dirt, several yards away from his thrashing animal. Their gaze cut between his outstretched hand and the rifle resting just beyond his reach. If his hand so much as twitched toward it, they were ready to fill him full of arrows. They spoke amongst themselves, arguing over who would claim the gun and the superiority it would give the owner.

Just as the first brave bent to retrieve the Spencer while his companions grumbled, one of the others toed the dead soldier with the turned-up toe of his moccasin.

He had only enough time to take a startled step back as the man flipped over onto his back to send a single pistol shot straight through his heart.

After recovering from the wind-sapping fall, Noble had known there'd be no time to find cover, not that there was any appreciable cover for miles around. He heard the fast approach of the Indian ponies and knew he had one chance and one chance only.

He'd seen his first possum while hunting with his friend Reeve Garrett when they were boys. His rifle shot had knocked it out of the tree but failed to draw blood. The hideous creature lay still on the ground, its thin lips pulled back in a deathlike snarl. It hadn't moved as he prodded it with his rifle barrel. Reeve had warned him to be careful, but sure of himself and his aim, Noble reached down to pick up the carcass. A carcass that came alive—suddenly, startlingly alive. The possum latched onto his sleeve with its sharp teeth, requiring Reeve to beat the critter off him with a stick. That morning Noble had learned that things aren't always as they seem.

Playing possum while three deadly hostiles stood over him was a sweat-trickling effort at control. A twitch, a deep breath, any response at all would give him away and see him as dead as his command would soon be.

Noble rolled, taking advantage of the surprise to fell the remaining two Indians just as swiftly. Then he scrambled up, and after putting the injured animal out of its suffering, limped to one of the restless Mescalero horses.

He wasted no time in vaulting astride and kicking his new mount into a full-out run.

Toward Fort Blair and a rescue he prayed wouldn't be too late.

Chapter 20

Hearing Anne Stacy talk about the attack upon her home and the death of her husband brought back a fear in Juliet that was never far from the surface. She could still hear the terrible war cries, the thud of arrows, could taste the terror at the back of her throat. She wondered if it was the same for her father, for he was keenly focused as the attractive widow told her story.

Or was his focus because the widow was so attractive?

Jolted from her morose memories, Juliet gave her father a long, hard look. Since her mother's death, she'd thought of him as father and soldier but not as a man—a man who might feel the same loneliness for companionship as she did. Was John Crowley being made aware of how much of life he was missing by the mere presence of the strong-willed widow?

Many times Juliet had thought about losing

her father to an Apache arrow, but never to one shot by Cupid. The idea startled, but did it threaten as well?

She glanced up at the portrait of her mother, a lovely woman with Juliet's fair hair and determined smile. More than a dozen years had passed since she'd heard that modulated voice and had felt the warm comfort of that smile.

No, she didn't begrudge her father future happiness, and she knew her mother wouldn't, either.

The thought of another woman sharing his life didn't upset her. It made her vulnerable. Since the time she was forced to hold down the household at a young age, Juliet considered herself responsible for her father's care. As she became marriageable, she'd hidden behind that duty, using the colonel as an excuse not to venture out on her own.

In doing so, she realized with a sudden sense of guilt and shame, had she been holding him back from finding someone with whom to share himself? Could gaining the approval of a colonel's daughter be as intimidating as winning her father's approval was for the many young men who'd stepped up anxiously to try over the years?

Had she and her father settled in like old spinsters, content with the complacency found in their easy relationship?

Was that why Crowley was so eager to marry her off, so that he could concentrate on his own love life while he was young enough to enjoy it?

How selfishly she'd been hoarding her father's love for herself all these years.

She watched him with Anne Stacy and recognized him as a man hungry for the companionship of a woman, not a daughter. And at that moment, she vowed that no matter how awkward or difficult it was, she would step back and give him the room he needed to reach out to another.

Feeling strangely isolated, Juliet slipped outside into the searing heat of afternoon. Looking off into the shimmering distance, as if hoping to find some answer there, she sighed and wondered what to do.

At first, she thought the desert was playing tricks with her vision. But gradually an approaching blur became a rider, and that rider defined itself as Noble Banning.

"Papa, Major Banning is coming in alone!"

Noble dragged the pony up in front of the Crowleys' adobe. He dismounted, his bad leg buckling. Without a thought or hesitation, Juliet slipped under his arm to support him as he faced her father with whatever news etched his features so starkly.

"The men are under attack in Bright's Canyon. We rode right into it, sir, and they started picking us off like flies."

"How is it that you survived to bring the news back, Banning?" Miles sneered in contempt as he approached with a handful of enlisted men trailing. "You were in charge. They're your men, yet here you are. Are you sure you didn't just run scared and leave them all to die?"

"You bastard," Noble hissed at him. "I don't have time to explain or to deal with you now, but I will. That's a promise. Colonel, I need a company to ride back with me. I've lost too many not to see the rest of them saved, if possible."

Juliet clutched at him, wanting to cry out for him to let someone else see to his responsibilities. How could she let him go again?

"Are you up to it, Major?"

"Yes, sir."

"Major Dougherty, assemble A Company and be ready to ride as soon as Major Banning gets some water and a fresh mount."

The last thing Juliet wanted was to release him. With her arm about his waist, feeling his solid strength, she could convince herself that he was here, that he was safe. But the instant he stepped away, she'd lost him to his duty, a duty that might not bring him back again.

"Major," Jane cried out, racing toward the Crowleys' home in a flutter of pastel silk and panicked nerves. "My husband, is he all right? I have to know."

"He took a bullet, Mrs. Howell, but he was holding his own when I left."

Jane paled, and Juliet was quick to embrace her.

"And my Tom? Is he all right, too?"

Noble took Pauline Folley's hands in his and looked somberly into her anxious face. The woman had followed on Jane's heel, obviously desperate for news. There would be no kindness in delaying the truth. "I'm sorry, ma'am. We'll try to bring him back with us."

Pauline gave a wail and fainted. Juliet bent over the prostrate woman as Jane raced for some water.

But there was nothing either of them could really do for Pauline Folley now.

As the newly widowed woman returned to consciousness, Company A of Fort Blair was ready to ride with a worn yet determined Noble Banning at its head. Still kneeling beside Pauline, Juliet looked up at him with a gaze stripped to bare emotions. He paused long enough to give her a faint close-lipped smile before raising his hand to signal the troops forward.

The three women huddled together for mutual support and prepared themselves for the waiting.

Juliet had little time to dwell on her worries. She helped Dr. Penny ready the infirmary for an influx of patients. They prayed the returning men would be more in need of medical attention than burial details. Once everything was finished there, Juliet began doing what she could for Pauline Folley and her children.

The army made no provision for the families of men killed in the line of duty. If an officer died, his family was stripped of its home and left to pay its own way to wherever it would go. A fine thank-you from the government for a wife's silent support, Juliet thought grimly. So at the evening mess, Juliet started collecting funds, numbing her heart and mind to thoughts of her potential loss.

After that, she wandered about the post feeling lost and melancholy. She couldn't get the sound of Pauline's shrieks out of her head. Her father was dining with Mrs. Stacy. Jane was taking her turn with the Folleys. She was alone and so lonely she wanted to wail, but the sobs dammed up in her throat until the raw ache was almost more than she could bear. But the dam broke the minute she heard the sound of Companies A and B returning.

They came in slowly, tired, dirty, with Miles heading them up, but too many gaps in the ranks. Juliet's gaze flew frantically along the single file line, desperate to catch sight of Noble, not seeing him—not seeing him—until almost the end of the column. He had a gravely injured Albert Howell doubling with him. Even as Miles reined up next to her, she was darting down the row of dusty riders, never even noticing, hurrying to where Noble Banning came to a stop at the infirmary. She was there to catch Albert as he began to slide from the saddle.

"Albert!"

Juliet stepped aside to let Jane take her place, watching anxiously as Noble helped her friend get the wounded man inside. But Juliet's inactivity didn't last long. There were other wounded to see to. She directed them according to severity of injury into the available beds. Those who weren't critical were laid out on the porch and given water by Colleen.

The longer Juliet worked beside Dr. Penny, the more faces she began to miss, some that had followed her father clear from Texas. But the only face she longed to see as she toiled far into the night hours was one thankfully absent from this scene of pain and death and the first one she saw when she reeled out of the infirmary closer to dawn than midnight, bleary-eyed with weariness and unshed tears. He stood, the movement awkward, making her wonder if he should be inside waiting his turn to see the doctor.

"How's Captain Howell?" he asked.

"Better than a lot of them. The bullet's out and he's resting fairly comfortably."

Noble nodded, his gaze dropping away before she could read what he wasn't saying in it. She didn't need the words to feel the pain. As she had on the night he'd brought in the slain deserters, Juliet stepped forward without hesitation, her arms encircling him, simply holding him on that darkened porch where no one was there to see. At the moment, she didn't care if they did. All that mattered was Noble and finding a way to express how much his return unharmed meant to her.

"This is the part of it you never get used to," he told her sorrowfully. "Even after three years of war, each loss feels so personal, making you wonder what you could have or should have done, when all you really can do is write the letters home."

"You need sleep, Major."

"So do you."

He moved back, freeing himself from her embrace but not from her care. His hand slid down her arm until their fingers meshed and held tight. Wordlessly, he led her to his quarters. Once inside the unlit room, he took her in his arms, crushing her against the hard wall of his chest, where their hearts beat together in what should have been passion, but wasn't.

His hand scooped under her chin, lifting her face in the cradle of his palm so that he could kiss her, again the fierce gesture speaking of desperation but not desire. Juliet answered with an equal yearning, with emotions too complex for the light of day but somehow just right in this place of shadows, at this moment of shared need.

She let her kisses express what she couldn't frame in words as she tasted his generous mouth, the aggressive bristles of his three-day-old beard, the salty line of his throat where the steady pulse of life provided inarguable proof that he'd survived the ordeal.

And she hugged him hard to make herself believe that would be enough. That she'd be able to let him go the next time duty called him.

But in her heart, she didn't know if she

could. She didn't know, after hearing Pauline Folley's sobs, that she could find that kind of strength to wave and smile as he rode out to meet an uncertain fate.

Maybe she was just tired. Or maybe she was tired out after years of smiling and waving. Or maybe she'd finally found someone so important to her daily existence that she selfishly wanted to say, *No more. Let someone else do this thankless job. I've sacrificed enough already.*

And when they lay down together on his narrow bed, the intimacy they sought wasn't one of breathless cries and hurried physical joining but rather of closeness, a closeness shared fully dressed, discreetly wrapped within each other's arms.

That was enough on this night, what was needed for them both to find a healing slumber.

At daybreak Juliet slipped into the house. She'd left Noble dozing fitfully but aware enough to return her kiss of parting with knee-weakening result. She needed to wash and change her clothing, and sought a few more hours of undisturbed sleep in the embrace of her own bed.

But her bed wasn't empty.

She must have made some sound of surprise. It was enough to wake Anne Stacy from her restless dreams—if she'd indeed been sleeping.

"I'm sorry," Juliet stammered awkwardly. "I didn't mean to wake you."

She'd started to back from her room when the older woman sat up to extend her own apology.

"Please don't go. I can't sleep anyway, and it wasn't my intention to occupy your room without your permission. Your father thought you'd be at the hospital for most of the night and said I might rest a while until you returned. I hope you don't mind."

"No." Juliet smiled, the gesture weary but genuine. "I don't mind. How are you feeling?"

"About how you look. Worn down to nothing but nerves. Every time I open my eyes, I expect to find myself in my bed with my Morris beside me."

Juliet nodded, not knowing what to say.

Anne sighed. "I suppose I'll get used to it."

"You will."

"I hear experience beyond your years in that voice. Your father tells me you lost your mother to the Apache at a young age." She smiled faintly, and in a strange way, that gentle smile reminded Juliet of the mother she still missed. "That gives us a certain kinship of sorrow, doesn't it?"

"A rather unfortunate alliance, one we share with far too many."

"And will share with many more as long as men are anxious to take what they want without asking for it. But you can't tell them anything they don't want to hear. You couldn't tell Morris that the land he bought and paid to settle really belonged to the Indians. He wouldn't listen to any words of caution."

Juliet came to sit on the edge of the bed, needing to share a moment of reflection with one who understood the turmoil in her heart. "How long had you been out here?"

"Five years. Five hard, long years. Hard enough to change an already disciplined man into one as unyielding as those buttes. Long enough for him to forget that we once were in love. I guess he felt he could show no weaknesses if we were to survive."

Juliet covered the woman's hands with her own. "I always thought one found strength through love, not harshness."

Sadly, Anne shrugged. "Even though the Apache took his life with their arrows, I'd lost the man I married years ago. Burying him seemed just a delay of the inevitable. Does that sound terrible?"

Juliet shook her head. She understood. "So, what will you do?"

"Your father has graciously allowed me to stay at the fort until he can arrange safe passage for the injured and for the other woman who also lost her husband. I suppose I'll go back to Massachusetts. That's where my family used to be. It's been so long since I've heard from them, I'm really not sure where they are now."

"You've no children?"

"A son, fighting for the Union cause. I'll try

to get a letter to him. My two daughters died of a fever when they were little more than babies. I'm afraid if I go back East, my boy, Ben will never be able to find me."

"He will. My father can see that your message gets through to him."

Anne sighed, her eyes going misty. "I'd be so grateful."

Feeling uncomfortable taking those teary thanks for doing so little, Juliet said, "Would you like some coffee?"

Anne smiled. "I'd love some. But only if you'll allow me to help in the kitchen."

"I'd welcome the company, Anne."

Together they went into the Crowley kitchen to begin a meal.

Noble Banning gave his report a few hours later. "I take full responsibility for what happened, sir. It was my ignorance that led us into that trap and cost us so many lives."

John Crowley regarded his second in command with a stern expression, but Juliet saw the empathy in her father's eyes. Miles and George Allen were also present at what could easily turn into an inquisition, but the colonel wasn't looking for martyrs or anxious to deal out punishments.

"Not ignorance, Major. Inexperience. Something, unfortunately, that one rarely gains without learning a harsh lesson."

"I'm not the one who's paid the price, sir."

Crowley smiled sadly. "Yes, you are, Major.

You'll pay every time you look back on this event and wonder what you should have done, when you take the blame for all the men we bury. No price comes as high as that of responsibility. I never fault a man for inexperience as long as he admits to it and learns something from his mistakes. God knows I've spent plenty of time in that school." He affixed his name to the paper in front of him.

"I'm satisfied that you did everything properly, that you acted to your best ability to secure the safety of your men. I consider this matter closed unless either of you officers has anything to add."

His look skewered Miles, who gripped his lips together and shook his head.

"I'm satisfied, sir," Allen volunteered.

"You're all dismissed then."

"Sir," Noble took a step forward. "I'd like a word with you in private."

Crowley nodded to the other officers. "Gentlemen, good day."

Juliet retreated to the kitchen to give them privacy but was perversely drawn to lean close to the door-opening so she could listen to what was being said. She told herself she would withdraw if the matters being discussed were personal, and she hoped she could keep to that vow. But just in case she had a stake in what was being discussed . . .

"What's on your mind, Major?"

"I lost a lot of men on this campaign."

She took the answering silence for her father's nod of agreement.

"I would like to know . . . I think I have the right to know if the man who betrayed our unit was among the fallen."

Juliet put a hand to her mouth to stifle her gasp. Would her father answer?

"If I told you yes, would you believe me, Major Banning?"

A pause, then, "Yes, sir."

"And if that answer was yes, what would your next course of action be, Major?"

"I'm sorry, sir. I don't understand—"

"With the reason for you bringing your men all the way out here gone, what would you do? Honor your word to me or the oath you took when taking up the Confederate cause? Which holds the higher priority? I'd be a fool to believe it was the word given to your sworn enemy."

He didn't answer right away, which showed how much respect he had for her father. He didn't try to bluff him with a quick lie, nor would he declare his intentions.

"I have served you well, Colonel."

"Yes, you have. But only because I had something you wanted."

"Does that mean you no longer have it?"

"That's not what I'm saying at all. What I will say is the day we hear that the war in the East is over, I'll tell you what you want to know. Then the matter will be between you and your conscience and off mine."

Juliet exhaled in wobbly relief.

Noble would remain at Fort Blair at least until the war's end—a bittersweet comfort because her relief was edged with doubt.

For as long as Noble held himself hostage to the truth her father denied him, she would never know the nature of his intentions toward her.

Chapter 21

"Tell him what he wants to know, Papa."

Crowley looked from the closed front door through which Noble had just exited to his daughter as she emerged from the kitchen. "You were listening." It was a mild accusation, proving he wasn't really surprised.

"Is that any greater crime than what you're doing by blackmailing that man for his loyalty?"

He frowned, pricked by her blunt phrasing and perhaps by his conscience. "This is Army business, daughter, and none of yours. It's a matter of honor."

"It is mine, whether you say so or not. This man you protect with your silence has no honor. He betrayed those who trusted him. Why do you feel obligated to shield the man who may have twice tried to take your life? Do you value your word to a liar, a traitor, and a possible murderer over your safety? Over mine?"

Crowley looked clearly surprised. "These matters are totally different."

"Are they? Who would have greater motive? Who would want you silenced more than the one who fears what you have to say? Tell Noble what he wants to know. Let him deal with the man. He's right, you know. He's earned the opportunity to see justice done."

"I will tell him."

"When it may be too late. Are you going to wait until this coward tries to take another shot?"

He waved a hand to calm her fears. "Jules, it's not the same man."

"How can you know that? Tell me. Make me believe it."

"I can't."

"Why? Why not? I may already be a target, so what difference does it make if you tell me now? Unless—" She stared at her father, assessing his immobile features, probing his hard glare. The truth she learned there rocked her. "Unless you're afraid I'd take the information to Noble. Unless you're afraid I'd betray your confidence."

He didn't look ashamed. He didn't look away. He didn't even blink as he asked flatly, "Would you?"

He couldn't have hurt her more if he'd slapped her and called her faithless.

She took a stumbling step back, struggling to speak the wounded assurances he waited impassively to hear. The words couldn't penetrate the anguish lodged in her throat. She swallowed hard, blinking back tears of fractured trust, a trust that never should have been doubted. Then, without giving an answer, she swept out the back door, leaving him shocked, angry, and unsatisfied.

The soil was hot, scorching waves reflecting off it causing Juliet to blink off drips of perspiration. And fight back tears of anger.

How could he suggest such a thing to her?

She snapped the failing leaves off her struggling seedlings, hoping to channel more strength to the rest of the plants. She didn't know why she bothered. She could already see they'd never thrive in this hostile clime.

She wiped a shaky hand across her brow and bent back to the futile task.

How could he question her loyalty? Hadn't she followed him from post to post, enduring hardship, loneliness, and fear without complaint? Hadn't he poured out his worries, his doubts to her on endless evenings, seeking her advice, her counsel above that of his officers? Had she ever, even once, betrayed that confidence? Had she ever given him cause to suspect her integrity?

She blinked against the burn in her eyes and tried to focus on the next small sprout. It lay withered and limp upon the ground, and with a cry of frustration, she tore it out by its insufficient roots, flinging it aside. Why was she wasting time on what would never grow?

And how could she ever repair the sense of trust once it had been uprooted with equal savagery?

Sitting back on her heels, she let the silent sobs shake through her shoulders, fueled by unwarranted blame and disappointment. All the years upon years she'd given to her father and his career. All the unflagging support and unbowed approval of his choices. How could he doubt her? How could he ask the state of her heart when it had always, always belonged to him?

Then her broken heart faltered, tripping on one wretched barrier that should have been easily cleared but somehow proved impossible to get over.

What if he was right to question her, to doubt her?

If her father had told her the truth in confidence, *would* she have taken that knowledge straight to Noble Banning?

She waited, expecting her mind to provide a quick denial, but it snagged on emotions too tangled up in Noble to lend a reliable answer.

"The poor wee things. 'Tis far too hot for anything to prosper."

Juliet rubbed at her watering eyes before smiling weakly up at Colleen. "I keep trying. I guess I don't know when I'm licked."

"Many a thing would never get accomplished if not for a bit of stubbornness."

Juliet had to nod, eager to distract herself from the disturbing turn of her thoughts. "Did

Mrs. Stacy get settled in with you all right? It's not too crowded, is it?"

"Crowded is eleven brothers and sisters under one roof. Cozy is what me and Mrs. Stacy are. She's a fine woman, and I like her just fine. Much better than the other one."

"Has Maisy bothered you, Colleen?"

"No. I've not seen her at all. She doesn't like the way the heat frizzes her hair."

Juliet smiled at the other's impersonation of the vain Maisy. Then she took a chance and asked, "And how is Captain Allen?"

The Irish girl's blush answered all her questions to that end. "Oh, he be a wonderful gentleman, so kind and considerate of others. He worries so over his friends' problems, taking them too much to heart."

"Which friends?"

"Major Banning mostly." Colleen put a hand to her mouth, fearing she'd spoken too freely. Nervously, she concluded, "I do go on."

"If you're to be a pastor's wife, you'll have to work on that," Juliet said with a warm smile."

Colleen's jaw dropped, her bright eyes going button-round. "Has he said something to you?"

Juliet stood up, brushing the dirt from her hands. "Sometimes words aren't necessary. I take it you're interested in the position."

Her features lit up like a Roman candle. "Oh, yes. Indeed I am. Now if there was just some way to get the gentleman to ask."

"Could be that's something we might work on together."

Juliet was surprised by the girl's sudden heart-felt hug. After all, why shouldn't she and the sweet-tempered George Allen enjoy romance? They deserved it. Love was something everyone deserved.

She stepped back, all at once overcome by the want to cry again. Gruffly, she promised to do what she could to help the meek lovebirds find happiness, all the while doubting she'd ever have any of her own.

She invited both Colleen and Anne Stacy to dine with them that night, partly because she enjoyed their company but mostly to provide a conversation buffer between her and her father. She wouldn't have survived the meal without them. As soon as possible, she escaped the house and walked Colleen home, leaving Anne with her father, hopefully to begin forging bonds like those that had been broken between them.

There wasn't much to do on an army post. After saying good night to Colleen, she stopped in to see if Dr. Penny needed her help, but Pauline had volunteered to take her mind off her own loss. The children were busy tearing bandage strips and dipping out water. She spent a few minutes visiting with Jane, but Albert had just returned to recover in his own bed. Jane was hovering over him anxiously, much to his delight.

It seemed everyone else had someone or some purpose until in her aimless wandering, she came across another lost soul.

"Good evening, George. If you could stand some company, I'd like to join you."

He waved her onto the empty porch planks beside him, his smile as melancholy as her spirit. "I was just contemplating how life gets more complex as we go along. I'd always thought it would be just the opposite, that the more we experience and learn, the more we are prepared to meet what befalls us." He laughed softly. "Funny. Things were so clear to me before the war. I knew exactly what I wanted. I wanted to be a vessel through which God could work to reach the lost. Now I am so lost myself, I don't know how much good I'll be."

She put her hand over his for a consoling squeeze. "I think it's through those trials and doubts that He shapes you to be a vessel He *can* use."

"You mean He's trying to break me in, like a saddle. If He's not careful, I'll be all worn out before I ever get the chance to do good."

"You've already done good, George, with Colleen, with Noble, with me. I've enjoyed our talks and I can't imagine anyone I would feel more comfortable confiding in."

He turned away, eyes downcast, as if he felt unworthy. "I thought my religious background would prepare me to help others make the right moral decisions and to advise them on the right paths to take. I didn't realize how confusing those paths could be, how unclear the choices. How can I advise when I'm not sure of my own answers?"

"That's where faith comes in, George, faith in your beliefs, faith in yourself."

"Oh, if it were only that simple."

"And in allowing others to have faith in you. Sometimes that's where the greatest strength comes from—from knowing others believe in you."

He glanced at her, his smile somewhat mystified. "You're a wise woman, Juliet."

"I've had a lot of experience with those dilemmas lately."

"And?"

"And I have no answers, either. Perhaps there aren't any answers, only choices. Choices that we have to decide how we're going to live with once we make them."

He sighed as if the weight of the moral universe rested upon his slumped shoulders.

"I know of one choice that you'd never regret making," Juliet said.

Curiously, he looked up at her. "What's that?"

"I'm not the one you need to be talking to." She nodded toward Colleen McDonnal's tiny home. "I think you may find some answers eager to be given."

With that advice, Juliet stood, smiling as she

saw a certain speculative gleam in the cleric's eyes. If only her own decisions were so clear-cut and sure to have a happy ending. As she continued her walk Noble fell in beside her.

"I saw you talking to George. Any particular topic of conversation?"

"Moral dilemmas."

"Ahhh," was all he said.

As they grew closer to her quarters, they could see the colonel's shadow as he smoked his cigar upon the porch. Juliet subconsciously widened the distance between them as they walked to make it more impersonal.

"Good evening, Colonel."

"Major Banning. Out for a stroll?"

"Just delivering your daughter safely into your care."

"She would be the first to say that was hardly necessary."

"But a pleasure, nonetheless." He gave Juliet a small smile.

"Join me for a cigar, Major?"

"Another time."

"I'll look forward to it. Good night."

"Good night, sir. Juliet." He nodded to his superior, but the look he gave Juliet was intensely personal. She glanced aside before her father could notice.

"You were gone a long time," came the colonel's tentative comment.

"And I'm tired. I'm going to bed." Her crisp claim left no opening for further discussion. But Crowley wasn't about to be ignored.

"Daughter, don't walk away from me."

His command brought her up short, her shoulders squaring before she spun to face him with an icy glare. "Excuse me. Am I to wait to be dismissed?"

Crowley flushed in irritation. "No, of course not."

"Then good night."

"Juliet, please. We need to talk."

"About what? I can't think of a single thing that needs to be said."

His voice softened with regret. "I can think of many things. I was unfair in my treatment of you earlier. I know you were only concerned for me and you know how I hate for you to worry."

"So you thought accusing me of disloyalty would be a good way to take my mind off it."

"Not a good way, obviously."

She scowled. "This is not a very good apology."

"I will gladly apologize if you will answer me one small thing."

Her eyes narrowed in suspicion. "What's that?"

"Are you in love with Banning?"

That was no small thing. Needing time to recover from the savage surprise, she demanded, "What does that have to do with anything?"

Gently, he explained, "It has everything to do with everything."

Still not ready to own up to those emotions,

she countered with a fierce, "If I am, that would excuse me from being reliable? I wasn't aware that love was the opposite of truth and trust."

"It isn't. If you're in love with him, I wouldn't want the knowledge I hold to come between you."

"But it does," she cried out in dismay, her behavior as good as a confession. "Don't you see? As long as you hold him here, I'll never know if what he feels for me plays any part in it at all. How can I ever trust him if you don't give him the chance to be trusted? How will I ever know if he cares for me unless he has the opportunity to show it?"

"And does he care for you?"

She turned away in anguish. "I don't know. I don't know what he feels. I don't know what I feel. Yes, I do. I feel trapped. I feel trapped between the two of you, and only the truth can free me."

Crowley gripped her by the shoulders, forcing her to look up at him. "But Jules, truth also has the power to imprison those who don't truly deserve the punishment. You don't know the full story or you would understand my silence."

Not understanding, she said, "Papa, please, give him the chance to show his loyalty. It's easy to call a dog your best friend when you keep it on a chain. Only when it's let loose can you know for certain. I want to know for certain. I need to know. Papa, I love him. How am I ever going to know if I can trust him or myself with him unless that trust is tested?"

Crowley hesitated for a long moment, indecision warring in his expression. "You love him?"

"Yes."

"Enough to risk losing him?"

"Yes."

"Then perhaps I should tell you—"

"Bastard!"

The wild cry interrupted their conversation. Both turned to see an unsteady Maisy Bartholomew weaving her way across the parade ground. Her hair was in disarray, her gown mussed, her eyes crazed and red from weeping. She was heading straight for them, her attention fixed upon the colonel.

"You're to blame. You brought us out here. You tore me from my home and friends when you forced my husband to betray his cause to fight for yours. Everything would have been fine if not for your interference."

"Good God, has the woman been drinking?"

Juliet shook her head. She didn't think so. She'd never seen Maisy touch a drop of alcohol. It wasn't strong spirits loosening her tongue. It was a weak and fracturing soul.

"I could have sat out the rest of the war and waited for Donald's release. But no. You come in and take 'em from where they were safe and you drag 'em out here to battle those red devils." She took a quick hitching breath, growing more agitated with each word. "You risk our lives for something we don't care anything about. Well, I'm not risking mine or my husband's anymore, you hear? No more warnings."

A terrible insight came to Juliet just then. "It was you, not your husband."

"Donald?" She spat his name as if it left a bad taste. "Donald would never do something so—heroic. He's too afraid of Major Banning." She glared at Noble, who was approaching her cautiously from one side. "Stay back. This is your fault, too. You and your holy causes."

"But why?" Juliet asked for them all. "Why attack my father? What good did you think that would do you?"

Maisy's smile held a crazy cleverness. "At first, to cast suspicion on our men. I hoped the colonel would be wary enough of them to send us all back. But when a warning wouldn't alert him, I had to take more drastic measures." Her gaze cut back to Noble. "I said get back."

"Now, Miz Bartholomew, you don't want to hurt anyone. I'll see you get safely back home."

"More of your silky lies, Major. Donald might believe them, but I don't. I'm taking matters into my own hands."

"Don't do that, ma'am." He was almost within reach of her. Juliet held her breath.

"We're going home. We're going home now!"

From out of the folds of her skirt she drew a heavy pistol, and before Juliet could cry out in warning, Maisy aimed it at John Crowley and fired.

Chapter 22

Noble lunged just an instant too late. Even as he caught the frenzied woman by the forearm and wrested the smoking pistol from her hand, Crowley staggered into his daughter's arms before crumpling to the porch boards. He heard Juliet's screams, the terrible, anguished sounds of someone losing the only person left that they loved.

"My God! Maisy, what have you done?" Bartholomew cried as he raced upon the scene.

"I took care of things, Donald. No more waiting. No more promises." Her features were now serenely composed, her task completed.

Noble handed her over into her husband's care so that he could check on the severity of Crowley's injury. When he knelt down beside Juliet, he could see it was bad: a nasty head wound. Its fierce bleeding discolored his daughter's gown and hands as she tried to stop the vital flow. She looked up at Noble, her gaze wild with panic.

"Help me! Help me!"

Between them, they maneuvered the insensible man to the infirmary, where Penny quickly made room and just as quickly shooed them away.

"But I can't leave! Not until I know he's going to be all right!"

"Major, please take her outside. I'll let you know his condition as soon as there's something to tell."

Noble took Juliet's elbow, but she continued to resist, her wide eyes fixed upon her father's still features, clinging to the sight as if it might be her last. Finally, with his arm firmly about her shoulders, Noble steered her away, out into the steamy night.

There she collapsed against him, reserve of strength crumbling into soft sobs of shock. He held her close, speaking into the tangle of her pale hair in a tender whisper.

"He'll be all right, darlin'. You just wait and see. He'll pull through just fine, just fine."

As he absorbed the reverberations of her weeping, he looked off into the darkness, praying, *Let him be all right, Lord. Don't do this to her now.* He'd seen loss and suffering in too many of its devastating forms to wish it upon this brave woman that he loved. If there'd been a way to take away her fright, to give assurances that she would never want for anything, that she wouldn't be cast away by the army that had commanded her life for so long, he would have given them. But there was nothing he could do or say ... except ask her again to marry him.

If the burden of her future was settled, perhaps then she could concentrate on willing her father well without worrying about what would become of her should he not recover. He held her tight, wondering if this was the right time, if he would be asking for the right reasons.

"He can't die," came her weak protest against the cruel inevitability of fate.

"Juliet, don't you go worrying now. I'll see you're taken care of. I'll see to it myself."

She shook her head in rapid denial, pushing her palms against his chest to emphasize it. "I don't want you to take care of me. I want him to be all right."

"He will be, darlin'. No one's going to take his place."

She ceased her struggles and once again accepted his embrace. And Noble said nothing more on the subject. He continued to hold her, closing his heart around a pain too mighty to explore while dealing with the priority of another's.

She didn't want him.

Eventually, her tears ran out and she calmed enough for him to coax her down onto the steps beside him. He kept his arm about her shoulder, a strong bolster of support.

"Why didn't I see it sooner?" she said to herself in an anguish of blame. "I should have seen how dangerous and determined she was.

All the signs were there. I just wasn't seeing them."

"Nonsense," Noble growled, trying to shake her from her self-flagellation. "None of us guessed. Not even her husband had a clue as to how far gone she was. It's not your fault, Juliet. You couldn't have known."

"But I knew he was in danger. I was so sure it was the same man who'd betrayed you. I'd finally persuaded Papa to tell me the man's name—"

"Did he?"

The sudden demand jolted through Juliet's misery. She looked up at his taut face, her stare accusing, agonizing.

"No. He didn't have time. But I should have known that's what you'd see as the important thing."

"No, Juliet, that's not—"

But she wouldn't listen. She shoved herself out of his embrace and stumbled to her feet. He watched as her inner courage strengthened her stance and put fire back in her tear-drenched eyes.

"Get away from here, away from us."

"Juliet—"

"Go! You're not going to hover over his bed like some vulture hoping to feed off his last words. You and your code of honor disgust me, Major Banning. How dare you try to take advantage of my pain! Get out of my sight and stay out of my life!"

Without listening to any further arguments,

she sprang up the steps and disappeared into the post hospital, where he had no right to follow, because he couldn't convince her that he was completely innocent of self-interest without confessing to emotions she'd already rejected twice.

John Crowley's condition fluctuated during the hours of the night. There were moments when Dr. Penny came close to losing him, but the colonel fought stubbornly. Perhaps it was the two silent sentinels at his bedside—his daughter and the widow who'd only recently caught his interest—perhaps it was his unwillingness to leave either behind that made him struggle against blood loss and trauma until by dawn's light, Penny pronounced him, with no little amazement, stabilized.

During those long, anxious hours, the two women learned to lean on each other. By the time Crowley was said to be out of danger, a strong bond had developed between them. Juliet felt secure enough to abandon her watch to Anne so that she could seek her own bed and some desperately needed slumber. She hadn't the strength to deal with the other matter pressing upon her heart—that of Noble Banning's treachery.

He'd just been using her. What more proof did she need?

She could ban him from her thoughts, but she couldn't keep the tears from soaking her pillow. Finally, she fell into an exhausted sleep, not awaking until late that same day to the smell of coffee brewing in her kitchen.

After quickly dressing, Juliet left her bedroom to find Miles and Jane patiently waiting. A pang of disappointment shot through her, but she refused to recognize it as a wish that it had been Noble seated in her father's chair instead of her old friend, Noble coming to apologize, to make some believable excuse to take the terrible sense of loss away.

But he wasn't there. And nothing he could say would ever make any difference.

Jane crossed to embrace her. "Oh, darling, I feel so awful for you!"

Juliet let her friend fuss and coddle her, needing the spoiling too much to protest. Finally, she forced herself to ask after her father's condition. Brother and sister exchanged a look.

Panic darted through Juliet as her private woes were forgotten.

"Is he worse? Please tell me."

"He's getting stronger by the hour," Miles assured her. Another glance at Jane had Juliet's belly knotting.

"But—?"

He cleared his throat, carefully putting his words together before speaking. "There's a problem with his eyes."

"His eyes? What problem?"

Miles shifted uncomfortably. "The bullet may have damaged his vision."

"Damaged how badly? Are you saying that he's blind?"

"In one eye, possibly both. Penny can explain it better."

But Juliet was already out the door, running toward the infirmary and answers she feared to receive.

"I'm not a specialist in these matters, Miss Crowley," Penny began with characteristic bluntness. "I'd advise you to take him to one. I can give you several names from back East. For the moment, he shows no response to changes in light and darkness. It may be temporary. I just don't know."

"How soon can he travel?"

Miles had come in behind her, his big hands settling on her shoulders. "We can have a protective caravan ready to go tomorrow. Would he be ready then, Doc?"

"I think so."

Juliet covered one of the major's hands with her own. "Tomorrow then."

"I'll escort you as far as the railhead myself."

She nodded, too frazzled to think of what else that would mean. It would mean leaving the only life she'd ever known behind her, perhaps forever. It would mean saying good-bye to Noble Banning.

Maisy Bartholomew got her wish. She was going home. Too sympathetic to the fragile woman's circumstances to insist she be punished, Juliet applied all her influence to arrange passage back to South Carolina, where

Donald's family would take her in and see that she received the help she needed. It was difficult to send her into enemy territory, but not impossible. The captain would remain in the West. He packed her belongings, delivering them and his wife without a hint of emotion to the sergeant in charge of her care. Maisy herself was placid to the point of being oblivious to her surroundings. She received her husband's brief kiss on her cheek without so much as blinking her eyes.

Juliet dismantled their home with a quick efficiency, storing each item, each memento with practiced care. As she was about to crate up her feathered friends, she paused in surprise at the sight of her garden. The sprouts were green and standing upright, showing every sign of prosperity. Something good would remain in reminder of her passing.

She placed their care in Colleen's hands, at the last minute adding the goat and chickens. There would be no place for livestock where they were going. Colleen accepted the responsibility for the gifts with grateful tears.

Then she presented Jane with her hanging plants along with an emotional hug.

"Write me, darling," Jane insisted. "Let me know how things progress."

"I will. I promise."

"Are you sure you have everything? You've been in such a rush."

Juliet paused to glance about.

The adobe was empty, awaiting its next occupant, now just impersonal rooms instead of a home. Her father had been carefully loaded into one ambulance for travel. Anne Stacy sat beside him. Pauline and her children would share another with Maisy Bartholomew and her military escort.

No, there was nothing left for her.

The entire regiment was lined up at attention. She took in their familiar faces: George Allen, Doc Penny, Albert Howell with his arm still in a sling. And at their head was the new commander of Fort Blair: Noble Banning. Despite the lingering pain of their last meeting, Juliet's heart gave a wistful lurch.

"Almost everything," she told her friend. Then she purposefully crossed to Noble.

He watched her approach, unreadable emotions flickering behind the pale blue of his eyes. She stood before him, part of her wanting to slap his face for so misusing her emotions, and another wishing to throw pride to the wind to have a last kiss good-bye.

She did neither.

"Convey my best wishes for a full recovery to your father, Miz Crowley."

How formally said, as if they were strangers. But because they were anything but, Juliet wanted to leave him with the one thing he desired most of all.

"This is your post now, Major. Hold it honorably."

"Yes, ma'am."

She pitched her voice lower so only the two

of them could hear what she would say.

"I lied before. Father did tell me this—he's dead, Noble."

Confusion clouded his features, then the spark in his gaze flared hot. "Who?"

"He died before you ever left Maryland."

She saw him digest that information. Saw the flash of questions, the moment of wondering why she'd chosen to reveal this only at this parting instant, and finally, the weight of acceptance. His quest was over. Now they were even. She'd given him back his life, and he'd taught her what it was like to live. And that was all there could ever be between them. She knew that as she waited for him to speak, for him to say anything that would give her a reason to stay, to hold out some hope....

"Have a safe journey, Juliet."

It wasn't enough.

"Thank you, Major."

His sword flashed up in a dramatic salute, his stare never leaving hers. And because there was nothing left for her to do but walk away, she did so with head held high, never looking back to the man who would always hold her heart at saber-point.

The ride was hard on all of them, but especially upon John Crowley. Juliet and Anne did their best to keep him comfortable, but fever fed his anxiety and made for a difficult trip.

Watching the other woman tenderly caring

for her father gave Juliet a glimpse of her future. A future alone. She'd never looked beyond a life tending the colonel, following the drum, but now it loomed before her, a vast unknown of independence and uncertainty.

And she was afraid.

She'd never been prepared for a life alone. Undoubtedly her father's condition would consume a great deal of their time. But once he'd either recovered or accepted his limits, where did that leave her? What would she do if Anne and the colonel set up housekeeping together? Though she was sure Anne wouldn't cast her out, her own pride wouldn't allow her to linger, a second woman in another's home.

They were heading for Boston, where one of the country's leading eye specialists would treat her father's blindness, a city like the one she'd stayed in while her father was involved in the Civil War. Thinking ahead to the crowds, the noise, the confusion, her spirit rebelled. She would suffocate in the press of narrow streets and confining manners. But what other choice did she have until her father had stabilized? And what after that?

One answer came to her as they boarded the eastbound train. As she saw to the loading of their belongings while Anne got the colonel situated in their private room, Miles lingered at her side. When she turned to him with a sad smile, he doffed his hat.

"Juliet, this doesn't have to be good-bye."

She could have agreed with him to spare

him pain, but it wasn't her way to give false encouragement.

"I'm afraid it will be, Miles. I have a feeling I'll never see the West again, and I don't know that I shall miss it. Even if Papa recovers enough to return to his commission, my guess is he'll be bringing another woman back to tend his house for him. There'll be no place in it for me." There was sadness in that statement but no resentment.

"Then you can come back with him and tend my house for me."

She'd expected him to make some last-minute declaration, but still it came as a bittersweet shock. Solid, unimaginative Miles, as limited in emotional intensity as he was in scope. He was offering her a future, one that would be familiar, predictable.

"You're a dear, dear friend, Miles."

He smiled miserably, for once reading between the lines. "But nothing more. I had held such high hopes that you would change your mind, Juliet, that you would see our future together as one. You can't blame me for asking."

She put her hand on his arm. "No, and I'm flattered. I truly am."

"I do care for you, Juliet. I would make you a good husband."

He would, she'd no doubt. He would give her exactly the same life she'd led with her father—no surprises, no changes, just worry and loneliness without love.

It wasn't enough. Not any more.

"I will think of you and Jane often."

She stretched up to press a fond kiss to his cheek. He understood it meant good-bye and sighed. For a moment, he held her close.

"I wish I knew of some way to persuade you to come back, Juliet."

There was, she admitted to herself at that melancholy moment.

If Noble Banning had done the asking.

"Good-bye, Miles."

With one last look around at the uniformed men, at the vast untamed sky and savage land, Juliet stepped on the train and headed for a new life.

Chapter 23

*Pride County, Kentucky
1865*

When he stepped onto the platform, the first thing he did was close his eyes and breathe deep. Even with the ash from the train, there was no disguising the rich, earthy smell of Kentucky.

Home.

Noble glanced around him, having to blink to clear his vision. Changes, yes, but enough similarities to make him feel embraced. He hadn't thought anything could affect him as profoundly as four simple words: "The war is over." But this did, this first, long-awaited glimpse of Pride.

Crowley had kept his promise with a reach that stretched all the way from Boston to New Mexico. When the South surrendered, Noble and his men were free to leave the post, where they'd continued to serve in Crowley's absence. He'd turned over his duties to Miles Dougherty with relief and no regret, and had led his men out of the desert.

And now he was home.

Time to put his life back on track, to put his future plans in motion. The war, the West... and all that went with it were behind him now. This was the moment he'd dreamed of as a boy, as a student far from home for the first time, on dark, dreary nights when artillery sounded like distant thunder, in a cold, lonely tent in Maryland. It's what he told himself he wanted more than anything while restless yearnings kept him from finding sound sleep on a lonesome frontier post.

Time to make good his promises, to vindicate his name, to right wrongs he'd once been powerless to alter.

So why was he feeling so unaffected by the attainment of that lifelong goal?

He knew the answer. It was wrapped up in one name, one face. Juliet. Having this without having her was somehow less than complete.

He shook off that thought because he'd vowed not to spoil his homecoming with hints of unhappiness. He was back where he belonged, and nothing would get in the way of that reunion. He needed to see his family, to reconnect with his friends and his former life. Then he would be strong enough to deal with what he didn't have—and perhaps rectify the situation.

He rode into the center of Pride on a rented

horse, his thrill at being back tempered by what he was afraid to find. How many of those he loved hadn't made it home from the war or survived its devastation? Anticipation and dread knotted in his belly until there on the walk, untouched by time or trials, were figures tied so tightly to his past that it was as if four long years were stripped away.

Reeve, Patrice, and Starla, along with a man he didn't know. They all spotted him at the same time.

He was hauled down from his rented horse and into Reeve Garrett's familiar embrace. Having his ribs nearly crushed by his best friend brought the reality home, but it was seeing his parents soon after that made him believe it.

"Welcome back, son."

He took the hand his father offered, giving it a firm shake. Judge Banning wasn't the demonstrative type, but brightness glittered in his gaze.

"It's good to be home, Judge. Mother." He bent so that the delicate creature whose loveliness remained unfading could touch a kiss to his cheek.

"You look well, dear, so tanned and strong. The West must not have been as awful as I imagined. When I heard you were in that prison, I—" Her voice failed her.

"No more talk of what's past," the judge ordered. "Noble is where he belongs, and soon he will be working with me out of my office as if these last four years never happened."

Noble's smile froze. But because his homecoming wasn't the right place to discuss his plans, especially plans that went contrary to everything his father stood for, he opted to let it go.

"Is there any chance you've kept any of my old clothes? I'm ready to get out of this stale uniform. Actually I'm more than ready to get out of uniform altogether."

His mother took his arm. "Of course, dear. Everything is just as you left it."

And more so. In his absence, his mother had made his room over into a shrine. His belongings were untouched and dust-free, as if he'd been amongst them every day for the past four years. All the awards he'd earned at the university, no matter how insignificant, were framed so that they hung proudly across his wall. He looked at them and at the accumulation of a lifetime and felt as though he were a stranger, intruding upon someone else's past. He was no longer the boy who'd won medals at church for memorizing verse to make his parents proud. He could no longer remember the debates that garnered him plaques or the horse races that brought him trophies. They seemed such a distant part of who he was now.

Civilian clothes fitted differently. After years of butternut and gray and then blue and brass, his tucked shirt with its detachable collar, the snug silk brocade vest and loose-cut fawn-colored trousers over high-top shoes felt unnatural, almost insubordinate.

For months he'd been obsessed with the pleasure of discarding the hated army uniform and the dreadful compromises it stood for. Now that the opportunity had arisen, he studied the Union blue of his jacket but could not cast it aside with contempt. Instead, he hung it carefully in his clothes cupboard until he could have it cleaned and folded away. Another memory of a life no longer his own.

The odd sense of detachment continued as he dined that evening with his friends at Glendower Glade. He'd practically grown up on those sloping green lawns with Reeve and his half-brother Jonah. Such high ideals he'd held then. He had been the epitome of the Southern gentleman—not at all like the man who sat before a wide-eyed audience, dispassionately telling of his adventures in the West.

Reeve leaned back in his chair to muse over their twists of fate. Noble remembered him as a restless youth, always on the outside, pretending that's where he preferred to be. But now he looked content, the master of his father's house, the husband of the only woman he'd ever loved. As it should be.

"So you were in command of a Union fort." Reeve smiled at the irony.

"Why didn't you just desert and come home?" Starla Fairfax demanded. She hadn't changed. Her impulsive nature centered on self. The gorgeous flirt had spent their adolescent years in shameless pursuit of him. He wasn't surprised that she'd come out of the war on top, dressed to the height of fashion, her beauty as flawless as ever. Like her brother, she seemed to have nine lives and the ability always to land on her feet. But what did surprise him was to see she'd taken a Northerner for a husband, and a banker to boot.

Hamilton Dodge had served with Reeve in the Union Army. They'd saved each other's lives and formed an unbreakable bond that only such desperate trials could forge. He was compactly built, solid in his work ethic, vocal in his opinions, and totally different from what Noble would have thought Starla would have looked for in a husband. Completely against the strict rules of society her father insisted upon. There was a story there, one he'd pursue with interest.

Though they'd exchanged only a few words, Noble guessed that he and the little banker would get along just fine. Reeve had good instincts about people. And Noble could see the sharp intelligence and innate honesty in one who'd be a future ally within the narrow fold of Pride.

His answer to Starla's question wasn't simple. It was a question he'd asked himself a million times, one he'd heard from his men, one echoed in his conscience.

Why hadn't he just deserted and come home?

"Because I'd given my word, Star, to the former commander, to his men, and to those children taken captive by the Apache. I couldn't just ride away from those promises and live with myself."

"Even if none of them was your responsibility?" Clearly, she didn't understand. But suddenly, he had a very clear picture of his own motivation.

"It was my responsibility because I was in a position to make a difference, and folks were looking to me to do just that. You can't have personal honor if you run away from those challenges just to make it easier on yourself or even on those you care for."

"I hear the lawyer talking."

He smiled at Reeve's indulgent comment and nodded. "I'd never once thought I'd be wearing a Yank uniform proudly, but when I led that patrol that rescued those little children and another white captive from the Indians, it was one of the finest moments of my life. I was glad to be released from duty when the war ended, but I felt no shame in having served with those men and I hope they felt none serving under me."

It was true. He knew it then. What he'd accomplished out on the frontier had done more for molding his character than any fancy school, than any past of privilege. It had taught him humility, pride and . . . and love. And all of those things together would forever shape the man he'd become: a man who would finish what he started, a man who'd learned to put others ahead of himself, a man who knew the benefit of belonging to a unit. A man who, despite having all those things, was still miserably alone even back where he belonged, even surrounded by his family and friends.

He thought he'd done a good job of concealing his sense of isolation, but amazingly, it was self-centered Starla Fairfax Dodge who picked up on his inner pain and cornered him about it as he gave her a ride back into town.

Don't give up on love so soon. It'll find you when you least expect it, she'd said.

He was terribly afraid that he had found it and it had already given up on him.

He wanted nothing more than to devote the evening to consideration of her statement. But his father had waited up for him with a cigar and a brandy and the discussion he'd hoped to avoid.

There was nothing but fondness and pride in his father's regard as they relaxed in the judge's study. Noble had no fear that either of those things would change, no matter what he said or did, but still he was reluctant to hurt the man who'd given him so much support.

"You were out at the Glade, I understand."

A neutral topic with hard-to-decipher undertones playing about it.

"I had dinner with Reeve, Patrice, Starla, and her new husband."

"The banker."

"Yes." Trouble there, Noble could tell.

"I'm not one to tell you whom to associate with, but you might want to heed public opinion in this instance. Garrett and his Yank friend aren't exactly well received."

"They will be by me, Judge. If you're saying I can't invite them here—"

"No, no, that's not what I'm saying at all." Of course it was. "This is your home and it's always open to your—friends. Only were I you, and jus' starting out, I'd be a bit careful with whom I ally myself."

"I don't plan to ally myself with anyone. I'm a lawyer, remember. I owe my loyalty to my client of the moment."

The judge mulled that over for a minute, re-clipping the end of his cigar to show his displeasure over the turn of conversation. Finally, he said, "Let's talk business."

Noble took a long drink and waited.

"Now that you're home, it's time I set you up with your own office and staff. No need to scramble around, digging up customers who couldn't pay enough to put new buttons on your coat. I've got enough work to keep you hopping for the better part of the year and I'm willing to set up a generous retainer. I wouldn't let any fancy city lawyers handle things for me. Told 'em I was waiting for my son to come home to take care of my interests. There's a building next to Sadie's that would make a nice home for your lawyering shingle. Your mama had it engraved as a surprise."

He presented the nameplate with a grin,

knowing how it would manipulate his son's emotions.

Noble Banning, Attorney-at-Law

Noble ran his fingertips over the recessed gold lettering the way a blind man would read. His voice was thick when he spoke at last.

"This is wonderful, sir. I'll hang it with pride."

And just as the judge started grinning wider, Noble clipped his expectations.

"But when I do, it'll be on my own office, not yours. I appreciate you wanting to give my career a boost, but we've discussed this before. I want to do it on my own, Judge, without having to make any compromises down the road."

Judge Banning's air of self-congratulation faded. "You don't want to taint your business with mine, is that it?"

"Judge, we don't see eye-to-eye on the way things should be, that's for sure. And because you matter so much to me, I can't allow that to come between us."

The judge stared at him for a long, gauging minute. Then his smile returned. "Very prettily said. Are you sure you don't want to be a politician?"

"I couldn't stand the constant strain on my moral conscience."

The judge laughed and put out his hand. "Welcome to Pride, son. You'll do a booming business here 'cause everybody thinks they're above the law and conscience doesn't enter into it. We're gonna need somebody as incorruptible as you to dig us out of our own messes."

Noble took his father's hand, relieved that for now things were resolved between them. "The voice of reason crying out in the wilderness."

"Jus' try to make me listen to it once in a while."

As he lay back on his bed, staring up at the ceiling upon which he'd painted the constellations as a child, Noble began to put his life in order. Firstly, he'd check on the building rents. Then he needed a place to live. He knew he'd always be welcomed within his parents' home, but he feared conflict of interest would arise sooner rather than later if he were to stay. Better he should claim his business and his personal independence at the same time.

Then he'd need clients. The money he'd set aside to begin his career wouldn't last forever, especially at the inflated postwar prices.

Staying neutral wouldn't be as easy as he'd made it sound to his father. He knew there were distinct factions in Pride. He could go with his father, which was where the money would be, or he could invest his time and energy for much less financial reward in the people of the county. It didn't take him a long while to decide which way he would go.

The wealthy men like his father didn't need

his representation. They were the ones the town needed to be protected against. And once he started down that path, he knew there'd be no turning back. While he'd hope he could retain a relationship with his family, he had to realize that might not be possible. It was a matter of loyalty over conscience. Nothing new there. He wasn't the only one being forced into that dilemma in this tumultuous world they'd created. But he wouldn't back away from it, either.

With his business intentions settled, there remained only one unfinished matter. What was he going to do about his personal affairs?

There was one thing his friends were good for. Their worth was measured in the value of their advice.

The next day he sat on the Glade's wide stone steps feeling the cool Kentucky breeze against his skin. Beside him sat the philosophical Reeve Garrett. Noble broached his subject cautiously.

"You and Patrice look happily settled in together."

"It's a fine institution, marriage. One I can highly recommend even to my most gun-shy friends." He laughed at the look Noble gave him, then asked, "What's her name?"

"Who's name?"

"The woman Patrice is sure even now is wearing your heart on her sleeve."

"Guess there's no keeping any secrets from a female, is there?"

"Darn few, my friend. Darn few."

"Her name is Juliet Crowley. She was my commander's daughter."

For the next hour, he tried to explain Juliet, to describe the essence of a woman who without being a great beauty was the most desirable creature he'd ever known. A woman who was the antithesis of the kind of wife he'd wanted for himself, who'd undoubtably be more of a hindrance to his career than a help because of her Northern background and outspoken ways. He didn't think he could survive another few weeks without having her at his side.

"So how did you manage to let her get away?"

"My mind was on the wrong things and she knew it. It wasn't so much a case of me letting her go as not knowing how to get her to stay."

"And you know that now."

Noble smiled wryly. "Haven't a clue."

"Well, to my thinking, there's not much you can do with her up there and you down here."

"That's my thinking, too."

"Have you told her that you love her?"

Noble blinked at him.

"Well, you might just want to start there."

He loved her. He loved her so dearly that he couldn't recall a time when she wasn't foremost in his heart, if not his mind. But he'd never said as much, not once even hinted at it, because it was easier to believe her claim of nothing serious than to express his thoughts and scare her away, perhaps for good.

He was a man given to decisive but not impulsive action. He liked to consider all the angles, weigh each possibility. But where Juliet was concerned, his motives were strictly linear. He wanted her as his wife, his mate, his companion, his friend. He couldn't begin to imagine that another female walked this earth that could come close to filling that position the way she would.

But to have her, he'd have to travel north and get her. If she was still free. No simple task. He knew well what she had thought of him during those last days. She'd thought him motivated solely by his code of justice to the sacrifice of all else.

Had she been wrong?

If he'd had his priorities in the proper order, would he have ever let her ride away without making some claim for a shared future? Would he have been so derailed by the knowledge that all his efforts for revenge had gone down a dead end that he wouldn't notice she was leaving—perhaps forever?

His decision to head straight to Boston to iron out their misunderstandings was postponed by his first legal case on behalf of Starla and her husband. All the while he was in his professional element, he couldn't shut off that part of himself that urged him to take care of the emotional, too. Only with them in tandem could he reach a balance in either.

Once Starla's woes were settled and he had

a lease on both a building and its small but airy upstairs living quarters, it was time to buy a ticket for the first eastbound train.

A plan once again delayed by the unexpected.

The last person he thought to see on his front steps was George Allen. He figured the country chaplain would be busy building up his church with all his new, hard-won wisdom and cementing his relationship with the Irish girl, Colleen. But here he was, hat in hand, looking younger and more uncertain in his civilian clothes and blatantly miserable.

"George, how the hell are you?"

"Can we talk someplace private."

Curious as to what had the youth so anxious, he led him to his new office, where the only furnishings were a big chair and some packing crates. He took a crate while George paced the cavernous room.

"What's on your mind, George?"

"It's not what's on my mind, Noble, it's what's weighing on my soul."

"The war is over, George. It's time to put it aside and move on."

"And you've done that? You've just put away all the things that made you travel halfway across the country, risking life and damnation to learn?"

Then Noble understood. George was talking about his search for the traitor. "That's ancient history. Juliet told me the truth before she left with her father."

George stared at him. "She did? And—and you decided to do nothing?"

"Nothing I could do. I couldn't bring a dead man back to life to punish him for my vain notion of justice. That ideal had already cost me more than I care to sacrifice again."

"A dead man? She told you his name?"

"No. And I don't want to know. It doesn't matter to me anymore. That part of my life is past, so if you're worried over the state of my soul, you needn't be. I've decided to leave that particular act of justice to your superior."

George didn't seem particularly happy to hear that. He stared at Noble for a long, silent moment, then said, "I want to ask Colleen to marry me."

"That's grand news. No surprise, but good news just the same."

So why didn't George sound happy about it?

"She's placed me on a pedestal like one of her home-country saints. She won't be convinced that I'm just a man, as susceptible to sin as any other."

"Once you've been married for a time, I'm sure she'll figure that out for herself."

He didn't smile. "I can't take her for my wife, Noble, nor can I accept the appointment to my church until I rid myself of the burden I've been carrying in cowardly silence for far too long."

Noble felt a prick of insight into an area he didn't want to penetrate. "You're a man of

God, George. Confess to Him and start over. Why are you coming to me?"

"Because it's you I've wronged. You and the other men in our troop."

George went to stand at one of the grimy windows, looking out over the past and its decisions as if they were even now spread out before him, while Noble listened without a word.

"I convinced myself that my act was one of moral conscience, that by pulling my friends out of the line of fire in an unholy war, I'd be saving their lives, their souls. I convinced myself that I had the right, no, the *duty*, to intercede. So many had died, Noble... my childhood best friend as he stood right beside me and others we shared meals and leaky tents and stories with. I felt I was doing God's will. But I know now that it was my own will behind my actions. I was afraid of dying, Noble. Nothing honorable about that. Just a coward looking for an easy escape under the guise of saving us all."

The shock wasn't as great as Noble thought it should be. Perhaps part of him had always suspected, but never wanted to be proven right. In all those conversations they'd had about moral issues and the state of the soul it wasn't Noble's fall from grace they'd been discussing, as he'd always assumed. It was George's own.

"Then all those men died in the camp. How could I tell you the truth then? How could I admit to doing something so horribly wrong?"

"Why are you telling me now, George?" Noble asked quietly. "Why confess when there was no one looking to blame you for the deed?"

"Because I want to start over, and I can't until I stand up to what I've done, in front of both of you and Colleen—and in front of my mirror. I haven't been able to meet my own eyes while shaving for better than a year."

To Noble's dismay, George bowed his head and began to weep. Watching him manfully accept the responsibility for treachery, Noble should have felt something akin to rage or vindication. He'd dedicated the better part of a year of his life to one goal only, to discovering who had betrayed them. But knowing didn't bring back the men they'd lost. It didn't relieve the guilt he would always carry as their leader. It was a hollow victory at best. Because he understood and sympathized, he was no longer qualified to judge.

"George, the traitor I sought died at Point Lookout."

Watery blue eyes lifted in confusion. "But I've just told you—"

"You've confessed a sin that we've all carried, one of pride and self-interest and fear. I can't judge what sits upon a man's heart when he makes a choice of conviction. It was my sin to think I could. I've served long enough to satisfy my conscience and now I'm ready to move on. George, it's time for you to do the same. Give my best to Colleen. Serve her and your congregation as well as you served me, and be assured that I could not have had a better man standing beside me."

Clearly, George didn't know what to say.

"You don't need my forgiveness, George, you need your own." Noble checked his watch. "Now, if you'll excuse me, I have a train to catch to Boston. It's time for me to make my own reparations."

Chapter 24

Juliet stood staring, unable to form a word or coherent thought.

It looked like Noble Banning standing at her front door.

He was just as heartbreakingly handsome as she remembered, even without the extra dash and drama of a uniform, so real, she was almost convinced she could reach out and touch him. But it couldn't be...

"Juliet, you're looking well."

The sound of his softly drawled syllables was enough to make her want to launch herself into his arms. But she held back, suppressing her joy, blinking away the wash of jubilation burning in her eyes.

Noble obviously hadn't come all the way to Boston to tell her how she was looking. She forced a smile.

"Papa will be so happy to see you. Come in. He's just come back from the doctor and could use some company that doesn't nag him unmercifully."

He frowned slightly at her overly cheerful tone. "Is he all right, Juliet?"

"If a professional soldier can ever be all right without a troop to order around. I'll let him tell you."

Noble followed her through the narrow group of rooms and out the back glass doors. John Crowley sat on the small patio surrounded by what little green and sky the city afforded. He looked well, perhaps thinner from the recovery process, but the black silk patch over one eye lent a debonair appeal. His face lit up with unashamed delight when he recognized his guest.

"Major—I should say Mr. Banning! What a surprise this is."

"I'm glad to see you in such good spirits, sir."

"Don't call me sir. My name is John. There's no need for formality, is there?"

"I guess not."

"Jules, fetch Noble some brandy and tell Anne we have company."

"Yes, Papa."

As she disappeared silently into the house, Crowley waved Noble into one of the wrought-iron chairs opposite him. "What brings you to Boston, Noble?"

"Some unfinished business."

Hearing his tone, Juliet guessed at his topic. She hurried anxiously to her father's study. How had Noble uncovered her lie? Was he here to demand answers from her father? Her hands shook as she poured out two glasses of amber liquor that would undoubtedly burn less harshly than the truth.

So he hadn't been able to let it go. The war was over, yet he still pursued retribution. With that kind of zeal, that kind of single-minded focus, what chance was there of him ever forgiving her for putting him off the scent for these past months.

Or had he immediately seen through her lie for what it was? Did he think of it as another trick, as another sleight of hand to deny him the information that weighed more than duty? Or would he believe her now if she told him the truth, *her* truth, that she'd only thought to give him peace of mind. Would he even care to listen to her explanation?

She'd heard nothing from him since she'd left the fort. His future was wide open now, and once he'd heard what her father would tell him, she'd never see him again.

He could get on with his life—and she with hers.

She swallowed hard and started back for the patio, carrying both glasses. Once there, she paused in the doorway, sidelined by surprise because of the easy way the two men were speaking together—like old comrades in arms, like friends. That was something she'd never expected.

"There you are, Jules. Bring those in before they get too warm."

She moved quickly to deliver the drinks,

careful not to lift her gaze as she handed one to Noble. But his hand slipped over hers as she tried to pass him the glass, and when he didn't let go, she had to look up.

She expected to see accusation, anger, even disappointment in his cool blue gaze but all she saw was a question. Afraid to interpret what puzzled him so, she forced a narrow smile and said, "I'll go tell Anne you're here."

His brows lowered. Not exactly displeasure. Definitely curiosity.

She slipped her hand out from under his. He had to let go or drop the glass. As soon as he did, she headed for the house, chiding herself for the way his touch left her nerves hopping like Mexican jumping beans.

But Anne had already heard Noble's arrival and swept past Juliet to embrace their guest as he stood.

"Mr. Banning, what an honor."

"Miz Stacy, a pleasure."

Anne stepped back, her cheeks pinkening prettily as she cast a secret glance at the colonel. "Actually, it's Mrs. Crowley now." She displayed her ring finger with girlish excitement. "For all of two weeks."

"Congratulations." He gave her another hug and a kiss on the cheek while his gaze cut to Juliet over the other woman's shoulder. Again Juliet read questions there, questions she didn't want to answer.

"That's not the only cause for a toast," Crowley stated with obvious pleasure. "Not only have I earned a wonderful wife, I've managed to regain my commission. I guess the government feels an old one-eyed warhorse with experience is better than a yearling right out of the gate."

Noble stared at him, his smile uncertain. "You're going back to Fort Blair?"

"Next week," Anne said, her satisfaction evident as she went to encircle her new husband's shoulders with the fond wrap of her arms. "I never thought I'd miss the dust and heat so much, but I can't wait to get back home."

Crowley lifted his glass. "To Fort Blair and the men who served her bravely."

Noble joined him with a "Here, here," and drank the brandy down in a single gulp. He toasted the couple, but his attention had another focus: the woman who stood, a passive observer, in the doorway. Noting the direction of his gaze, Crowley patted his wife's hand.

"I must see to my eyedrops. Anne, would you be kind enough to fetch them for me? Juliet, keep Noble company for about an hour until my vision clears. Then we'll enjoy a bountiful meal instead of the poor excuse for fodder that we dined on at the post."

Juliet looked far from enthusiastic, and Noble wondered why. Had he waited too long? Had she found someone else? He had to get her alone to ferret out those answers.

"Perhaps we can walk. I'd like to reacquaint myself with some of the sights. I've some fond memories from when I attended Harvard."

"If you like. We won't be gone long, Papa."

Crowley gave her a piercing stare and an order to "Take your time."

After the heat of the West, Boston's air held a decided chill. And so did Juliet Crowley. He was prepared for the first but uncertain how to protect himself from the other.

"So your father married Anne."

"Yes. She's good for him. They make each other very happy."

He advanced to the next step. "And returning to Fort Blair."

"Yes."

"And you?"

"What about me?"

"Will you go with them?"

"No. There's nothing for me there. Anne will take good care of Papa."

"What about . . . your friends?" What about Miles Dougherty, was what he wanted to know.

"Albert's father, the senator, got him and Miles transferred into the Seventh Cavalry under Custer. Apparently that's where the ambitious go to earn notice. With the Apache menace all but over, the Southwest is all but forgotten. The army is looking toward the Black Hills these days."

"And Jane?"

"She knows Libby Custer. She'll have someone to gossip with, and she'll be with Albert, so she'll be content."

"And you?" he asked again. "Are you content?"

Still she hadn't looked up at him as they walked side by side like cautious strangers. She shrugged philosophically. "One doesn't live on the frontier without learning to make the most of what one has. I'll be fine." Before he could ask for more details, she asked, "What about you? Do you have your law practice established?"

"And have already won my first case."

She smiled faintly. "Good for you."

They walked for a while in silence. Noble felt her tension and waited to hear what was on her mind.

"And what about the other matter?"

"Which matter is that?"

"The unfinished business that brought you here to see my father."

His steps faltered in his surprise. How had she guessed? He studied her taut profile and wasn't encouraged by what he saw. Her lips were compressed, her jaw tightly clenched as if in a struggle to hold back her opinions.

"It's been concluded satisfactorily. At least on that end."

She stopped and whirled to face him. Anger and agitation brightened her glare. "So now what? Now that you know I lied to you, what are you going to do? Hunt the poor soul down and make him pay for tarnishing your vanity?"

Before he could answer, she continued in an emotional rush, "I don't suppose you even care why I told you what I did. Why should you believe that I wanted you to have the chance to regain your pride in yourself and your confidence in your men, that I wanted you to be able to see your future clearly without the taint of retribution? What good would it have done you to learn the truth? You can't make amends for your father by becoming everything he's not at the sacrifice of who you really are."

"I know."

His soft-spoken reply threw her off stride. She took an uncertain breath and added, "So what good would it do for you to blindly seek justice without knowing the reasons or the circumstances—"

"None."

She hesitated again, her breath suspended, her gaze searching his in confusion.

"The past doesn't matter anymore, Juliet. I came to make my peace with your father, to tell him that I finally understand why he did what he did and that I admire him for the difficult decision he had to make. But that's the past. It's the future I came to ask him about."

Her luscious, kissable lips formed a silent O.

"If you're not going West with your father, do you plan to stay here?"

She blinked, scrambling to come up with an answer. "No. I don't know."

"You hate the city," he reminded her gently.

"Perhaps I'll travel, see some of those places I've read about in books." Her reply sounded breathless, and to him, unconvincing.

"Why don't you come down to Kentucky and see if all you've heard about it is true?"

She flushed slightly as a combative spark returned to her eyes. "What's in Kentucky that I could possibly find to be of interest."

"Me," he said simply.

She blinked again, this time because her eyes were swimming with unshed and unwanted tears. "If you're asking just because you feel you owe something to my father or because you feel sorry for me—"

He laughed. "Darlin', the last thing I feel for you is pity."

Her gaze intensified. "Then what do you feel?"

His hands captured her upturned face between them. Her eyes remained wide and fixed upon his, asking for no less than the truth. Then they fluttered shut as he bent to capture her mouth in a kiss sweet enough to make her weep with joy, with hope, with love.

He raised his head at last to make an anxious study of her flushed features, concerned about the cause of her tears. When her eyes opened, her gaze was solemn, giving him momentary pause until she demanded, "Tell me in words."

"I have nothing unless I have you."

She snatched a quick, shaky breath.

"Come home with me, Juliet. Let me show

you the things that I love enough to be willing to fight and die for. And if you think you can find contentment there, I want you to stay as my wife."

She tried to speak, but the first sound came out as a squeak. After clearing her throat, she tried again, the words gruff with feeling. "Is that what you came to ask my father?"

"I thought it best that we come to an understanding if we're going to be related."

A smile trembled upon her lips. "And what did he say?"

"He said his mind was set upon it the first time we sat down to dinner together but that you were considerably harder to convince."

"Did he?"

His thumbs stroked away the dampness on her cheeks. His voice was an equally tender caress. "Well, what do I need to say to convince you?"

She fitted her hands over his, stilling their movement while she studied his face, the face that had filled her nightly dreams and waking thoughts. "I've spent my entire life traveling from place to place out of duty. Just once I'd like to go where my heart leads me."

"And where is that?"

"Wherever you go, if it's for the right reason."

The right reason. Noble's thoughts scrambled for the answer she waited to hear. Then he found it in his best friend's advice.

"I love you, Juliet. I want to make a life with

you, a home with you, children with you. Marry me and make me content." When she continued to stare at him in silence, he asked, "Were those the right reasons?"

"You state an excellent case, Mr. Banning. You are going to be a very successful lawyer."

She started to put her arms about his neck, but he held them aside for a cautious moment.

"And your reasons, Miz Crowley? Tell me in words."

"As if you didn't know them, you arrogant man."

"Tell me anyway."

"I love you, Noble, and I want all those things with you."

"You'll give up following the drum without regret?"

"Only to follow my dream."

A dream that came true with Noble Banning's kiss.

Avon Romantic Treasures

*Unforgettable, enthralling love stories,
sparkling with passion and adventure
from Romance's bestselling authors*

✻✻✻✻✻✻✻✻✻✻✻✻✻✻✻✻✻✻✻✻✻✻✻✻✻✻✻✻✻✻✻✻

MY WICKED FANTASY by *Karen Ranney*
79581-7/$5.99 US/$7.99 Can

DEVIL'S BRIDE by *Stephanie Laurens*
79456-x/$5.99 US/$7.99 /Can

THE LAST HELLION by *Loretta Chase*
77617-0/$5.99 US/$7.99 Can

PERFECT IN MY SIGHT by *Tanya Anne Crosby*
78572-2/$5.99 US/$7.99 Can

SLEEPING BEAUTY by *Judith Ivory*
78645-1/$5.99 US/$7.99 Can

TO CATCH AN HEIRESS by *Julia Quinn*
78935-3/$5.99 US/$7.99 Can

WHEN DREAMS COME TRUE by *Cathy Maxwell*
79709-7/$5.99 US/$7.99 Can

TO TAME A RENEGADE by *Connie Mason*
79341-5/$5.99 US/$7.99 Can

Buy these books at your local bookstore or use this coupon for ordering:

Mail to: Avon Books, Dept BP, Box 767, Rte 2, Dresden, TN 38225   G
Please send me the book(s) I have checked above.
❏ My check or money order—no cash or CODs please—for $_____ is enclosed (please add $1.50 per order to cover postage and handling—Canadian residents add 7% GST). U.S. residents make checks payable to Avon Books; Canada residents make checks payable to Hearst Book Group of Canada.
❏ Charge my VISA/MC Acct#_____Exp Date_____
Minimum credit card order is two books or $7.50 (please add postage and handling charge of $1.50 per order—Canadian residents add 7% GST). For faster service, call 1-800-762-0779. Prices and numbers are subject to change without notice. Please allow six to eight weeks for delivery.
Name_____
Address_____
City_____State/Zip_____
Telephone No._____   RT 0698

We've got love on our minds at
http://www.AvonBooks.com

Vote for your favorite hero in "HE'S THE ONE."

Take a romance trivia quiz, or just "GET A LITTLE LOVE."

Look up today's date in romantic history in "DATEBOOK."

Subscribe to our monthly e-mail newsletter for all the buzz on upcoming romances.

Browse through our list of new and upcoming titles and read chapter excerpts.

Dear Reader,

As you're getting deeper and deeper into the holiday hustle and bustle, don't forget to take some time out for yourself—by indulging in an Avon romance! Is there any better way to enjoy a precious few moments of time for yourself?

Avon's Romantic Treasure for December comes from Karen Ranney, whose emotionally intense and wildly passionate love stories are sure to warm up the coldest December night! In *Upon A Wicked Time* a young beauty transforms a wicked English duke into a man worth loving. This is a story that will go straight to your heart!

Contemporary readers won't want to miss Patti Berg's delightful *Looking for a Hero*. What would you do if a devastatingly handsome man washed up on your beach and into your life? And what would you think if he insisted he was a real, live 18th Century *pirate?* Fans of warm, wonderful, magical love stories won't want to miss this "keeper!"

Readers just can't get enough of *The MacKenzies* by Ana Leigh, and the latest MacKenzie is here—*Peter*. These heroes are hot, and Ana Leigh's writing is filled with the passion and humor—and western setting—I know you all enjoy!

And if you like your romance stormy and sensual, then don't miss Margaret Evans Porter's *Kissing a Stranger*...where a beautiful heroine travels to Regency London, desperate to marry for money. But she ends up with more than she ever bargained for...

Until next month, happy reading.

Lucia Macro

Lucia Macro
Senior Editor

Avon Romances—
the best in exceptional authors
and unforgettable novels!

THE HEART BREAKER	by Nicole Jordan
	78561-7/ $5.99 US/ $7.99 Can
THE MEN OF PRIDE COUNTY:	by Rosalyn West
THE OUTCAST	79579-5/ $5.99 US/ $7.99 Can
THE MACKENZIES: DAVID	by Ana Leigh
	79337-7/ $5.99 US/ $7.99 Can
THE PROPOSAL	by Margaret Evans Porter
	79557-4/ $5.99 US/ $7.99 Can
THE PIRATE LORD	by Sabrina Jeffries
	79747-X/ $5.99 US/ $7.99 Can
HER SECRET GUARDIAN	by Linda Needham
	79634-1/ $5.99 US/ $7.99 Can
KISS ME GOODNIGHT	by Marlene Suson
	79560-4/ $5.99 US/ $7.99 Can
WHITE EAGLE'S TOUCH	by Karen Kay
	78999-X/ $5.99 US/ $7.99 Can
ONLY IN MY DREAMS	by Eve Byron
	79311-3/ $5.99 US/ $7.99 Can
ARIZONA RENEGADE	by Kit Dee
	79206-0/ $5.99 US/ $7.99 Can

Buy these books at your local bookstore or use this coupon for ordering:

Mail to: Avon Books, Dept BP, Box 767, Rte 2, Dresden, TN 38225   G
Please send me the book(s) I have checked above.
❑ My check or money order—no cash or CODs please—for $_____ is enclosed (please add $1.50 per order to cover postage and handling—Canadian residents add 7% GST). U.S. residents make checks payable to Avon Books; Canada residents make checks payable to Hearst Book Group of Canada.
❑ Charge my VISA/MC Acct#_____Exp Date_____
Minimum credit card order is two books or $7.50 (please add postage and handling charge of $1.50 per order—Canadian residents add 7% GST). For faster service, call 1-800-762-0779. Prices and numbers are subject to change without notice. Please allow six to eight weeks for delivery.
Name_____
Address_____
City_____State/Zip_____
Telephone No._____

ROM 0598

Bestselling Author
CHRISTINA SKYE

"CHRISTINA SKYE IS SUPERB!"
Virginia Henley

BRIDE OF THE MIST
78278-2/$5.99US/$7.99Can

Urged by a psychic to visit England's Draycott Abbey, magazine editor Kara Fitzgerald is thrown into a passionate encounter with one Duncan McKinnon—an encounter laced with fiery desire and ancient rivalry.

A KEY TO FOREVER
78280-4/$5.99US/$7.99Can

SEASON OF WISHES
78281-2/$5.99US/$7.99Can

BRIDGE OF DREAMS
77386-4/$5.99US/$7.99Can

HOUR OF THE ROSE
77385-6/$4.99US/$5.99Can

CHRISTMAS KNIGHT
80022-5/$6.50 US/$8.50 Can

Buy these books at your local bookstore or use this coupon for ordering:

Mail to: Avon Books, Dept BP, Box 767, Rte 2, Dresden, TN 38225   G
Please send me the book(s) I have checked above.
☐ My check or money order—no cash or CODs please—for $_____ is enclosed (please add $1.50 per order to cover postage and handling—Canadian residents add 7% GST). U.S. residents make checks payable to Avon Books; Canada residents make checks payable to Hearst Book Group of Canada.
☐ Charge my VISA/MC Acct#_____ Exp Date_____
Minimum credit card order is two books or $7.50 (please add postage and handling charge of $1.50 per order—Canadian residents add 7% GST). For faster service, call 1-800-762-0779. Prices and numbers are subject to change without notice. Please allow six to eight weeks for delivery.
Name_____
Address_____
City_____ State/Zip_____
Telephone No._____ SKY 0698

Experience the Wonder of Romance
LISA KLEYPAS

STRANGER IN MY ARMS
78145-X/$5.99 US/$7.99 Can

MIDNIGHT ANGEL
77353-8/$5.99 US/$6.99 Can

DREAMING OF YOU
77352-X/$5.50 US/$6.50 Can

ONLY IN YOUR ARMS
76150-5/$5.99 US/$7.99 Can

ONLY WITH YOUR LOVE
76151-3/$5.50 US/$7.50 Can

THEN CAME YOU
77013-X/$5.99 US/$7.99 Can

PRINCE OF DREAMS
77355-4/$5.99 US/$7.99 Can

SOMEWHERE I'LL FIND YOU
78143-3/$5.99 US/$7.99 Can

Buy these books at your local bookstore or use this coupon for ordering:

Mail to: Avon Books, Dept BP, Box 767, Rte 2, Dresden, TN 38225   G
Please send me the book(s) I have checked above.
❏ My check or money order—no cash or CODs please—for $_____ is enclosed (please add $1.50 per order to cover postage and handling—Canadian residents add 7% GST). U.S. residents make checks payable to Avon Books; Canada residents make checks payable to Hearst Book Group of Canada.
❏ Charge my VISA/MC Acct#_____Exp Date_____
Minimum credit card order is two books or $7.50 (please add postage and handling charge of $1.50 per order—Canadian residents add 7% GST). For faster service, call 1-800-762-0779. Prices and numbers are subject to change without notice. Please allow six to eight weeks for delivery.
Name_____
Address_____
City_____State/Zip_____
Telephone No._____   LK 0798